The Heart Doesn't Ask

Michael Slayter

Dedication

In memory of the late Johnnie Edna Hartwig…

If all boys and young men had a grandmother like her, the world would be a better place.

Acknowledgment

First, to my wife, Jane, for her flexible and creative thinking that keeps me grounded and connected to my readers.

And to my grandson, Noah Slayter, who designed the cover. His talent will take him to many places, I'm sure.

About the Author

I am a retired officer from the U.S. Army Veterinary Corps. My kaleidoscope lifestyle has provided me with a wealth of real-life experiences to fuel my creative urges.

I have three books: *Journey to Understanding and Kisatchie Voices*, both of which were released around Christmas of 2023, and a third book, *The Brothers Harper*, released in May 2025.

Jane, my wife of 53 years, and I keep busy with our two grown sons, their wives, and six grandchildren. My family roots are in Louisiana, and Jane and I live in Northern Virginia. The story that follows is based on true characters and events within my own family and extended family.

Chapter 1

April 2008 – Alexandria, Louisiana.

Cash Ratliff's name made the back-page headlines after police dragged him off to jail, charged with public intoxication, assaulting officers, resisting arrest, and, in an almost cinematic twist of irony, joyriding in a stolen car that turned out to belong to the city's Chief of Police.

But his hell-bent spiral didn't begin there.

Three hours before his arrest, Cash stood, swaying, in the apartment doorway of Julie Thompson, his first and only serious girlfriend for the past eight months. The sagging smile on his face told her everything.

"Cash, I told you not to have another drink!" she shrieked, her voice ricocheting off the walls like a siren. Neighbors cracked open their doors, drawn by the noise and familiar drama.

"Get out! And don't even *think* about coming back until you're sober!"

She had been a temporary glimmer of hope for him, a portal into a world where everything was gentle and clean – too clean, too gentle, too otherworldly for him. Her family was fueled by old money passed down through generations, and her father dabbled in local politics. Cash had met the man only once during a sober moment and gave him an impressive portrayal of solid, well-mannered manhood. Julie saw the other side.

Stumbling along in an aimless direction, something crossed his mind through the alcohol haze - she had not said *never*. But he knew her forgiveness hinged on something he was not ready for, at least not now. Why should he surrender anything that brought him instant absolution in a world that always seemed destined to find fault with him?

He ambled along, plodding for blocks with his shoes untied and his smudged, sweaty shirt unbuttoned until he found himself in front of a police precinct station. It took a few seconds for his eyes to focus and realize that in front of him stood a late-model Ford Explorer parked in front of the building with the motor idling. Call it poetic justice.

Answering an unwritten invitation, he grinned, opened the driver's door, and climbed in. The owner came running out just as Cash pulled away with a howling laugh and a screech of spinning tires. After thirty minutes and a chaotic chase, it took three patrol cars to pull him over and six Alexandria policemen to subdue his gangly, 6'2", sinewy body.

When it ended, a stream of blood made a streak in his tousled blond hair, and his shirt hung in tatters. A sober man would have been screaming in agony from the beating they gave him, but his blood alcohol was high enough to blot out most pain sensations. The arresting officers, however, did not escape a collection of painful bruises, contusions, and loosened teeth.

In lock-up, when he regained what appeared to be an imaginary degree of sobriety and awareness of his situation, he opted for his one and only phone call. Julie answered the phone with a blunt tone.

He tried his best not to slur his words. Very slowly and with carefully measured diction, he said, "Hey there, sweetie–ah, look, I'm sorry about all this." He paused a few seconds to hear what she had to say, but heard nothing. "Okay, look, here's the deal. I - I need some dough, you know, money for a, well, you know, a friend of mine." He turned and asked the officer with a question mark on his face. "How mush did he shay?"

"The judge said two thousand dollars," the officer yelled from the other side of the room.

Julie's voice became suddenly clear and vivid. "Cash, who said that? Did I hear something about a judge? Wait a minute, how much? Cash, where are you?"

He thought he heard a brief sob as she hung up the phone. A rancid bolus of bile rose into his throat, and he swallowed hard to keep it down.

A fleeting glimmer of thought told him he didn't deserve her. But only a brief, small glimmer. To hell with her. Never liked her that much anyway, right? He could live through anything. What's a little jail time? Free rent? With that thought, he aimed a wad of bloody spit into a trash can, saw it hit the floor instead, then turned to his jailer and asked, "When's brikfash around this place? I like my eggs over easy."

He stopped and peered closely at the man. His double vision seemed to be self-entertaining. As the guards firmly led him back to his cell, he said loudly, "I'm going to write to my congressman about this. You're mistreating a disabled veteran!" The iron gate closed with a heavy clank as he leaned against the wall, laughing like a wild man.

Not until the next day did he vaguely remember the passenger in the back seat, something he hadn't noticed during his haste to avoid capture. During a quick arraignment the next morning and with his brain still in a hung-over fog, Cash foolishly declined the services of an attorney and agreed to a non-jury trial.

Three weeks later, a judge found him guilty and sentenced him to five years in the State Penitentiary at Angola, located in south

Louisiana. Many considered the sentence too light, especially Bob Preston, Alexandria's Chief of Police, owner of the stolen car, and husband of the equally inebriated woman in the back seat.

A public defender had been assigned after the fact by the wishes of an unknown benefactor, and promised to have the sentence reviewed in view of Cash's heroic service in the U.S. Marine Corps. Less than four years before, under blazing enemy fire during his second deployment in Afghanistan, he had reached three wounded marines and dragged them to safety, one by one, only to have a fragment of grenade shrapnel slice open his neck like a saber and send him on a one-way ticket back to civilization.

The attorney's strategy centered around convincing the appeals court that his intoxication resulted from unintentional self-medication for depression and post-traumatic stress disorder related to combat injury, a situation that had allegedly been undiagnosed and overlooked. Cash and the attorney both recognized the explanation as a thin stretch of the truth, bordering on imaginary.

In a hearing one year after the initial sentencing, the judge, being a former Marine, allowed the dice to roll in Cash's favor as he considered a plea for leniency. This judge was not new to the bench and remembered encounters with Cash as a youth, although his record of juvenile offenses and school truancy remained incidents held in a sealed file.

Additionally, right after he finished high school, no one could pick him out of a police line-up in a case of breaking into a private residence, even though the detectives knew of his reputation for picking locks better than most. Although it all happened years before with lots of mind-changing and lingering suspicions having since gone under the bridge like flood waters, the judge invoked his long memory and gave Cash the benefit of a doubt. The results of the appeal, however, took a slow turn in reaching him.

The initial conviction brought on mixed reactions at the State penitentiary in Angola. Warden Faircloth came to his cell on the first day and said, "Just so you know, that sentence was way too light! No justice in it. We'll be looking for ways to add something to it. You just fart wrong, and we'll be on you like stink on shit, you got that?" On first impressions, the warden had reminded Cash of 'Boss Hogg' on *Dukes of hazard.*

Years before, after high school graduation and one year on his own with some boring, random trade school classes in business and auto mechanics, taken at his grandparents' insistence, Cash looked for a real adrenaline rush and enlisted in the Marines. His classroom performance in trade school had not been a challenge, but he had a remarkable rate of retention with minimal effort and earned high marks, just like in high school, which stood out in his entry record when he enlisted. It showed he had an acumen for business and was a born mechanic. But his instincts were always veiled in self-interest, relentlessly hunting for any edge, no matter how ruthless, that would put him a step ahead, while leaving everyone else in the dust, something he learned the hard way as a preemptive tool, ready for anything that confronted him.

After boot camp, he found himself assigned to a motor pool where his greatest adventure was confined to changing oil and tightening fan belts. Here he learned to push the limits of acceptable public behavior, including a new appetite for alcohol.

On a drunken dare from his comrades in arms, he applied for marine reconnaissance training and found his name on the list of accepted candidates. He finished near the top of his class and celebrated graduation day from Basic Reconnaissance Course with two of his buddies as they polished off a bottle of Scotch that evening, hitchhiked to a local watering hole, picked up some local girls, and headed for a private moonlit place on the edge of town in the girls' car. They killed another bottle of the cheapest booze they could afford while they tried their luck with the girls and howled at the moon.

While the evening was still unfolding and the promise of more adventure remained just out of reach, they somehow found their way to a tattoo parlor and, as the girls watched, each came away displaying some version of a dragon on their shoulder with U.S.M.C. in fiery letters floating on the dragon's breath. The girls thought it was a blast and urged them on. They were set to leave for jump school the following day, but as Cash and his friends stepped out of the tattoo parlor, they were ambushed by a trio of jealous boyfriends—young men who had spent the night scouring the streets in search of their favorite tarts and trying to find out who had disrupted their own plans for the evening.

Traditionally, the Basic Reconnaissance Course made boot camp look like a church social, and those tough enough to finish it learned some dark stuff intended for a combat enemy, not a local encounter in a blue-collar town where the good ole boys had mixed feelings about bombastic military swaggering, especially if it infringed on their female companionships. When the encounter ended and the screams died down, the girls stuffed their bloodied boyfriends into their own car and drove them to the nearest emergency room, leaving Cash and his two buddies walking and hitchhiking to a safer spot.

One ride was in the back of an old pickup truck that bounced so hard one of them threw up in the truck bed. They didn't bother to tell the driver about the mess and hopped off in the next town.

There, they made a phone call and waited for someone in a familiar uniform to come help them avoid the cops. Help came by way of military police who whisked all three of them back to base, where new deployment orders waited with the ink still wet.

The next morning, the local police combed the deep woods of North Carolina, while Cash and his hangover, along with the rest of his new marine company, climbed to 40,000 feet on their way to Afghanistan. Change of plans. For the time being, jump school would have to wait, but fate had another agenda that would unfold a few years later.

His arrival in Angola greeted him with uncertainty, not that trepidation was foreign to him, but this was a different kind of uncertainty, a palpable doubt, fear almost. In Afghanistan, he was surrounded by a reassuring circle of brethren trained to look out for each other. But in this hellhole, he wasn't sure what to expect. Different smells and sounds lurked in shadowed corners. The suffocating ambiance of the place made him truly frightened for the first time in a decade.

But his self-esteem would not allow him to remain immersed in a pool of fear for long. The common thread among the inmates included distrust of anyone in your line of vision. He never had the same cellmate for more than four weeks. No one could tell him what prompted the changes, but the rumor was that prison policy did not allow two inmates to bond for too long for fear they would start making sinister thoughts and plans.

One of his many cellmates answered to the name 'Rusty.' No last name, just 'Rusty.' He spoke of no surname and had no history he cared to share. Cash had learned to detect and avoid all kinds of dreadful personalities over the years, but Rusty was both an enigma and a likable sort. He seemed to find something comical around every corner.

"I'm about to get my ass out of here," Rusty announced one day out of the clear blue. He carried a broad, beaming grin on his face. "I'm going to Camp Beauregard."

Cash asked, "I think I've heard of it. What's there? Your time's not up, is it?"

"Naw, it's this place up in Pineville where they send perfect little angels like me so we can get used to being around normal folks again. They think we forget what that feels like." He ended with a clown face and a sneering chuckle that sounded more like a snort.

"Is it better than here?"

"Hell, it can't be any worse!"

"How long you been in?" Cash asked.

"Almost six years. I got just a few months to go."

"How'd you work that deal? You kiss someone's butt twice a week?"

Rusty laughed out loud. "Naw, just stay out of trouble. If you're not doing hard time, like ten to twenty, they might put some fairy dust on you and let you go."

"Who? Who's *they*?"

"I dunno. Some dumbass board that meets every so often. I can't remember what they call it. Just a bunch of suits and briefcases. Maybe the local Bishop sits on it, who knows? Just keep off the Warden's shit list and hope they pick your record out of a hat." Cash had his doubts.

Pineville – he knew about Pineville. It lay right across the Red River from Alexandria.

And so, for the next two years, he danced on a razor's edge between Jekyll and Hyde. To the warden and the guards, he gave the appearance of a model prisoner, all stiff and polite. He had one face for the Warden and guards and another when the lights went out.

Among the inmates, they all learned an unspoken rule about Cash Ratliff. If you value your pearly white teeth, don't cross him or get in his way.

Minor scuffles among inmates went unnoticed, but Cash had a way of making quick mincemeat of anyone who challenged him, and he did it so it wouldn't show. No one enjoyed having their head stuffed in a toilet bowl. He could make a punch in the gut feel like a deep knife thrust, but without the blood. Word about him got around soon after his arrival.

A couple of ringleaders made the mistake of trying to put him in his place, after which no one challenged him again - ever. In the meantime, he knew how to depart from his natural image and take on whatever appearance allowed him to blend in harmlessly.

Some called him the chameleon. His clothes were always spanking clean and starched. He had friends in the laundry detail who knew how to get it done in exchange for a little protection and other unsavory favors. He could be a foul-mouthed slob or a diplomatic stateman. He had the vocabulary for both. Don't make trouble for any of his friends unless you want the wrath of Ratliff heaped on your head.

It happened on a weekend, a Saturday morning, when one of Cash's cellblock buddies came running to him during outside exercise time.

"Hey, Cash! Did you hear?"

"Hear what? Slow down, what's going on?"

"They're putting all of cellblock D on lock-down."

"That's right next to ours. What happened?"

"Some visitors came in with food for guys on block D and they had a bunch of homemade, uh, you know, bread loaves. The guards thought that was weird, so they cut into one of them. They found a hacksaw blade."

"You're kidding!"

"Naw, then they cut into some more and found all kinds of hardware shit. The Warden's on the warpath! He's thinking about shutting down our cellblock, too! Cash, can you do something? I've been in solitary before and it ain't fun!"

Cash boasted a walking encyclopedia of alibis, rationed out as favors to others in return for whatever he needed to add some sanity to his own prison life. By the end of the day, he had convinced the Warden that any kind of lockdown would not prevent future incidents and that visitor restrictions might be a better answer. The Warden bought it.

Soon after his arrival, he found that working the system appeared so obviously easy, he wondered why more inmates hadn't discovered it as well. He had a certain smile and nod of the head that conveyed docile and obedient innocence. He grew up knowing how to use it. He began volunteering for various jobs around the prison and found no act of mild groveling beneath him to stay in good graces with the guards. He stayed away from any trouble that didn't fit into his current, ongoing scheme of things, but always with a clear view of those involved and for any angles that may play out for himself.

Something distinctly unique that helped his appeal started in the fall of the second year. He was looking out through the library window after supper and saw two inmates getting into a car with guards that he recognized, but the guards were in civilian clothes. He timidly turned to one of the duty guards with a question.

"Say, ah, those fellas down there at the front gate – where are they going?"

The man in uniform walked over, glanced out the window, and said, "Oh, they're going to that, uh, that AA meeting. It's at a church just outside of town, I'm not sure where. Something the Warden just started. Why do you ask?"

"Just wondering." But the wheels in Cash's brain were already turning. He immediately made an appointment to see Warden Faircloth.

As usual, the Warden was always looking for an underlying motive when special requests came his way.

"Why you want to go to an AA meeting?"

"Well, sir, you know why I'm in here. If I hadn't been drunk, I could have stayed out of trouble and now, all these weeks and months, sometimes when I still feel the urge to drink, I just can't… "

"You just what? Do what?"

"Sir, I know there's alcohol in the infirmary and it's just right there and I know if I tried to get to it… "

"You'd be in a shitload of trouble."

"Yes sir. I've tried really hard to show I'm a changed man and I regret what I did, but old habits are so hard to break. It's like a Jezebel woman telling you to come into her bedroom. Hard to say no. I just think an occasional trip to an AA meeting would help." He waited for the Warden to say something. When nothing came, he tried a different approach. "I saw some other guys going, and I just hoped that you might understand." He paused and added, "And the Governor would appreciate your efforts to help inmates rehabilitate spiritually, don't you think?"

Faircloth was beginning to appreciate what Cash was saying until he mentioned the Governor. He stood up from his desk, took a long draw on his cigarette and flipped the ashes on the floor. "You let me worry about my own damn career, you hear me? Now get outa' here!"

The next afternoon, Cash had a visit from the guard on his cellblock.

"Hey, Ratliff! Put on some decent clothes. Warden wants to send you to a meeting somewhere. You know anything about that?"

Cash just smiled.

And so, thus started a series of trips that got him out of the cell block and back around normal people. It was refreshing, to say the least. At one meeting, a local minister came to give a motivational speech, and Cash took the time to talk to him. May as well keep up the façade, he figured. Usually, the escorting guard appeared in a hurry to leave, but the minister saw a chance to sprinkle a dash of God's Word on them both, so Cash milked the system for a few more precious moments away from his cell.

The speaker harkened to the name of Reverend Isaiah Watchword, and the sound of it immediately made Cash skeptical. Among the crowd gathered there, the preacher's three-piece suit stood out in stark contrast to the others dressed in various modes of attire, as if they had just come from work. Always on his best behavior, Cash usually arrived with a small towel draped over his hands to conceal the handcuffs. That night, the towel had been overlooked by the guards who guided him to the back seat of the car. A man in handcuffs at an AA meeting did not go unnoticed. At the end of the meeting, Rev. Watchword approached and shook Cash's hands with both of his like a martini shaker, almost as though granting absolution.

"Can you tell me how God brought you to this meeting?" the Reverend asked. His voice dripped honey-sweet and sanctimonious. "Did you hear his voice?"

Cash had not stepped into a church since age twelve, after both parents died in a head-on collision driving home to Houston. The juvenile court gave custody of him to his paternal grandparents in Colfax, Louisiana, both in their late 70s, and somehow, church attendance did not appear on the family agenda anymore.

Furthermore, the law, not his grandparents, made him go to school. The grandparents had raised his father and two other children, but their aging energy level couldn't keep up with a rambunctious boy entering puberty.

Day by day, he learned to stay alive in a tough neighborhood. He ran with a crowd that entertained themselves by looking for any excuse to start fights. He knew how to get out of a tight spot, and he learned how to lie with a straight face. He found out about girls by himself. At age fourteen, Amy Spencer enticed him to run his hand under her blouse for five minutes, and thus began a never-ending treasure hunt driven by libido and a thirst for adventure with a risk attached. God's voice was not in the script.

In his estimation, everything the Reverend Mister Watchword had said that evening was total bullshit. According to the preacher, the world reeked with evil, and life harbored original sin around every corner, a statement with which Cash agreed, but the preacher's droning voice said the remedy was to love everybody. To Cash, it sounded as appealing as drinking dirty dishwater. The

Reverend liked to use the words 'discernment' and 'atonement' over and over. Cash wondered if the man could preach about anything if those two words were not in his vocabulary.

He waved the bible around, but never opened it. Maybe the Reverend's flawless ducktail hairstyle that covered his ears and his dripping, weepy pulpit drama that finally overshadowed the sermon made the theatrics look valid, but who cares? It got Cash a few hours of reprieve from the big place. He could play the game and took advantage of every minute it offered. He found no problem wading through a few minutes of pulpit sewage if that's what it took. He really didn't give a flying crap about any religion because he felt no one else really did either, if the truth be known.

But Cash answered the man's question quickly with a Cheshire grin. "Yeah, preacher, I heard the voice. I couldn't really say I heard it, but I felt it. Yeah, I felt it. Felt good!" The crowd milled around them, saying goodbyes as they headed for the door, each carrying their own personal load of mental baggage.

The preacher responded like a prophet and shouted, "I knew it when I saw you come in the door! I knew you were one of His chosen. Hallelujah, my boy! Thank God you're here!" The man flashed a big, toothy smile that revealed an array of gold crownwork.

"Yeah! Hallelujah!" Cash almost shouted. He tapped the guard's shoulder, nodded positively, and the guard quickly mouthed 'Hallelujah' with a look of confusion. Cash concluded his visceral response by raising his hands toward the ceiling, bringing his handcuffs upwards while his whole body trembled to a point of vibration. It was the stuff that brought on Academy Award Nominations. A few faces in the crowd gawked briefly to see the commotion.

"Maybe you could come speak at the big house," Cash said when he pretended to regain his composure. "You want me to say something to the Warden?" The preacher smiled broadly and agreed, and Cash was impressed with his own brand of sales pitch. He never mentioned it to the Warden.

The group met every week, but the Warden said he couldn't spare the overtime or personnel to accompany him that often. Cash knew just how far to push the man without jeopardizing his progress, and they finally agreed to a schedule of once every three weeks. Doing small favors just short of kissing the Warden's butt didn't hurt either. It got him what he wanted.

For the next few months, Cash attended the meetings when he could and pretended to listen to Watchword's pontifications. The drive took thirty minutes on each leg, there and back, to the old church where the group met. His official escort changed each time, usually one of the older men who did nothing but desk duty. So far, they all had projected a sour attitude, making Cash think they did not like being given what amounted to a babysitting detail. Conversations with them consisted of grunts and three-word sentences.

One odd, old buzzard would not let Cash use the men's room before the return trip. He told Cash he could hold it because he wasn't waiting for a pit stop or any other delaying tactic to keep him from getting home to watch his favorite TV show.

On the most recent trip, however, the guard was a young man named Stanley. It seemed he had drawn the short straw to be driver and escort for the next several trips. The older guards had probably stacked the deck. *Must be on the bottom of the pile where the shit rolls downhill,* Cash thought.

Stanley stood by the driver's door in civilian clothes and spit out a large wad of tobacco from his mouth as another guard put Cash in the back seat. He noticed Stanley's pants fit a bit tight in the waist, and the cuffs stopped about ankle high.

The young guard had a round, youthful, pudgy face with light complexion, a peach fuzz moustache, a flattop haircut, and the residual, fading signs of persistent teenage acne. His contrast with the older guards made it immediately obvious that he had just started the job and probably didn't know the flavor of the Angola culture yet.

Glancing in the rearview mirror after a few minutes of driving, he asked Cash, "You been in the place long?"

Cash had relaxed in the back seat with his head resting on the window when the question caught him off guard. Not impressed with the young man's interest, he moved only his eyes toward the voice and said, "Long enough, why?"

"Just wondering. What did you do before, ah, you know, before, uh, coming here?"

"Umm, self-employed."

"Oh yeah? Doing what?"

Cash adjusted his posture and squirmed in his seat. He cleared his throat and mumbled, "Whatever. Why do you ask?"

"Sorry. Just filling the time with conversation."

Cash always reserved his milk and honey diplomacy for older, more seasoned guards. Stanley didn't fit that profile.

He growled, "I don't make a habit of talking to guards."

Stanley gripped the steering wheel a little harder. "Okay, I'll just drive. How's that?"

"That's your job. How's that?"

The rest of the ride remained silent except for the sound of the tires on the road and the occasional car traveling in the opposite direction.

Cash settled back to gaze at the swamp on both sides of the road while moonlight shone on telephone poles and Spanish moss that hung from cypress trees in the water. In the silence of the back seat, he wondered if this ongoing façade appeared valid and convincing. Would it really make a difference?

During the next trip on the return leg back to Angola, Stanley stared long and hard in the rearview mirror before speaking. The wire mesh barrier between the two men made conversation mildly awkward. As usual, Cash lay half-dozing when Stanley's voice jabbed him like an ice pick.

"Ah, I was just wondering, what did you think about that preacher's comments tonight?"

Cash barely raised his head up and opened one eye. "Say, what?"

"I said, what did you think about what that preacher said?"

Clearly irritated, Cash opened both eyes and muttered, "About what?"

Stanley cleared his throat and hesitated, trying to summon the right words. "All that forgiveness stuff. You know, loving your enemy – that kind of stuff. He acts like he knows just what God's thinkin' all the time. Just how does anyone know what God's thinkin'?"

"Hell, I don't know. Does that stuff bother you?"

Stanley thought for a moment and said, "No, it just makes me wonder."

"About what?"

"You know, where do you go when you die, what's it like – that kind of stuff."

Cash gazed out the window for a full minute and finally said in a monotone, "My only thought is I never trust preachers who wear expensive clothes. Sounds like he's never been through a real shit storm, y'know?"

Stanley remained quiet for a few seconds, then said, "Yeah, maybe next time I'll ask him about that." No words passed between them for several minutes and then Stanley interrupted the silence again. "I heard you was over yonder in Afghanistan, huh?"

Cash shifted in the back seat and continued to look out the window. Memories began to cloud his thoughts. Stanley's sudden desire to talk seemed unavoidable. Cash asked gruffly, "Is tonight any different than the last time we sat in the car together?"

"Oh, that's right. You cut me off the other night. Sorry."

But the young man's last question still echoed in Cash's thoughts, so he relented and replied, "So, you been checking up on me. Yeah, I was over there. Two tours."

"Was you in the Army?"

"Hmm? No, Marine Corps."

Stanley sat up straighter in the driver's seat and said, "No shit? So was my brother."

"Is that supposed to impress me? Where is he now? Shacked up somewhere?" Cash ended with a deep chuckle.

The young man ignored the coarse humor, took a long breath, and sighed. "Yeah, he was in the Corps. One tour over there – well, almost one tour. Came back in a body bag. That was a few years ago, maybe a bit longer. My daddy never got over it. Failure to thrive, the doctors called it. He just gave up. He died not long after

Whip's body came back."

Cash abruptly turned from the window, feeling the hair on his neck stand up. He leaned forward and snapped, "After *who* came back?' His intensity caught the young guard by surprise.

"Uh, Whip, my brother. That was his nickname. He was older than me, and I never could get him to tell me why he caught that nickname. But everybody called him that, even as a kid. Must have been a reason."

Cash leaned back and stayed silent, rubbing his chin with both hands. The handcuffs made a soft rattle. He started to say something, but Stanley interrupted his thoughts.

"Yeah, about seven or eight years ago, maybe longer. I can't remember exactly when. They told me he was in a Hummer on the highway between Kabul and Kandahar. Whip was driving, I think. I never got the whole story."

Cash asked carefully, "What happened?"

"I really don't know. They say the whole damn thing just – like - blew up. They said he probably never knew what hit him. They never found his left foot."

Stanley's account of his brother's death awakened Cash's memory of a time focused on real survival, that of coping with bone-grinding reality, and he could sense his own protective walls coming back into focus. Trying to maintain his callused attitude, he returned to his gaze out the window and mumbled, "Hell, nobody lives forever anyway."

The cold sarcasm didn't make an impact on Stanley. Maybe he hadn't clearly heard what Cash had said. He continued, "I got to thinking about all that stuff the preacher was talking about, like loving your enemies and being humble. I don't see how anyone over there could do that. It just don't make no sense. If I had been over there, I'd be so pissed all the time, I just, I - I don't know."

Cash replied dryly, "Yeah, well, a lot of folks went over there and didn't come back. I don't think about it much." He noticed a slight quivering tone had developed in the voice coming from the front seat. Against his better judgment, Cash rubbed his eyes, inhaled deeply, and leaned closer.

"Yeah, so - okay Stanley, you got me thinking and I have a question. Is that okay? I mean, it's a bit personal, if you don't mind."

Cash's question took him by surprise. Stanley took a deep breath and focused his eyes on the mirror while trying to keep his attention on the road. Slowly, he said, "I guess that all depends. Go ahead."

Cash moved closer. "You've been my escort these past few weeks and you're always in civilian clothes, so you don't wear a name tag. They told me your name was Stanley, but nobody told me your last name."

For a moment, Cash could hear no response. He could see the young man's face in the mirror, veiled by indecision and outlined by the faint glow of the dashboard lights.

Cash spoke gently. "Hey Stanley, is it okay for me to ask? If you don't want to tell me, that's okay."

The inside of the car became quiet as a tomb. A slow rain had begun, and the smell of wet asphalt penetrated the car's interior. The sound of the tires changed to a wet hiss. Both men seemed to be collecting their thoughts. Stanley finally answered, "I'm not sure. Like I told you once before, we're trained not to get too close to inmates. We can't give out no personal stuff like phone numbers, stuff like that. I probably done told you too much already."

Cash leaned even closer and asked in slow, deliberate tones, "Stanley, is your last name Langston?"

He felt the car immediately veer off onto the shoulder and then swerve back onto the road again as Stanley tried to turn his head and look back at Cash.

"Whoa, cowboy! Sorry if I distracted you."

Stanley began driving slower. He adjusted the rearview mirror to give a better view of Cash in the back seat. A minute passed.

Finally, the young man responded, "Yeah, my name is Langston."

Cash hesitated before continuing. "Langston from Morgan City?"

Then, with a sudden decisiveness, Stanley steered off the road into a gas station parking lot.

"Why are we stopping?"

Stanley killed the engine, turned, and looked back at him. "Maybe you just crossed a line you ain't supposed to cross. We're stopping so I can talk to you without running off the damn road. Now, why do you want to know stuff about me? How did you know I was from Morgan City?"

"So, that's where you're from, right? How many Langstons are there in that town? That's not a common name in Cajun country. I was just wondering if I knew your brother."

Stanley looked at Cash, who could easily see the tears starting to well up in the younger man's eyes. Cash tried to defuse the moment. "Hey look, don't get all mushy on me. It was just a simple question."

Cash felt shocked and surprised by the sudden transition in the young man's demeanor, whose voice now clearly trembled. "I don't get it! First, you sound like you don't give a rat's ass about my brother, then you start asking personal questions. What's with you, huh?"

"Hang on, hang on, sorry if I hit a nerve. I was just pickin' up on the conversation you started. Sorry. I'll just sit here and be quiet."

Stanley glared at him and roared, "Hey, don't give me that bullshit! You're going to tell me why you're asking!" In what seemed to be one motion, he pulled the keys from the ignition, stepped out of the car and reached for the rear door handle. He jerked the door open, and Cash could see his face had turned red and his hands clenched in fists. Raindrops dripped from his nose.

He poked his head into the backseat interior with his hand on the Glock pistol still in its holster. Cash leaned away from him as the young man shouted, "Look - I'm just a country hick from South Louisiana, but I'm not completely stupid. We been taught to look out for inmates who try to get too close. We were talking about my brother and now you want to know all about me and my family. How come, huh? You sorry bastard, speak up!" Stanley unsnapped the cover on his sidearm. His eyes bulged as he talked.

Cash's eyes darted in all directions, trying to form a response, but he could come up with nothing but the need to tell the truth. Maybe the thoughts about his brother, with the preacher's remarks running in the background, were just too much of an overload. Without the cuffs, he knew he could easily put a crease in this young man's head and be gone, but right now that was out of the question. He slowly slid away from the open door.

"Uh, yeah - alright, I'll tell you if you just calm down. I didn't have the least bit of interest in you until tonight when we started talking about your brother. I knew a guy in the Corps whose nickname was Whip. Toughest guy in our squad. He was from Louisiana, and he saved my life once."

Stanley wiped his eyes and frowned. "So? You haven't answered my question. Why are you wanting to know all about my family?"

"Not your family, just your last name."

Stanley cleared his throat and finally said, "Yeah, it's Langston. I'm Stanley Langston."

"And the guy I'm thinking of was Gerald Langston. We knew him as Whip Langston. Grew up in Morgan City. Say, can I get out of the car so we can go inside somewhere and talk?"

Stanley reached again for his sidearm and said, "In the rain? Hell no! You think I'm crazy? Was that what you were trying to do? He started to close the door, but then he continued, "You probably saw my name on a sheet of department orders. So, give it up, man. What are you not telling me?"

"Okay, okay, I'll stay put. Just let me finish what I was saying, okay? Calm down. Whip told us he had a brother, a younger brother. And this younger brother's nickname was Smurf."

The look on the guard's face suddenly changed to a mixture of joy, anguish, anger, and pleading. The two men looked at each other in silence as unspoken words clearly passed between them while the rain kept pounding.

Stanley finally closed the door and sat back in the driver's seat. He took a handkerchief from his back pocket and wiped his face. He looked straight ahead through the windshield and said, "Nobody could have known my childhood nickname unless my brother had let it out." He swallowed hard and spoke through the handkerchief. "Was you there when he died?"

Cash continued, "No, I wasn't exactly there when it happened."

He glanced back at Cash and jabbed, "What do you mean, *not exactly there*? Either you was or you wasn't!"

Cautiously, Cash continued. "I had just gotten there on my first deployment. We were in the middle of a firefight when the wind kicked up and dust was blowing all around us. Couldn't see for shit! Hot lead is flying all around us. We knew the ragheads were somewhere out in front of us, but we had no idea if they were pulling back or coming at us. Turns out, one of them was so blinded and disoriented, he tripped over our sandbags and fell right on top of me. He stood up and was about to club me with his rifle butt when Whip put a .45 round right through his ear hole. Almost blew the guy's head off. Blood and brains all over the place."

Stanley had now turned to face the back seat and managed a smile, then a grimace. Then he said, "But you haven't told me what you meant by *not exactly there*. Where was you when he died?"

"Okay - The wind finally stopped, we got rid of the dead body, and cleaned up our space. The platoon leader asked me to get in the Hummer that had just arrived and go help load a pallet of ammo we had been waiting for. Your brother made a joke and said he thought I probably couldn't lift anything without wetting my pants. He was probably right. So, he went instead. He got in the Hummer, and that's the last I saw of him. He was doing me a favor, and it cost him."

The silence stretched into a minute as the two men stared off into empty space. For what seemed like an eternity, neither man said a word.

"Why did you get out?" Stanley finally asked.

"I had just checked out of the VA hospital, and I got into an argument with a young, silly-ass lieutenant."

"An argument? That's all?"

"Well, after I punched his lights out, they gave me a choice. Written apology with dishonorable discharge or time in Ft. Leavenworth."

"No shit? Man, I can see why you and Whip got along so well."

Then, as if reading each other's thoughts, Stanley rubbed his eyes again, put the car in gear, and pulled out onto the road.

Three weeks later, they both returned to the AA meeting. As they left the building at the end of the meeting, Cash noticed Stanley talking intently to Reverend Watchword while the preacher gestured wildly. He was apparently preaching a private sermon while Stanley pointed his finger at the preacher's chest as though unloading a ton of bottled-up feelings and emotions.

On the drive back to Angola, Cash mustered up the courage to ask Stanley what the preacher had been telling him.

Stanley's response was visceral. "Oh, I told him all right! I told him all this holy bullshit was nothin' but just that! Bullshit! Why did my father have to die? Huh? He lost Whip, but he still had me! Don't I count for nothin'? I asked the preacher what God thinks about that, and he couldn't answer me. When it comes right down to it, he ain't got the answers to nothin'!" Stanley's words sprayed droplets on the windshield in front of him. "And I'll tell you something else, Warden Faircloth can just kiss my ass if he thinks I'm going back on another one of these baby-sitting trips!"

Cash worded his next question cautiously. "Did that preacher really get to you?"

Stanley's line of vision repeatedly shifted from the road to the rearview mirror, and Cash could see the rage reflected in his eyes, eyes that had a vocabulary and message all their own.

Ironically, the next day, Cash's sentence was reduced to three years with the strong possibility of finishing the last six months of his sentence at Angola's Work Release Center nestled on the quiet grounds of Camp Beauregard, a National Guard Post, in Pineville. He remembered what Rusty had told him about it. If that possibility indeed materialized, he would be within a ten-minute drive from the very place he had been arrested. Alexandria glowed brightly just across the Red River bridge from Pineville.

He saw his lucky break when the news came weeks later. The Warden called him into his office and said with piercing eyes, "Well, you got your wish! You're going to Camp Beauregard and damned if I know why! I'm not buying it for one second," Faircloth had said bluntly. "That marine hero crap doesn't float with me, and I know you'll fall off the wagon and do something stupid. You've kept your nose clean around here, but I've seen your record, and you're no angel." He had not a hint of compassion on his face. "I'll take even odds that you'll find a way to screw yourself." He stopped and looked at Cash as though what he had said was so monumental as to require time to sink in. Cash started to speak, but decided to let the man believe his own words. He gave the Angola Warden a weak smile and a nod, suggesting that he heard and understood the prophecy. It amounted to one last placating gesture before he left.

For the first time in what felt like forever, he held a hand worth playing. The season had turned—late spring was in the air, thick with the scent of second chances, and his thoughts flew to Julie like a reflex, sharp and sudden. His letters to her had vanished into silence, some returned unopened, others swallowed whole by the Angola abyss. He hadn't dared to call. Two and a half years had passed like a bad dream. Was she still out there, somewhere? And if she was, would she even turn her head, notice him?

Camp Beauregard occupied slightly more than 12,000 acres, surrounded on three sides by deep piney woods, untouched for decades. Legend spoke of a Confederate cemetery somewhere on the premises near the back perimeter, secluded in the underbrush, lost in the memories of the dead. The entrance to the Post faced the main highway that led to urban civilization in Rapides Parish, blessed with pine and hardwood forests and salt-of-the-earth people whose lives were not in any mad rush.

The Director's house was a short distance inside the main gate and surrounded by two acres of lawn, azalea beds, and sprawling old live oak trees, probably older than the house itself. It seemed larger by comparison to other houses Cash had seen in the surrounding neighborhoods during the ride there. The house rested on low pilings, had a high peaked roof, a porch that wrapped around two sides, and a porch swing at each corner. Wide flower beds graced the edge of the house along its entire perimeter. He saw tennis courts and a stable beyond the backyard.

The Work Release Center required only a short walk from the Director's house. It consisted of about five acres surrounded by a six-foot chain link fence, not meant to provide security or confinement, but to remind the residents that their temporary home had boundaries, just like Angola. A cluster of small, frame, shotgun-style buildings stood watch inside the fence, as well as weather-worn picnic tables, paint-chipped Adirondack chairs and two asphalt basketball courts. Torn, rotten netting draped the hoops, reminders of years past. Cash saw a few men in official-looking uniforms, but none of them carried guns.

The mission of the Center allowed inmates the opportunity to work out in society each day, returning to the security of the fenced enclosure each night, a halfway step to be rid of the emotional memories and encumbrances left behind at Angola and to gain a gradual renewal to a normal role in the public's eye. Before coming there, they carried the stigma of being inmates. At Camp Beauregard, they were trustees. The Center was not at full capacity when he arrived and only housed about a dozen men.

When Cash arrived, he reported to the office of the Director, a retired Air Force Major by the name of Christopher Hamm. The Louisiana State flag and the Stars and Stripes hung loosely in opposite corners of the office behind his desk. On one side wall, Cash saw a bookcase filled with three-ring binders and books on Louisiana law. Pictures of military aircraft with flight crews covered most of the back wall. The atmosphere in the office had a smokey aroma like pipe tobacco, molasses, and old leather. The faded finish on the floor held a spiderweb of cracks.

Cash stood in front of the Director's desk with an alertness and clean-cut manner, very focused and attentive to the man who stood now in charge of his life, a man who carried the distinct demeanor of a ground-pawing rodeo bull that required cautious measure of every word spoken, every move considered, a man who instilled fear of stepping over an imaginary line. He had closely cropped grey hair invaded by a receding hairline. His bulldog face was full with the beginnings of a pendulous jowl supported by a thick, muscular neck. His eyes rarely blinked.

Hamm sat behind his desk and never took his piercing gaze off Cash as he spoke. His voice came forth in a raspy, penetrating tone that Cash found familiar. He harped, "My name is Hamm. H-A-

M-M. Major, United States Air Force, retired. My last assignment was over there across the river in Alexandria, a place called England Air Force Base. I helped to close it down. Thankless job. As of today, my goal is to teach you how to put things behind you. You've almost finished your time and you're here now and that means you belong to me, in a sense of the word, and I expect you to learn what's required of you and follow it to the letter. Understand?"

Cash nodded. Hamm continued, "We have a listing of local businesses that hire the likes of you, and we will find you a position. In Angola, you had no choices. Here you do, in a limited sense. But you step out of line just one degree, and you go back to the big house and none of the time here is counted as good time. I have a direct line to the Warden down there and I won't hesitate to use it. Understand?"

"Yes sir," Cash replied without hesitation. He looked down, shuffled his feet and then peered at the man behind the desk. He carefully asked, "How do we address you, sir? Is it Major Hamm?"

The Director looked at him and formed his words with unmistakable clarity. "How does Mr. Hamm sound to you, sonny?"

"Sounds wonderful, sir." Cash rocked slightly on his heels and smiled.

Hamm picked up a half-smoked cigar from his ashtray, and Cash immediately went to his pocket and brought out his lighter, igniting the flame all in one motion. The Director looked at him cautiously as he slowly accepted the gesture and said, "I haven't read your file completely, but there's something about you that gives me cause to wonder."

"About what, sir?"

Hamm took a puff on his lit cigar and studied him even closer before speaking. "Your reputation precedes you. The Warden said you could smooth-talk your way out of a throat-cutting. I'm waiting to see how you'll fit in here. I know why you were in, but now, listening to you, I can tell you're different."

Cash considered that's probably what he told all new arrivals. However, it was an open door to a dialogue that might prove useful someday. "How so? Am I in trouble already? I didn't think I was much different from anyone else around here, such as it is."

"How so? Such as it is? Nobody here talks like that. You're one of the few around this place who even knows how to make complete sentences."

Cash folded his arms and looked at the floor. He tried to stifle a slight grin.

Hamm cleared the cigar smoke with a wave of his hand, but without shifting his stare and said, "Never mind. You seem to act like a guy who's pretty damn sure of himself, hmm? Don't let that get out of hand, not around here. I'll give you a straight path to follow and there's no mercy for anyone who strays off it, such as it is!"

"Yes sir, I'll keep an eye on that."

"See that you do," he said flatly. "And one more thing, I'm not Warden Faircloth, so suckin' up to me will get you nothing but trouble. Got that?" Without waiting for an answer, he stood, looked past Cash, and yelled, "Rodney! Get in here!"

Within seconds, a tall, black man about fifty appeared in the doorway. He wore a fresh pressed gray shirt and trousers, and a tattered Houston Astros cap turned backwards, which he immediately took off before speaking.

"Yessuh? You call me?"

"I did. Show this fellow, uh, Ratliff, where the beds are. Help him find one and make sure there's an empty locker for him." He pulled the cigar from his mouth and gave Cash one last glaring look. "You don't mind a barracks environment, do you?"

"Not at all, sir. Quite familiar with it."

Cash could feel the eyes of the Director on his back as he left the office and followed Rodney. The Warden's words of doubt, spoken so recently, suddenly went rampant through his thoughts, playing tag team with Hamm's remarks. Clearly, he had something to lose here, something Angola could not have offered.

Chapter 2

Rodney took Cash to the next building, one supported on pilings that elevated the floor about three feet off the ground, silently calling attention to the decades since it was built. The wooden steps leading to the entrance begged to be replaced.

Through the squeaking screen door, Cash felt himself stepping back in time where soldiers trained and waited for orders to Europe, the Pacific, or Korea.

Two restrooms, one on each side of the main door, created a tunnel-like entrance. One of the doors opened and unleashed the sound of a toilet flushing. A man stepped out, fumbling with his zipper. Cash peered through the open door and saw austere porcelain features with abundant stains and rust, and with no stalls for privacy.

Beyond the restrooms, the sleeping arrangement resembled that of a classic World War II movie with one large, open room filled with thirty bunks, fifteen lined up on each side, and a center aisle down the middle of a freshly painted, gray wooden floor. The steel frame head of each bunk abutted the outside wall, accompanied by a moderately sized locker next to a window.

A handful of men lounged on their beds, reading magazines and smoking cigarettes. No one bothered to look up when Cash walked in. Half the beds looked unused. There was no air conditioning, just fans, a big one in two corners and one hanging from the rafters. After three years in a cell with closed boundaries, the openness of the room with multiple beds seemed out of place.

"Which bunk you want?" Rodney asked politely. "We got plenty."

Cash looked for one in a corner away from the others and found one that suited him. The mattress lay curled up at one end of the frame. "This one, I guess."

"Hang on a second," Rodney said. "I'll get you some sheets."

Staring at the naked mattress, he said flatly, "No thanks, uh, Rodney. May as well just tell me where they're stored, and I'll get 'em."

Rodney replied with an air of pride, "No suh, that's my job. Boss tells me to fix you up, and that's what I do. I can't have him see you doing what he told me to do. You just wait here and I'll be right back."

Cash nodded, unrolled his mattress, and sat on his new bunk. He pulled his duffle bag up on the bed beside him and began pulling out what few clothes he had and stacking them in a wadded, wrinkled pile, along with a couple of magazines and a few toiletries. It summed up all that he owned, his entire collection of earthly possessions. Hopefully, it would be a beginning. He leaned down, slid the empty duffle bag under the bed, and raised up to see three of his future bunkmates standing ten feet away, sizing him up.

"Howdy," he said quietly without making direct eye contact. "My name's Cash."

The three stood motionless, as though their feet were nailed to the floor. One took a long draw on his cigarette and blew smoke from his nostrils. Another chewed on a toothpick. After several seconds, a third one said, "We go by last names around here with the new guys. We'll let you know when we want to know your first name."

Cash glanced upward at them and said, "Okay, my last name

is Ratliff. What's yours?"

The one nearest declared, "That's for you to find out when the time comes. And just so you know, we ain't nobody's woman around here. We left that back in Angola."

Cash never moved his eyes from the one who had spoken. He wiped the back of his hand across his nose and said with no expression, "Sounds fine to me. The thought of it never occurred to me. I can get with the program as easy as anyone." He finished with a wide grin that provoked no response.

As he turned his attention to the pile of clothes on the bed, he sensed that two of them had taken a step closer. With that, he unbuttoned his shirt and peeled it off along with the sweaty t-shirt beneath it. The fiery Marine Corps dragon on his shoulder blade and the thick scar on his neck sent a silent message. Slowly, all three backed away while keeping their eyes on him.

Cash returned his attention to the small stack of clothes on the bed. "Nice talking to you," he said casually without looking back.

The locker assigned to him was twice the size he needed. He always traveled light and not by choice. Within minutes, Rodney appeared with sheets, blanket, and a pillow.

"I hope you'll be comfortable here," Rodney said. "I should tell you, everyone here is always careful around new people."

"Even you?"

Rodney just nodded.

"How long you been here?" Cash asked.

"Three months. So far, so good."

"Sounds like everyone makes it to the end, right?"

"Almost everyone. Once in a while, somebody goes sour."

"Like how? This seems so much better than back at the other place."

"Some people just don't get with the music. Last month, one guy had a furlough for three days." Cash looked at him with a question on his face. "We get furloughs every now and then if Mr. Hamm approves it. But anyhow, five days later, this guy with the furlough, he calls Mr. Hamm from somewhere out of town and apologizes, saying he'll be back the next day. Mr. Hamm was really pissed and told him to git to the nearest Sherriff's office and turn hisself in. Man, you could hear Mr. Hamm screaming from here to Shreveport! That guy, he never came back. He's back at the big house now and he was just three months away from getting out."

"What was his name?"

"Rusty."

Rodney's short epistle about Rusty held Cash's attention like a magnet. He saw immediately that he needed to learn which way the wind was blowing if he wanted to finish the course.

The first few days went by with no opportunities for conversation with the others. From their viewpoint, they had little to talk about, even though Cash was bursting with questions about the daily grind. He excelled at reading body language and the message clearly told him that new friendships would require some coaxing and patience, maybe even more than he needed at Angola. He spent time perusing what thumb-worn reading material he found lying around in the game room and the rest of the time just ambling around inside the fence enclosure, watching the grass grow. Outside the fence, the nearest tree line grew several hundred yards away like a spiritual mirage except for an occasional sentinel oak or pine tree up closer, but the audible breeze through the crowns of the distant pines sounded like faraway angels whispering. Further down the road and past the enclosure stood several old Quonset hut buildings with tall weeds growing around them, each one with its own story. The whole scene seemed uncommonly quiet with only occasional bird calls, croaking frogs, and practically no traffic noise. As yet, Cash did not have an outside job, but he could wait for the assignment. This was easy time. Every day, with or without employment, brought him one day closer to his release. The only person who said much of anything to him was Rodney and that was only when absolutely necessary. Usually, he got up each morning, went to breakfast, walked around outside, and went back to his bunk to stare at the ceiling. His time after lunch and supper were no different.

Finally after a week, a new arrival came through the front door of the sleeping quarters, with Rodney close behind, as usual. Cash estimated him to be about six feet tall, close to 250 pounds, with a headful of fiery red hair that matched his shaggy beard. He chose a bunk in the corner opposite Cash's and, with one hand, dumped out the voluminous contents of his overstuffed duffle bag. He didn't seem interested in anyone else, even when he stripped down to his underwear, pushed his pile of clothes aside, and climbed onto the bed. That's when Cash saw that he had arms and legs like an Angus bull. He looked to be in his early 30's. From beneath the heap of clothes, he pulled out a magazine that displayed a cover photo of a hunter with an eight-point buck draped across the hood of a Chevy pickup truck. Cash waited several minutes while the man read, and then walked over to him to introduce himself.

"Hi, my name's Cash Ratliff," he said with his hand extended. The newcomer slowly lowered his magazine and answered, "Kelly, Oscar Kelly." He raised his magazine back up to eye level and resumed his reading.

Cash rubbed his hands together and said, "Nice to meet you, Oscar. Maybe we'll talk later."

The man answered with a long sigh and a flip of the pages.

That evening, everyone gathered for supper served on long, plantation style tables. Cash was the last one in line, and he saw all the residents seated on one side of the room, except for Oscar Kelly, who sat on the opposite side surrounded by empty chairs. Seeing his opportunity, Cash loaded up his plate and found a seat directly across from the redhead. The two sat in silence for five minutes until Oscar finally spoke without lifting his eyes from his plate.

"Okay, I'll take the bait. What do you want?"

"Want? Nothing really, just trying to be friendly."

"Humph, why do I need to be friendly?"

"You want me to move?"

"Suit yourself."

"Okay, in that case, I'll stay." Cash had half-stood as if to leave but now settled into his chair and tried to engage Oscar in conversation again. "Where are you from?"

Oscar raised his head and looked at him with eyes dissecting into Cash's brain. He finally answered, chewing a mouthful in slow motion, "Lafayette. But that was a while back. Why?"

"No reason, just wondering."

Oscar continued to study him and remarked, "Naw, everyone's got a reason. What's yours?"

Cash waited a few seconds before answering. He turned and looked at the other side of the room, then leaned forward and mumbled discreetly, "A guy has to know who he can trust. Can't figure out who that is without a little conversation, you know?"

Oscar put his fork down and grumbled with a frown etched on his face, "Nobody. I don't trust nobody. That makes it easier. I'd advise you to do the same." He picked up his fork and stabbed another bite.

Cash continued to lean forward and whispered, "You know, you're right about one thing. Just a lot of talk doesn't mean anything. I guess you need to watch what people do before you can trust them."

Oscar just grunted. He shoveled in the last bite, chewed with his mouth open and looked at Cash. He swallowed, wiped his lips with the back of his hand and stood to leave.

"You doin' anything after supper?" Cash asked.

Oscar leaned across the table and snarled through his teeth, "What is it with you, fella? Can't you tell I just want to be left alone? Huh?"

"Well, everybody's got to depend on somebody, you know? So far, I haven't found anyone here that fits that idea."

Oscar's voice suddenly boomed throughout the room. "And you think I just might be your bosom pal, right? Where'd you get that idea? Well, get this through your head!" He slammed his open palm on the table so hard it made the dishes rattle. "I don't want your company, I don't want to be your buddy, I don't want nothin' but to be left alone!" He looked across at the other side of the room and bellowed, "That goes for all of you!" With that, he turned and left.

After a few moments, Rodney and three other men from another table slowly got up and strolled across the room to where

Cash sat, digesting what seemed to be the rules of the house. The oldest one spoke first.

"Say, uh, my name's Tom Fontenot." He looked to be in his sixties, skinny as a rail with baggy pants. He began pointing to the others next to him. "This here is Lionel Richard, and that young feather merchant over there is Wendell Stokes. We call him Squirrel. You already know Rodney Hart."

Cash raised a few inches from his chair and shook everyone's hand. "Cash Ratliff. Pleased to meet you."

"Yeah, we know your name. Mr. Hamm told us right after you came in."

Cash motioned toward the door and asked, "Say, what's with him, the one with the wild red hair? What's his problem?"

Tom answered, "Who knows? He seems to have a lot on his mind."

Rodney stepped forward and said, "Give him time. He'll come around. I remember him from Angola. This ain't nothin' new. He'll soften up when he feels like it. Probably off his medications. Something simple as change of weather can do that to his kind."

Cash asked, "What do you mean by 'his kind'?"

"He's one of them kind that has fits, I forget what they call it."

"Epilepsy?"

"Yeah, that's it, except he has the kind where they don't have fits, they just zone out and can't figure out where they're at."

Tom chimed in, "Yeah, one time he got off his meds down in Angola and walked off the exercise yard and into the wrong cell block. He had no idea where he's supposed to go. Takes him a while to come out of it, but he does. Every time. He scares me, though."

"Scares you? How?"

"Anybody that big and that strong who goes out of control is like having a pissed-off gorilla in your bedroom. Never know what he might do."

"Has he ever hurt anyone?"

"Not that I know of."

Another three days went by, and nothing seemed to change in Cash's routine. He saw men leave around 7:00 in the morning and come back after 5:30 in the evening. No one talked about where they went or what they did. That weekend, he discovered that the fenced-in grounds included a horseshoe pit, some picnic tables, and a small tool shed. A nearby building appeared to be nothing but storage, but when he stuck his head in the open door, he saw one large corner cleared out to make room for a set of free weights for anyone wanting to pump some iron. That's where he found Oscar. He was curling weights that looked like wheels from a freight train. In one corner he saw a bench with a barbell rack at one end. The bench pad had black, cracked plastic coverings with bits of dirty, white stuffing peeking out. Cash found a chair and sat down.

"You lookin' to do some bench press?" he asked. "I'll spot for you."

Oscar looked at him for a moment and said nothing.

"It seems you've done this before."

Oscar just grunted.

Cash waited a few seconds, then moved his chair closer. "Say, ah, I didn't mean to bother you at dinner when you first got here. I'm just not one to sit in a corner and say nothing to a new face."

Without saying anything, Oscar went to the bench press and

began threading discs on the lifting bar. When he had racked up what he wanted, he looked at Cash and gave a subtle shrug. Cash took the hint and stood at the head of the bench, ready to hand the weight down to Oscar. He looked closely and then realized Oscar had loaded 150 pounds on each end.

"You gonna' bench 300? I don't know if I can lift that off the rack for you."

Oscar reached up and picked the bar off the rack with no help from Cash. Four rapid grunt-filled repetitions later and he parked it back on the rack and sat up.

Cash walked around to the foot of the bench and made sure Oscar could see his broad smile of approval. "My god! How did you do that? You've been doing this for a while, haven't you?"

Oscar remained straddling the bench and took in a deep breath. He studied the floor as though in deep thought. Finally, he answered meekly, "Yeah, sort of. Well, a few years back anyway. I started with a set at home. My dad bought it for me before he died."

Oscar's sudden willingness to talk surprised Cash, but he did not want to push his luck by asking too much. "I lost my dad a few years back. My mother, too. I know what it's like."

Oscar's voice had a challenging tone. "You sure about that? You know what it's like?"

Cash saw his opening for more conversation and asked, "So, what happened to him?"

Oscar studied him closely before answering, making Cash feel conspicuous and a little uneasy. "Oil rig blew up. Out in the Gulf. First day on the job."

"Man, that sucks. How old were you?"

"Fifteen, going on thirty, maybe," he mumbled.

"Must have been tough. Any other folks in the family?"

Oscar's face suddenly seemed to darken. He slowly stood and walked to the door just as three other trustees entered. He brushed past them in the doorway with the finesse of a bull elephant.

"What's his problem?" one of them asked. They turned and watched him amble toward the main buildings.

"Let it go," Cash said. "I just asked him a heavy question."

The two in the door chuckled and one of them asked, "Did he say, 'not guilty' or 'go to hell'?"

"Huh?" Cash didn't quite grasp the meaning.

Squirrel answered, "That's what eventually comes out around here. You ask someone what they're in for and they'll tell you what the court said, but no one here says they're guilty. We're all innocent."

The others snickered quietly. The group seemed to be in a jovial mood. A few more faces came through the door, following the sound of soft laughter.

Cash continued, "No, we were talking about something else. I think I pushed the wrong button."

Squirrel continued, "So what did you do to get in here?"

"Well, I am guilty as hell," Cash said flatly. "Got drunk, found a car with the keys in it and took a ride. Seems like every police car in town was after me. I finally stopped and should have gone quietly, but I was too drunk to think straight. A couple of those boys in blue ended up in the ER."

Tom spoke up and asked, "Where'd this happen?"

"Across the river right over there in Alexandria. They finally caught me in the parking lot by the Alexandria Mall."

"Who would be dumb enough to leave the keys in the ignition?"

Cash scratched the back of his head and chuckled. He looked up and said with a big grin, "The Chief of Police. It was his car, his family car. I guess he had stopped to just run inside for a second."

A stream of laughter burst from the entire group which had now grown to more than ten men, all listening.

"You stole Chief Preston's car?" one of them asked with an astonished look.

"Yeah, he probably thought it was safe where it was."

They all looked at him with eyes that begged him to finish the story.

"So, where was it?" Tom finally asked.

"In front of the Police Station."

Cash could tell from the roar of laughter that he was now a welcome member of the group.

"And what's more, I didn't notice his wife passed out drunk in the back seat. I pulled over and stopped when she started bangin' on my head with her purse."

At this point, most were rolling on the floor, laughing. It occurred to Cash that Angola was never like this. Given the chance, men will find something to bring them together in a spirit of hope.

Tom continued, "Yeah, and that police chief knows the names of every one of us in here. Cash, my man, you're in deep shit if you think you're going to find work in these parts."

"Don't worry about me. I'll manage."

That evening, approaching 9 PM, Cash felt like having a moment of solitude and walked along the inside of the fence line, deep in thought about his future. From somewhere in the darkness, he heard a voice in forced whisper tones.

"Psst! Hey, Cash!"

Cash stopped and peered into the ink black night. After several seconds, he took two more steps.

"Psst! Hey, over here!"

He stopped and looked again. Nothing. "Whoever you are, come out where I can see you."

From behind a large pine tree outside the fence, he saw an emerging silhouette coming toward him. The mystery man stayed half hidden in the shadows, but his fair complexion and red hair made Oscar Kelly stand out in the dark like a roman candle.

Cash hissed under his breath, "What are you doing out there? Man, you better get back inside the fence before Hamm sees you! How'd you end up out there?"

Oscar whispered back, "The gate was open during the day, and I didn't know they locked it at night. I tried to get back in and now I'm stuck."

"No, you're not. There's a gap in the fence about a hundred feet from here. C'mon, I'll show you. Hurry up!"

Cash quickly led Oscar to a spot where the bottom of the fencing wasn't tightly secured to the post. Both men struggled to raised it up and Oscar almost slipped through, snagging his pants on the wire.

"I'm caught!" he whispered loudly.

"Hang on, let me get my hand in there."

Voices came from the shadows in the direction of the sleeping quarters.

"Hurry, man!"

With a strong jerk, Cash freed Oscar's pants from the wire snag, ripping a small hole in the fabric. Like a returning prodigal, Oscar scrambled through looking highly relieved.

"Oh, my God! That was a scare! Thanks, man." He turned and started to walk toward the sleeping quarters, but Cash stopped him.

"Where did you think you were going? I think you owe me an explanation. Why were you out there?"

"I told you. I didn't know they locked the damn gate."

"Bullshit. Where were you going?"

"Look, don't tell nobody. I just screwed up, ah, just a stupid move. I wasn't going nowhere. Honest. I just saw an open gate and I walked through it."

Cash looked at him through skeptical eyes. "Okay, now listen to me. We're gonna' walk back to the building slow and casual like. Just walk like you don't give a damn about anything. Look at the ground and kinda' shake your head a little, like you're thinking. The guards will see us, and they'll think we're just strolling along and talking. If you look worried, they'll start asking questions. Hang on, let's brush the dirt and grass off your clothes." Seconds later, Cash continued, "I could get in a little trouble for letting you back in, and only a little, but they'd be haulin' YOUR butt back to Angola if they figured out what you were doing. Just stick with me, okay?"

By now, the darkness was even more intense. Curfew loomed just seconds away. As they approached the buildings from out of the shadows, one of the guards said, "You two are cutting it close.

Better get inside."

Both men waved and smiled.

Cash had a new friend. About an hour later, he had to ask the question. "Oscar, you seem like a different person from what I saw earlier. What happened?"

"I found my meds," he said. "I been on them for years and they got stuck in my bag somewhere during the move to this place. I couldn't find them."

Cash studied him for several seconds. "You seemed to be bothered when I mentioned family. What's the deal?"

Oscar rubbed his eyes, peered off into the distance, remembering. Finally, he said, "After my dad died, my mom remarried a little while later. The guy she married had been a good friend of my dad, but it turns out he was a real wimp. My dad could say BOO and he'd back off. But he turned out to be a real sonofabitch and he beat my mother. She wouldn't go to the cops, so I took care of business myself."

"You look like you probably could do that," Cash said with a weak smile.

"When I was done with him, mama got all teary eyed and took his side. That was my first trip to juvenile court. Later, the two of them kicked me out of the house when I was sixteen. I lived with friends, one after another, until I graduated from high school. But, before that, I got picked up for shoplifting when I was seventeen, did some community service, and then later I stole a credit card from one of the guys I was living with. That one got me two years. I stayed clean until this guy I was working for - I was doing sheet metal work - he accused me of taking money out of the petty cash drawer in his office. I had no alibi and he had witnesses who didn't

46

like me. So, here I am. I'm finishing up five years. When I get out, I'm going to find those lying bastards and…"

"Not so loud! Don't talk like that here! They look for excuses to send people back to the big place."

The weekend passed, Monday morning blossomed, and Mr. Hamm called Cash into his office. The Director's words had an unexpected tone. He seemed pleased about something. "I got something for you. Hope you don't mind yard work."

Cash crossed his arms and looked at the ceiling. "Yard work? Sounds like that would be really redeeming."

"You want to be a wiseass? This is honest work and it'll get you out into the community. That's why you're here."

Cash hooked his thumb in his pants pocket and muttered, "Yeah, I'll bet."

"Or I could get you a job washing dishes. There's plenty of those around."

With a disgusted look, he said, "Okay, tell me about it."

Hamm stared at Cash cautiously, then continued, "Argyle landscaping. Got an office in Tioga, just a few minutes from here. Tioga, that's over by – oh, that's right, you already know your way around these parts." He sifted through some papers on his desk. "Grab a chair and start signing these pages where you see the 'X' on it. You're finally getting some legitimate work to do!"

"Argyle, I never heard of that one. That's a funny name for yard work."

"Yeah, but don't tell the old lady you'll be working for. She's a piece of work. Been a widow for a few years. But stay on her good side and she'll treat you right."

"Anyone else from here ever worked for her?"

Hamm looked up from his desk and said, "Yeah, but that one didn't work out."

"What happened?"

"Never mind. You don't need to know."

"What about Oscar? Found anything for him?"

"What do you care? He'll get work when we find something that fits him."

I guess that means yard work is what fits me, Cash thought.

He turned to go but looked back at Mr. Hamm and said, "By the way, there's a spot in the fence that could use some repair. It's up in the northeast corner. Barely hooked to the post."

"Hmm, checking the fence, are you? How'd you know about it?"

Cash knew he could tell the truth with a clear conscience. He had seen it just a few days ago. "Oh, I was just walking around the grounds with nothing to do. You know how it is."

"Hmmm, anything else I need to fix around here?"

"Well, there is -"

"Get outa' here!"

Later that day, Oscar rushed up to him with a worried look and said, "They found it! That hole in the fence! They found it and they're fixing it now! What if they start asking me questions and -"

"Relax! I told Hamm I saw it earlier, which is the truth, actually. I was just suckin'up to him. You gotta' lighten up, man. Life's too short to worry the way you do." He looked directly at Oscar and asked, "But you haven't really told me why you were outside the fence."

Hearing his own words, it occurred to Cash that maybe Oscar

did had reason to worry.

That evening, when the rest of the men sat outside listening to the crickets, Rodney said, "I heard you got a place to work."

Cash turned in his direction and snorted, "Yeah, some old biddy with a landscaping company. Just what I need, an old grey mare with one foot in the grave, telling me to push a lawn mower."

Rodney cocked his head and asked, "Argyle?"

Cash answered, "Yeah, how'd you know?"

"Never mind, you'll find out soon enough."

Sophia Blessing, a widow in her late seventies, toughened by time and circumstances, opened a whole new paradigm for Cash. Her husband started a lawn service forty years ago with used and overhauled equipment shortly after his discharge from the Air Force, while she worked as a nurse at the Baptist Hospital in Alexandria. He built it into a thriving business, eventually overseeing ten mowing crews and one tree service crew. He died of a heart attack twenty years later and Sophia was determined to keep the business alive, even though the current work force had shrunken down to five mowing crews. Larger landscaping contractors had underpriced her on her commercial clients, leaving only private yards and one cemetery that the competitors didn't want. Most business owners would have given up and moved on. Sophia didn't. She had nowhere else to go.

When Cash arrived, he noticed her house looked about fifty years old, like a left over from another era. Old and tired. The paint peeled in long curling shards at various corners, and he noticed the deck boards of the front porch showed warps and cracks that usually arise after half a century of neglect. Many needed to be replaced. There were a few shingles missing from the roof.

She stood in the front yard when the car stopped and watched Cash get out. The driver told him to be there at 5 PM for his ride home unless he wanted to hitchhike back. He added that Mr. Hamm didn't appreciate people who couldn't keep a schedule, so he needed to be mindful of that and be on time.

Cash wasn't quite sure what to make of her on first sight. She wore big, faded green jeans, baggy around the legs and hips, with the cuffs rolled up several turns. Her top was a dirt-spotted LSU sweatshirt with loose threads at the wrists and neck, and a large, straw sunhat tied under her chin with a scarf. Her grey, curly hair complimented her complexion, a pale ruddy brown from lots of sun, but she sported a wide swath of bright red lipstick accented by large glasses with thick lenses. Cash couldn't decide if she reminded him of someone's old aunt or an old movie actress from a black-and-white film. When he finally spotted her footwear, he decided that old aunt fit the best analogy he could make. The shoes were a large, floppy, canvas variety with rubber soles and so worn out that her toes poked through the tips. They looked comfortable. He saw a thin line of black under the edge of her fingernails but tried not to stare. The cigarette between her fingers held a long ash that seemed determined to not fall off.

"Are you the convict they sent to work for me?" Her voice had the sound of a rusty bucket handle.

"I'm a trustee, yes ma'am. That's what they call us."

"Humph! We'll see about that. My name is Sophia Blessing. What's yours?"

"I'm Cash Ratliff. Nice to meet you."

She did not extend her hand, but rather looked at Cash like his clothes were on backwards. "C'mon, I'll show you what I want you to do."

As she led Cash around to the workshop in her back yard, he noticed her unsteady gait and a certain ramble in her stride which required that one watch her take several steps to determine exactly what direction she was headed. Her intent became obvious as she plodded toward a large shed with an open garage door across the front and a small standard door on the corner. The driveway looked sun-bleached with cracked asphalt. Through the door, he saw several large riding mowers parked and in various states of disassembly. The floor consisted of aged concrete with a patina of spilled engine fluids, accumulated over many years. When he stepped inside, he immediately noticed that the room harbored a faint smell of grease, oil, and grass clippings. Cash saw an elevated ramp that allowed the mowing machines to be at eye level while working on them.

"I need the oil changed in those three," she motioned toward a group in one corner, "And take the blades off of those over there and sharpen them." She then pointed to a tool cabinet that was home to every variety of wrench ever invented, plus what seemed like a few hundred different screw drivers. "The oil is in those boxes on the bottom shelf. I had to put them there so I could reach them myself."

Cash tried to be reassuring and said, "Can't be much harder than working on a Humvee, right?"

Sophia paused and stared at him with a blank gaze. "Am I supposed to be impressed with that?"

"No, ma'am, I just don't want you to worry about what I'm doing. I can handle it."

For the next few seconds, she stared at him like he stood on some kind of slave trading block. She put her cigarette out on the floor and finally said, "You'll spend a couple of weeks working here at my house before I let you go out with the mowing crews. I gotta' know what I'm dealing with." She turned toward the house but stopped and looked back. "Let's see if you turn out any better than the last one they sent me." As she continued toward the back door of the house, she muttered, "Trustee, my ass."

Cash took that to mean he would be on probation for a couple of weeks before she could trust him. No problem, small steps at first. Easy money.

At noon, Sophia came back to the shop to check on Cash's progress and found him reading a magazine he had discovered in a pile of discarded rabble. She immediately took alarm at his apparent inactivity but then stopped for a closer look. All the assigned work seemed to be done, and there was a certain semblance of order to much of the surroundings. On the pegboard, previously empty, hung all the tools according to function and size, and he had tossed all the empty cans and cartons in a large trash barrel.

"You sharpen those blades like I told you?"

"You could shave your legs with 'em now, ma'am."

Sophia squinted at him with an intense look that slowly changed into a devilish grin. "So, they sent me a smart ass, huh? Wash up and come to the house. I'll fix you some lunch."

"I have a question," he asked as she was about to go. "You said before that you had put the oil where you could reach it. So you could reach it? Why you?"

It took a split second for Cash to realize he had stepped over a line he should have seen and avoided.

Her voice seemed to boom coming from such a frail body. She approached him and stopped within inches of his nose. Then she said with undeniable authority, "Who in the hell do you think does the work around here when everyone else is home watching football or playing bedroom canoodle? Huh? I know every inch of these machines! Now you've gone and put things where I can't find them anymore when you're gone!" With that, she turned and headed back to the house.

Minutes later, Cash stepped through the back door and into the kitchen—and found himself caught off guard by the sheer scale of it. The room was enormous, more like a ranch cookhouse than a widow's kitchen. A wide center island dominated the space, its worn wooden top scarred with years of chopping and meal prep. Suspended above it, an iron rack hung heavy with a dozen or more pots and pans—cast iron, copper, steel—all swaying slightly with the door's closing draft, like a culinary wind chime.

Against one wall sat a stove so large it looked fit for a firehouse or a roadside diner—eight heavy gas burners on top and an oven below that could have easily roasted a whole hog, maybe two. The exhaust fans hissed faintly, as if alive and waiting. At the far end, a door stood ajar, revealing a walk-in pantry spacious enough to serve as a spare bedroom—though the shelves inside were mostly bare, dotted with a few cans and mismatched jars, like forgotten soldiers in retreat.

Cash gave a low whistle, half-impressed and half-surprised. "Hell of a kitchen," he muttered.

As if on cue, Sophia entered the room, stopped and looked around as though seeing it for the first time. She cleared her throat loudly and said, "Yeah, there was a time when it wasn't big enough. I had five growing kids and a bunch of work crews to feed. Now the kids are all grown and gone, and the work crews – well, that's another story."

"So where are the kids now?"

"Never mind that. I'm going to fix you a sandwich and then you're going to tell me all about yourself. You're on a trial period right now, you know."

Cash made an exaggerated frown with arched eyebrows at the sound of the word 'trial' and said, "I hope it's a short one. How many witnesses you got?"

"You got a sense of humor, I see."

"So, who was your last trustee here? The one that apparently didn't work out?"

"Never mind."

With that, she focused her attention on the center island and in what seemed like less than a minute, had two hefty ham sandwiches stacked and on the table. She handed Cash a glass of iced tea and picked up a small, empty glass for herself. Before Cash could take the first bite, she returned to the table with her glass filled with ice and an amber-colored liquid. Cash took note of it but said nothing.

"So, why were you in the joint?" she said with piercing eyes as she took a long, slurping sip of Johnny Walker.

An hour later, Sophia was working on her second glass of scotch.

"So, your parents are dead, you grew up in Colfax, did some time in the Marine Corps, got in trouble, and now you know how to kick ass. Anything else I should know?"

"Nothing much," he said with a shrug.

"You expect me to believe that? There's always something more."

Cash was convinced this woman could not be overwhelmed,

but now he saw his opening.

He leaned forward as though he had a big secret to tell her. "Okay, if you ever lose your car keys, I can show you how to hot wire your car to get it started."

Sophia never blinked an eye. "You ever go to college?"

Cash sat back and rubbed his chin. Then he chuckled and said, "Never saw the need. Why pay money to get a piece of paper that doesn't mean much of anything? I saw college guys in the Marine Corps, and they didn't act any smarter than the rest of us."

"You don't think much of yourself, do you?"

Cash shifted uneasily in his chair. "What do you mean?"

Her voice had the blare of an old bugle. "I'm looking at someone who can't see past his own nose. What are you going to do when you get old and tired like me?"

Cash tried to sound solid. "I saw my grandfather retire to a rocking chair, watching the world go by and swatting flies on the front porch. He had a college degree, worked all his life, and what did it get him? I think he died of boredom."

"And your answer to that was Marines and jail time."

"Never a dull moment," he concluded with a grin. "Some jealous boyfriend is probably going to get me in the end."

"Is that your story? Nothing else?"

"Yes, ma'am, plain and simple. But you haven't told me much about yourself."

"Hey, I'm asking the questions here! You'll get to know me better as time goes by." She took another draw on her cigarette. "I can't believe you stole Bob Preston's car! For a guy who thinks he has all the answers, that was a purebred, registered case of supreme dumbass! Does he know you're back in town?"

"That was three years ago. You think you could cut me some slack?"

"I asked if he knows you're back in town?"

"Shouldn't I be getting back to work now?"

"Answer my question first."

Cash shifted in his chair. He wasn't used to being backed into a corner like this. Especially not by someone like her. "Well, he's across the river, so yes, I would guess he has his connections with that kind of information."

She looked at him warily and said slowly, "Right. So, we're done talking. You need to get back out to the shop. Hurry up! Look at you! First day and you're already a slacker!" She laughed hard and ended it with a cough that sounded like an old cappuccino machine. In a nearby trash can, she spit out a large wad of blood-tinged phlegm. While probing and searching in her pockets, she raised up, looked around, and said, "Where are my damn cigarettes?"

Chapter 3

The next morning started as a routine day in the breakfast line, unremarkable, almost peaceful. Cash found himself looking forward to his second day on the job. Granted, Sophia was a quirky sort, but in a disarming, charming sort of way. She seemed genuinely interested in Cash's past and had an almost intuitive grasp of his present state of mind.

Cash and the driver left Camp Beauregard on time and, in minutes, turned the corner toward Sophia's house. As her house came into view, cold shivers snaked down Cash's spine and old memories sprang to life. Red and blue lights flashed everywhere.

"What the hell?" the driver exclaimed. "Three Sheriff's patrol cars and an ambulance?"

In her night robe, Sophia sat near the back of the ambulance while an EMT technician tended to something on her forehead. Police-band radios hissed and crackled in the background. Cash and the driver got out of the car and stood back, watching several deputies canvassing around the shop, sifting through the shrubbery, inspecting the grass near the driveway.

Cash let a long minute elapse, then stepped forward and spoke to Sophia. "Are you okay? What happened? What's going on here?"

"Someone tried to break into the shop last night, in the wee hours of the morning, about 5 AM. I could hear them rattling around out here trying to get the damn door open. I walked out with a flashlight and yelled at them. I think there were two of them."

Cash looked closer at her scalp wound.

"I'm fine," she said. "These youngsters want me to go to the ER, but I'm not going. What will they do? Give me some pain pills that put me to sleep, and then send me home? No, I'm not doing it."

He pointed to the cut on her head. "How did you end up with that? What happened to your head?"

"I came out here to see what was making the noise and just stumbled into them. It was dark, and I don't know what they hit me with, maybe a tree limb or a brick." She rubbed her head as she spoke. Her voice remained calm but with steel beneath it, unshaken, in total control.

Cash watched the deputies as they continued looking. One of them picked up a small linear-shaped metal item from the grass and looked at it with squinted eyes.

Cash said openly, "Say, you know what that is, don't you?"

The deputy looked at Cash, irritated at being interrupted. "Piece of wire. It's nothing, just some kind of trash or something," he said.

He was about to toss it back into the grass, and Cash stopped him again. "Don't throw it away. That's a lock pick. Here, I'll show you."

He took the pick from the deputy and, within seconds, had the shop door open, then casually handed it back to the man.

"You seem pretty good at that," the deputy said as he stared at Cash's face. After a few seconds, he continued, "Say, don't I know you?"

Cash turned to walk away.

"Hang on a second. You look familiar. Turn around so I can see you."

Sophia had stepped away from the ambulance and came closer to listen.

The deputy sounded irritated, "Hey, you! Come back here! We need to talk!"

Cash ignored his words and stepped closer to the shop door. He pointed to the glass window on the door and said, "Look at this smudge. Someone leaned his face against the glass to see inside. Can't you get DNA off that?"

Two other deputies leaned in to follow the conversation. The first deputy continued, "Hang on a minute. I used to work for the Alexandria Police Department. Your face is so familiar to me. Yeah! Now I remember!" With that, he grabbed his handcuffs from his belt and bellowed, "C'mere, fella'. I don't know how you got here, but you're going with me!"

As he tried to grab Cash's arm, Cash deftly gripped the man's thumb and gave it a twist. The deputy grimaced with his mouth open in a silent moan. The other two deputies jumped in and pinned his arms back. Wisely, Cash didn't struggle.

Sophia yelled, "What the hell are you doing?" She pulled on the second deputy's sleeve. "Hey, I'm talking to you! Yes, he works for me! Let him go!"

The first deputy massaged his thumb and answered, "Okay, but first, I need to see something." While the others had a firm grasp on him, he unbuttoned the top buttons of Cash's shirt and pulled the collar down over his shoulder. The thick scar on his neck and his Marine Corps tattoo showed like a flag waving.

"I know you. We met a couple of years ago. I'm still seeing the dentist because of you. They gave you five years. What are you doing here?"

Sophia had heard enough. Her thin, frail body suddenly penetrated the middle of the small crowd of men. She pointed her finger at the deputy and said, "If you don't let him go, you're going to be in such deep shit, you won't be able to dig your way out before Christmas! You can stop right now!" She pulled her cell phone out of her robe pocket, dialed, and waited. The deputies paused when they heard her say, "This is Sophia Blessing. I need to talk to Christopher Hamm. Yes, right now!" A few seconds passed, and she resumed. "Good morning, this is Sophia Blessing. We have a police problem with Cash Ratliff. Can you talk to one of these deputies and set them straight? Your driver? I don't know. Maybe he didn't hang around. I don't see him."

She handed the phone over and stepped back. When the call ended, half-hearted apologies flew in all directions, and she knew the lame excuses would follow.

"Stop, I don't want to hear any of that crap," she exclaimed. "Find out who tried to break into my shop! That's why you're here." She started to walk away, but turned and took a moment to look at each of the deputies. "A wise, old woman once told me there's no such thing as a smart cop. I never believed her until today. Don't make it any worse!" She turned toward the house, and Cash followed her like an obedient child.

They never found the suspects.

For the next two weeks, he tackled Sophia's growing list of menial tasks. Several times a day, she made a point of drifting by the door to check on his progress. Cash immersed himself in organizing the shop so it felt like home to him. It had been a long time since he had had the privilege of arranging his surroundings the way he wanted them.

Occasionally, Sophia would question his actions, and he would gently reassure her that he only changed a few small details to make his own work go easier. She seemed pleased to hear that, although Cash still sensed a note of skepticism in her voice. Personal conversation was sparse until one day she brought him a lemonade and sat down to talk. As the dialogue deepened, he learned that she grew up in Virginia. Her five grown children ranged in age from forty to fifty-two, three boys and two girls. They were scattered all over the country, from Northern California to Tampa. John, her youngest, lived in Atlanta and worked for a computer software company. Sophia seemed to mention him more often than the other children.

She spoke with a tone of disappointment, "It's tough when you have children you raised, watched them grow up, get married, and then one day, POOF! They're gone, and their childhood just seems like a dream, like it didn't really happen. Sometimes I wonder why we raise them just to give them away to someone else."

Cash listened carefully and could sense her feeling of loss, the victim of circumstances she couldn't control. It occurred to him that loneliness does not confine itself to the walls of a prison. Not all prison walls are made of steel and stone.

As he moved from one day to the next, he felt a gradual freedom from the constant scrutiny of the correctional system. He finally had the space to reflect and confront the fragments of his past that he had long since abandoned. He was slowly making peace with his regrets, accepting the immutable truth that the past could not be rewritten. With each passing day, a quiet confidence took root—he started to believe in himself again. Yet, one unresolved matter clung to him, persistent and unrelenting. At last, summoning a big dose of courage, he drew a steadying breath, turned to Sophia, and asked, "May I use your phone?"

"You want to use my phone?" she croaked. "Don't you have a cell phone?"

"No ma'am. They're not allowed at the Center. We're only allowed to use the office phone, and they monitor who we call."

"So, if I let you use my phone, will I be breaking some kind of rule? What happens to me if I do?"

"I just want to contact an old friend I haven't spoken to in a while. Nothing dishonest, I assure you."

"Long distance?"

"No ma'am. Local."

"Someone you're supposed to avoid?"

"No, nothing like that. Nothing with criminal intent. Just a friend."

"What's her name?"

Cash broke into a weak smile. "Her name's Julie. We haven't spoken in almost three years. I wrote to her a bunch of times when I first arrived in Angola, but I never heard anything back. I'd like to give it one more shot."

"Wait a minute! If you think I'm giving you time off to go see her, you're crazy!"

Cash began to sound apologetic, perhaps a little pleading. "I'll be free and clear in a few months, and I just thought I might, well - you know - just five minutes on the phone, that's all I need."

Sophia stared at him with a familiar look, one Cash had become accustomed to.

"Go ahead. Five minutes, no more."

"Great! Thank you so much! I'll just finish up a couple of things here and then -"

"No, do it now. I'll be right here in my lawn chair. Five minutes, no more. Use the shop phone."

She ambled across the floor of the shop, sat in a worn-out folding chair, and lit a cigarette while Cash cleared a spot for himself on the workbench where the phone rested. From his wallet, he pulled out a crumpled scrap of yellowed paper and held it up to the light. He punched in the number, and after it rang twice, a woman's voice answered.

"Hello?"

Cash felt his pulse go up at the sound of Julie's voice. He cleared his throat and tried to respond without sounding apprehensive. "Julie?"

"Yes, who's this?"

"Julie, it's Cash, Cash Ratliff. Julie, please don't hang up. Please don't. I just wanted to hear your voice. I hope you don't mind. I'm just checking to see if you were still around."

"What? Why now? Aren't you still in prison? Wait - oh my God! You're out, aren't you? I can't talk to you! I just can't!"

"Hang on, hang on, I'm not out, but I am, sort of. I'm at this place where I work during the day and - and I'll be finally out in about five months, and so, I just thought I'd call and -"

"Cash, it's been a long time."

"Yes, it has been a long time. I wrote to you."

"I never got any mail from you."

Damn prison system, he thought. "Are you still in Alexandria?"

"Yes, I'm still in town." Her tone of voice had begun to grow barbs. "Cash, I don't know what you're thinking right now, but what did you expect me to do three years ago? Did you really think

I would just sit around and wait for you? I couldn't wait for you. You were in jail, Cash! When we were together, you were drunk most of the time. I don't know the real you, the man I might have been interested in. You brought this on yourself. Now, leave me alone!"

"Julie, I just – I just hoped that -"

"Cash – Cash – listen to me carefully. I'm married." A long silence followed.

"You hear me? You understand? I have my own life now." Her voice suddenly carried a gentle, firm tone. "Don't call me anymore." The line went dead.

He slowly lowered the phone from his ear and glanced over at Sophia. She puffed on her cigarette and spoke through a cloud of smoke, "Sounds like you just got shot down, buster. Spin, crash, and burn, by God! And here I thought you were tougher than that." She hesitated and looked for a response. Hearing none, she said, "Finish your chores and come inside. We've got time to talk before your ride comes to pick you up."

Cash spent ten minutes methodically putting the tools away, though he barely noticed what his hands were doing. His mind had bolted to another place, still stunned by the blow Julie had dealt. I'm married. The words echoed like a door slamming shut. Why hadn't she just given him five minutes? Something in her abruptness sounded like fear, perhaps avoiding a deeper conversation that might have pulled them both into an emotional undertow. And if that thought harbored any truth, then maybe, just maybe, there was still a crack in the door. Maybe he could reach her. But the finality in her voice - cold, practiced, unshakably firm- told him not to try crossing that threshold.

Sophia sat waiting in the kitchen. She watched him take a seat opposite her at the large breakfast table. For several moments, they both said nothing, and Cash nervously studied the palms of his hands. Then she finally spoke.

"Come sit over here next to me, you big clown."

Cash rose from his chair and stepped over the long bench where she sat. He slid down to within a few feet of her and said nothing.

"So, her name is Julie. I got that much from what I could hear. What's her problem?"

He shrugged and said, "No problem. Sounds like she's doing just fine."

"But you're not. What did she say?"

Cash cleared his throat. "Sophia, I had a drinking problem before I got arrested. I met Julie at a bar where a bunch of LSU students were having a party, and I sort of crashed into it. I guess I appealed to her at first because she didn't hesitate to go out with me the next night. We had a great time for a few months.

Sophia got right to the point. "Did you sleep with her?" She never did bother with fluffy details.

Up to that point, Cash had locked his eyes on the table in front of him until Sophia's question jarred his attention. He looked at her with a bit of amazement at her brazenness.

"Yeah, twice."

"How was it?"

"What do you mean? We had sex, okay? It is what it is. What more can I say?"

"Were you sober or drunk when you did it?"

Cash inhaled a long breath and let it out slowly.

"That's what I thought. A drunk man can't pay attention to a woman's needs. He's just thinking of himself. Were you drunk both times?"

He nodded slowly.

"So, she comes away thinking you had to be drunk to appreciate her value in bed. Nice going. Got no one to blame but yourself."

"Yeah, that's what the judge said when he read my case folder. He said it was time for me to face up to the consequences of my lifestyle."

"What have you had to drink since then?"

"Nothing. Never had the chance for a drink since then. The urge still hits me, though, once in a while."

"Stay out of my liquor cabinet, fella'. There's nothing in there for you."

"I don't even know where it is."

"So, what do you want to do about this ex-girlfriend?"

"Nothing. That bridge burned a while ago."

"Giving up so soon? I can't believe you would - "

"She's married. That's the end of it all. I need to move on." He started to get up from the bench.

"Sit down, young man! I'm not done talking to you." Sophia had a frown and a tone of voice she might use on a ten-year-old. "As I understand it, your time at the Work Release Center will be up before you know it. What will you do then?"

"Beats me. You got any ideas? Do I keep working for you?"

"On what little I pay you? Ha! Right now, the State of Louisiana takes care of your room and board. All I'm giving you is pocket change. I can't afford what you're going to need."

"You've got mowing crews that you can afford. What's the difference?"

"I've been baby-sittin' you. If you want to work for me, I need you out there with the working crews. They need to know if they can trust you."

"So, when do I meet them?"

"I need to talk to Mr. Hamm about letting you out of my sight all day. What do you think he'll say?"

"I have no idea. I can only hope." A slow smile came over his face. "I'd say he'll agree with whatever you've already told him."

That is when Cash realized this crafty woman had left the subject of Julie far behind them in the dust. He saw her drawing a picture of his future, and apparently had been since the day they met.

Cash wanted desperately to change the subject. "I have a quick question," he asked. "Where did you get the name 'Argyle' for your business?"

A slow smile came across her face. "My husband came up with that ridiculous idea. He loved Argyle socks, and I hated them. Without asking me, he had all the signs and cards made up with that name just to get my goat."

"And I'll bet you had something for him, right?"

"You bet your ass I did. We were taking a trip to Las Vegas, and the night before we left, I sewed the fly shut on all his underwear! We got on the plane, and he had to use the restroom. He came back to the seat, thinking he had put them on backwards. He had to wait until we landed and got to baggage claim. He almost wet his pants trying to hold it! Yes, sir, I got him!" She finished with a raspy laugh.

This is going to be a fun job, Cash couldn't help thinking.

The next morning, he walked out to the car for his usual ride to work. The driver said, "Mr. Hamm wants to see you. I'll come back and pick you up later."

Christopher Hamm sat at his desk with a pile of documents and notebooks in front of him. He clamped his cigar tightly in his teeth as he sorted through the paperwork. Cash knocked on the doorframe before entering.

"Ratliff? Oh, yeah. C'mon in. Mrs. Blessing wants to put you out in the public's eye with her working crews. Think you can do that?"

"I don't see a problem."

"It won't happen right away. She wants to change your hours so you're there when the crews first show up and they can get to know you. Your job will be to help them load up their trucks and see how their schedule works. That means you'll have to be up early to get there before they leave. Then, after a while, you go in later and stay later. That way, you'll see them when they come in at the end of the day, help them unload, clean up the equipment, and so forth. If that works out, you'll start going out with them a couple of days a week, then we'll bump it up to full-time. In the meantime, you just keep doing what you're doing at her shop. Understand?"

"Absolutely."

"How's she doing, by the way?"

"Seems fine. She's lonely, likes to talk."

"Lonely? She got friends all over town."

"Well, none that I've seen."

The next morning, he looked forward to seeing Sophia again. In a strange way, he felt a clear connection growing between them. Strange because of their age difference and also because she was unlike anyone he had ever known. Was the attraction just a novelty? Could the whole thing be just a matter of entertainment, something to fill a void in the half-empty lives of two people from totally different views of the world? No, there was something else with a pulse, something deeper, but he couldn't grasp what to call it. Two other trustees rode in the car with him that morning and were dropped off at an auto repair shop. He had seen this shop a few times before during his daily ride to and from Sophia's. He could see and smell and hear all the familiar bits and pieces of a mechanical shop and wondered why, for some reason, he had not been assigned to something like that. Maybe the system did not show that he had experience in that field. It didn't matter because he felt happy with the current plan. Today, that plan centered around meeting Sophia's work crews as they loaded their flatbeds and headed for neighborhoods where the hum of machinery would cut, trim, and otherwise manicure vast lawns of the rich folks in Alexandria.

Each crew seemed to be a diverse, miniature replica of the United Nations. He had found out that Sophia had a deep appreciation for the work ethic of other cultures, and they appreciated the chance to make themselves useful and showed pride in their work. He wondered if any of them were of illegal status.

Each trailer carried three mowing machines and several string trimmers with about a dozen gas tanks. The busy crews positioned every item in its exact place on the trailer beds and every time Cash would try to be helpful, he found himself simply in the way or just watching.

At one point, a small, slender worker almost dropped a two-gallon gas can, and Cash managed to catch it. In the process of handing it back, he saw the employee's sun hat fall backwards and reveal a bright young female face. She couldn't be over 100 pounds and handled things like a grown man twice her size. She smiled at him, dipped her face in a gesture of thanks, and continued with her task. Her driver uttered something that sounded Arabic, but Cash couldn't be sure. Upon hearing it, the young girl rushed to find a seat on the truck.

When the last truck pulled away, he stood there feeling totally useless. Sophia approached him from behind.

"What do you think?"

He turned, and his answer sounded distant. "They move like we did in boot camp. No wasted motion. I like it."

"So, you're probably wondering what you'll be doing the rest of the day. Is everything caught up in the maintenance department?"

"Yeah, I guess I could just stick a broom up my…"

"Watch your mouth, sonny boy! There's plenty to do. I need my own yard done. There's a push mower behind the shop and you've seen where the edgers are. Shouldn't take you long. Mind you, my yard goes all the way out to the main road and around the corner."

"Is this some kind of punishment?"

"Aw, quit your bitching. You've got all day. You'll be done and gone before the trucks get back."

Twice, while he maneuvered the 24-inch mower, she stood waiting at the nearest spot where he made the turn, holding a glass of ice water for him. He finished an hour later, with the sidewalk trimmed to boot. The azaleas had finished blooming, so they needed pruning and a dose of fertilizer. That filled out his afternoon.

Two weeks went by, and he found himself checking the schedules of each crew the day before and then looking to see if they had the right equipment the following morning. He also learned quickly that these crews needed no supervision. They knew their own routine, appreciated the employment, and worked hard to keep it.

Wednesday rolled around, and Sophia finally did something that surprised him. She called him in from the shop when the last truck had left and said, "Come in the house, I want to show you something." She led him into a room he had never seen before and sat him in front of a large rolltop desk. Faded floral curtains hung from the windows. One curtain rod dangled from brackets, ready to fall to the floor at any moment. Scraps of paper covered the desk along with other desktop items, and Cash wondered how she managed to stay organized. Everything seemed centered around a large notebook. Sophia pushed all the loose paperwork aside with one swipe.

Pointing to the notebook, she said, "This is our scheduling book. We need to make some changes, and I want you to call the customers and tell them. Let's see how you handle it."

Cash was still hot from being outside and wiping perspiration from his face as he listened to her instructions as best he could. "You want me to talk to customers?"

"Yes, I do. I think you'll be good at it."

"What makes you say that? What do I talk about? Any single women on the list?"

Sophia didn't miss a beat. "You see? That's the kind of imagination I'm looking for. Christopher Hamm told me you were a good talker. C'mon, you can do it."

"I'll have to thank Mr. Hamm for that recommendation when I see him. You know, I learned all this fancy bullshit talking stuff in the Marine Corps. I might slip and say something unmentionable."

"No, you won't. You're not that stupid."

"Thanks, but old habits are hard to break." He shook his head and said, "What if I get some whiny old woman on the line? I can't stand that."

"Look, you want to work for peanuts the rest of your life? Huh?" She tugged on his sleeve. "Answer me. No, answer me, don't look out the window."

"Sophia, I'll probably lose customers, and if they start asking me questions I can't answer, I just don't think -"

Sophia ignored his jailhouse excuses. "Okay, let's start with a simple one. This lady likes her yard done on Tuesdays or Thursdays. Right now, those are becoming our busiest days, and she is the farthest away from here. We need to convince her to change to Friday. Her name is Mrs. Guillot. There's her number. Call her and put it on speakerphone."

This had not been in the game plan, but the unexpected from Sophia did not surprise him anymore. She dialed the number, handed the phone to him, and he let it ring five times. Just as he was about to hang up, a woman's small voice answered with a thick Cajun accent.

"Hello?"

Cash cleared his throat and looked at Sophia with desperation on his face. "Ah, Mrs. Guillot, this is Cash Ratliff from Argyle Landscaping. How are you today? Is this a good time to talk for a second?"

"Yes? What's the matter? Didn't you get my check?"

Cash's eyes darted around the room, and he answered, "Oh, yes ma'am, I'm sure we did, but I wanted to talk....."

"You don't know for sure? Is that why you're calling? My daughter wrote the check, I'm certain. I watched her do it last weekend. Maybe she forgot to mail it. Can I call you back?"

"No, no ma'am, there's no need to do that, I'm sure it's stuck in the mail somewhere. You know how those postal workers are."

Her words were suddenly slow and very direct. "Listen to me, my husband was a retired postal worker, God rest his soul. He did that job for thirty years. He never lost a single letter. They gave him a certificate when he retired."

Cash looked at Sophia and saw a small hint of a grin. Yeah, two can play this game. "Okay, Mrs. Guillot, because your husband was such a good worker, we're going to start doing your yard on Fridays so it will look nice on the weekends. Is that when your daughter comes to your house?"

"Why yes, it is."

"I can see the look on her face now when she sees your beautiful yard."

"Oh, that would be nice!"

"Good, we're so glad to do that service for you. It will be just a couple of days out of the usual sequence, but once we get started on Fridays, it will be that day every week."

"From now on?"

"Yes, ma'am. From now on."

They both said thank you and hung up. Cash looked at Sophia and saw her doubled over, straining to suppress her laughter.

"Wonderful! You had that old woman eating out of your hand! Quick thinking! I like that! You see? You're good at this. Okay, here's another one. Same deal. We do hers on Wednesdays, and we need to switch to Fridays. Go ahead. Her name is Mrs. Caslick."

This call picked up after just two rings.

"Yeah? Who's calling?" The voice has fangs.

"Mrs. Caslick, this is Cash Ratliff from Argyle Landscaping. How are you today?"

"Who's this? Are you selling something?"

"No ma'am, we're the mowing company that takes care of your yard. I wanted to talk to you about a change in schedule."

"Okay, make it quick. I'm expecting a call from someone important."

"Of course, I'll get right to the point. During the peak growing season, we've been mowing your yard on Wednesdays, and we need to change it to Fridays."

"What for? No - wait, can't do that. I work from home, and in my business, I make all my conference calls on Fridays, and I can't have those noisy machines outside my window. No, that won't work."

Cash looked at Sophia, and she first shrugged, then gestured to Cash to talk some more. He read the word 'charm' on her lips.

"Mrs. Caslick, I must divulge a bit of a private matter in this situation. One of our supervisors has a sick wife who can only be treated on Wednesday, and we're trying to clear out his schedule, or we will have to let him go. His wife is really sick, and he has no insurance, and with four children, well, I don't know how he's going to manage. None of his crew speaks English, and they all agree they can work on Fridays. It's just a pitiful situation, and….."

"Good God! So, that's it? Fridays or nothing?"

"What time of day do you make your calls?"

"We start at 10:30 in the morning."

"What if we promised to be done by then?"

"You sure?"

"Absolutely."

"Okay. Oh, that poor woman! What does she have? I mean, what is she sick with?

Sophia clutched at her sides and motioned for Cash to continue. Tears of silent laughter rolled down her cheeks and she started to cough.

"Well, ma'am, she's right here in the office with me and I would put her on the phone to talk to you, but she has a terrible cough."

The timing could not have been more perfect. Sophia let loose with one of her familiar wrenching hacks that sounded like an old washing machine. Cash could almost feel the empathy ozzing through the speaker phone.

He struggled to suppress his own laughter and did the best he could to continue. "Okay, Mrs. Caslick. We'll be there on Friday and done by 10:30. Yes, you have a nice day as well."

Sophia recovered from her coughing spell in less than a minute, but still could not stop laughing. Every time she thought she had her composure under control, she would look at Cash and start again, tears and all.

Finally, she said with a clear voice, "I need a drink! This was great! You're hired!"

Cash sat back in the chair, looking smug, when she came back with a glass of scotch on ice. "I mean it," she said. "You're hired!"

"For what? What about me working with the crews?"

"This is your job from now on. You're going to be my office manager. That, and taking care of the machines like you've been doing. I'm stuck here all day long because I'm afraid to miss any calls from new customers. We need to grow this business to the level it was before it was -" Her voice trailed off.

"Before what?"

"Never mind." She took a long sip of her drink and repeated, "Just never mind. I need you here, not out there riding mowing machines. That is, unless you don't want a raise!"

The next morning came, and Cash arrived with an eager spirit, hoping to build on the personal equity he had found with Sophia Blessing. Faint, weak memories of his business class came to the foreground in his thoughts as he imagined more and more ways he could improve Sophia's revenue flow.

The driver dropped him off in front of the house, and his eyes immediately locked onto the child standing next to Sophia on the porch. She wore a simple cotton dress with a floral print, a narrow collar, and no sleeves. Her dark brown eyes and hair matched the ebony glistening of her skin. Both the child and Sophia shaded their eyes from the morning sun as Cash came up the front walk.

"Cash, this is Shauntae. Her parents work for me on the mowing crews. They're from Ghana. Shauntae is going to spend the day with us."

Cash slipped his hands into his pockets and strolled at a slow pace toward the steps with his eyes on the child as though she had to be approached cautiously. He wasn't sure of the brand of diplomacy needed in this situation. He leaned forward and looked at her, then at Sophia.

"Her parents had a slight glitch in their daycare arrangements," Sophia explained in a light, affectionate tone. "They had to bring her here. We've done this before. Not too often, but Shauntae and I are old friends, aren't we?" She looked down at the little girl and was rewarded with a broad smile that showed beautiful, straight, white teeth.

"How old is she?" Cash asked.

"I'm five years old and I'm going to be a doctor someday," the child said in perfect English. "And Miss Sophia said you're going to work on my coloring book with me."

Her response caught Cash completely off guard. His line of interest or experience certainly did not include children. This child, however, had an alluring magic about her that captured his attention like the first azalea bloom of the spring.

"Is that right?" he said. "How did you know I liked coloring books?" He looked at Sophia as the question gave Shauntae a moment to pause and think. Then he continued, "I have some work to do first, and then we'll talk about it."

The child's face dropped, and he could see a pout forming as the bottom lip started to protrude. Cash looked at Sophia, at a loss for words.

"Shauntae, Mr. Cash just got here. Let's give him a chance to get organized first." She gave Cash a wink and led the girl back inside. Cash made a beeline for the shop.

Thirty minutes later, Sophia came to the shop door and said, "I guess I sort of ambushed you this morning. Her parents had come to this country just months before she was born. Her father had been a schoolteacher, and her mother worked in a bakery. They arrived with Shauntae's maternal grandmother, who lives with them in a two-bedroom apartment.

"Shauntae is with us, that is, with me, because her grandmother is sick today and can't watch her. She's no trouble, and she'll be gone by late afternoon."

"Cute girl. How old is she, really?"

"She's five, just like she told you. And plays the piano."

Cash was holding a wheel from a mower parked on the work ramp, and he stopped talking long enough to heft the frame up and slip the wheel back onto its axle bearing. He gave it a few quick turns with a box wrench and then turned to Sophia.

"So, how are you going to keep her entertained all day?"

"She brought some books. She'll entertain herself. When you're ready to take a break, I'd like you to come to the house for a short while."

"Sure, what's up?"

"Details to follow," she said as she shuffled back to the kitchen door. Cash did not see the faint smile on her face.

An hour later, Cash cleaned his hands and went to the house as instructed. Shauntae was sitting at the breakfast table with a stack of books and a box of crayons, all crowded into a small space the size of a placemat.

Cash spoke up and said to her, "Here, let's give you some more room," and started to unstack the pile of books and spread them out over the table.

"No, thank you," she said, "I'm efficient. I don't require that much room."

He looked at Sophia and asked in a half-whisper, "How old did you say she was?"

Shauntae gathered her materials back into the stack she had created and walked into the next room. She returned, struggling with a portable keyboard about three feet long. Within seconds, she had it plugged in, and her little fingers flew across the keys like Liberace. All Cash could do was sit and watch in amazement. When she was finished, she turned and gave him a huge grin.

"Ah, Shauntae, that was nice. So, what was it?"

"That was Clair de lune. It means moonlight in French. I'm still learning parts of it. My teacher has me playing it in the key of G, but I think it sounds better in F."

"Ah ha! Yes, you're right! I can see that." His face was in a painted smile as he turned and looked at Sophia with a clown's grimace.

Shauntae continued, "Did you know the lyrics of Amazing Grace can be played with the same rhythm as House of the Rising Sun? The lyrics fit right in, it's the same tempo."

Doing his best to look engaged, he said, "No, I never would have imagined that! What a coincidence!"

He looked at Sophia again and mouthed, What is it with this kid?

Finally, Sophia came to his rescue. "Shauntae, you should go back to your coloring books. I have to talk to Mr. Cash."

The two adults walked into the living room. Cash noticed that she had her car keys out. "I have to go to the grocery store," she said. "I don't have her favorite item for lunch, and I really should get it. She loves peanut butter and jelly sandwiches."

"Okay. Yeah - but wait, while you're gone, who's going to – oh, wait a minute, I never agreed to be a babysitter. No ma'am, this isn't going to work. I'll go to the store and -"

"In those greasy clothes? Think again, buster."

"Sophia, I just can't take responsibility for a five-year-old child. I've never done it before. Oh, please, don't make me do this!" He felt like a five-year-old himself, begging.

Sophia spoke calmly, "As you can see, she's not a typical child of that age. She's stayed with me before and she's no trouble. She'll entertain herself and I'll be back in thirty minutes."

Seeing no alternative, Cash agreed, threw his arms up in surrender, and walked back into the kitchen. He was almost thinking out loud, How much longer do I have?

Shauntae turned and looked at Cash. "You want to color with me?" she asked.

Forty-five minutes later, Sophia returned, as promised, although a little late. She walked into the kitchen and found it void of human life. She checked the bathroom and down the hall – nothing. The coloring books were neatly stacked at one end of the table. She felt panic beginning to rise.

"Shauntae! Cash! Where are you?"

A man's voice answered that sounded like it came from a world away. She looked again in every room in the house and finally went out on the back porch. The shop door was open, and there was gleeful chatter coming from that direction. She walked quickly to the door and saw Shauntae standing on a step stool with a kitchen apron wrapped around her, a socket wrench in one hand and a spark plug in the other. The apron was smudged with streaks of grease.

"We're changing spark plugs!" she said with a voice of authority.

Cash shot a sheepish grin at Sophia and said to Shauntae, "Okay, put it right there in that hole and tighten it down like I showed you. Shauntae carefully gripped the plug in her fingertips and twisted it onto the threads. She looked at Sophia with a smile of accomplishment.

Cash pointed to a screwdriver laying on the workbench. "What's that?" he asked her.

"Phillips head," she responded.

"And this one?"

"Flathead," she said.

"Okay, let's finish with the air filter on this one. Where did you put it?"

She quickly hopped off her stool and retrieved the air filter from the box it came in.

Sophia's previous level of concern became one of benign amusement, watching the two of them thoroughly enjoying each other's company.

"We'll have her driving a John Deere in no time!" he said approvingly.

Sophia finally intervened and said, "Okay, Shauntae, let's go clean up and have some lunch. I got your favorite." The two of them, one skipping and the other shuffling, made their way to the back door and disappeared.

Cash joined them a few minutes later for lunch. When they finished, Sophia told Shauntae to go into the bathroom and wash her hands.

"She's a precocious little thing, isn't she?" Sophia remarked to

Cash.

"I guess so, whatever that means."

"She speaks Twi as well as English."

"Huh?"

"Twi is one of the languages of Ghana."

"I thought you said she was born here?"

"She was, but her grandmother still speaks only Twi around the house."

He returned to the shop and couldn't take his mind off what he had witnessed that day. Time passed quickly until his ride came that afternoon. He stuck his head in the kitchen door and yelled, "Hey, I'm done for today. I'll see you tomorrow!" Shauntae and Sophia came out of the living room and Sophia whispered something in the child's ear. Shauntae ran over to Cash, held her arms up, and gave him a big smacking kiss on the cheek when he bent down.

"By god, I think you made him blush, child!"

The next day, Cash arrived halfway expecting and hoping his new work partner would be there again. No such luck. Her grandmother must have recovered from whatever ailed her the day before.

"Too bad Shauntae isn't here today," he said.

"Yeah, she has a way of getting under your skin," Sophia replied. "Want some coffee?"

"No thanks, I've had mine already."

"That's okay, come and sit with me for a few minutes."

Cash took a seat across the table. He was beginning to see that Sophia needed daily conversation as much as she needed a worker around the machine shop. She took a sip from her cup and asked, "You've never been around little kids, have you?"

"No, I didn't have any brothers or sisters, and I was the only child when I was with my grandparents."

"So, your grandparents raised you?"

Her question sounded more like a statement. Cash wondered how she would know.

"I went to live with them when I was twelve."

"Because?"

Cash took a deep breath and looked out the window for a few seconds. "Do we have to talk about this?"

"No, I was just wondering. Where were your parents?"

He could see she wasn't going to leave the topic entirely. Clearly, she wanted to use a different approach. He rubbed his eyes and cleared his throat.

"Both of my parents were killed in a car wreck. I was with them. I came out with a broken arm, but they…"

"And so, you went to live with your grandparents. Your dad's parents?"

He thought, How would she know that? Lucky guess?

"Yeah, they were really getting up in years, and my mother's parents were even older."

"What do you remember about your parents?"

His eyes shifted around the room as though looking for something lost. Twice, he opened his mouth to speak, but hesitated.

"I'm sorry. I think I hit on a sensitive subject," she said.

"No, that's okay. It's just that – I just haven't, well, I don't think about them much."

"We can talk about something else."

"No, I don't mind. It's been so long ago. I remember my mother would cry a lot. Just out of the clear blue, I start crying. She took a lot of pills. I never knew what they were."

"How did your dad react to that?"

"I don't remember. He would take her into the bedroom, and I could hear them talking. Dad was soft spoken, so I couldn't tell what he was saying. Mom would start yelling, and then I could hear her crying again. It happened about every couple of weeks."

"When did it start?"

"I don't know. I can't recall when she wasn't like that."

"Sounds to me like you recall more than you care to remember."

Cash had said enough. He stood to leave and said, "So, you're wondering how I got to be in this situation, like, in prison and all that? Is that what you're working up to?"

"All I asked was who raised you. Sounds to me like you have lots to talk about."

Cash stood, scratched his head slowly, and said, "No, nothing I can't figure out myself." He gazed at the floor before continuing. "In answer to your question, it would be a safe bet to say I raised myself." He tried to act casual while Sophia never took her eyes off him. Suddenly, he found himself unable to look at her directly.

She seemed satisfied for the moment with his answer. Several seconds passed before she broke the silence. "Okay, I've kept you from your plans for today. Go out to the shop, get caught up, and come on back inside. I want to talk some business with you."

Later in the day, Sophia suggested that Cash spend the next

few days calling customers and introducing himself. He decided to use that opportunity to ask what they thought of the service. His alter ego appeared to have kicked in as he really seemed to have found a niche for his gift of gab and salesmanship.

"Have you considered how you want to attract new customers?" he asked her one day.

Sophia replied in a sober tone, "I wouldn't know where to start. I've been treading water for the past twenty years or so, just to keep what customers we have. We've lost all our commercial clients. The big guys simply outbid us. We couldn't function with the low prices they charge."

Cash thought for a minute, then spoke, "What about churches? Did you lose any churches?"

"No, I don't think we ever had any church clients."

For a moment, he was surprised that she wasn't sure about her answer. He said thoughtfully, "Let me see what I can do. I have a few ideas."

Sophia gave him a look that showed a mixture of relief and suspicion.

It took a great deal of calling and inquiry, but Cash found out that volunteer groups maintained the grounds of many of the small churches in town, and the larger ones were serviced by Sophia's competitors.

During one conversation that day, an idea came to mind. He found the number and called a large community church on MacArthur Drive and asked to speak to the office manager.

After a minute, a woman's stiff voice came on the phone. "This is Gladys Perkins. How can I help you?"

"Hi, this is Cash Ratliff from Argyle Landscaping. I wonder if you have time to talk for a minute?"

Gladys replied abruptly, "I suppose, what's up?"

Cash took her abruptness in stride. "We're trying to build up our clientele list, and we heard that you use one of our competitors for your yard service. We can make you a sweet deal if you're willing to hear it."

"Yeah?"

"Yeah, we'll give you a decent fee, and for every new private account you send us, we will chop two percent off our base price to you. Would that work for you? Send us enough and we'll be doing your grounds for practically nothing."

The discussion ran on for another fifteen minutes and they struck a deal. He walked into the kitchen to tell Sophia the good news.

"What?" Sophia shrieked. "You want to give away our service? Are you crazy? Are you out of your mind? What have you been smoking?"

Cash calmly responded, "It will give us visibility, something we don't have right now. Most of the people I've talked to have never heard of Argyle Landscaping. I'm sure lots of folks have moved out and lots of new ones have moved in over the past twenty years. We can buy little cardboard signs with our company name to stick in the ground after we mow."

She shook her head decisively. "I don't know about this. You really think it'll work?"

"I think it's worth trying. The risk is minimal. Next thing is to find where we're wasting money."

Sophia waved her hands and shook her head. "We're operating on a shoestring here. How can I cut back any more than we have?"

"Where do you buy your gas?"

"Whatever is closest to where the crews are working. Why"?

"Classy neighborhoods generally have more expensive gas stations."

Sophia nodded.

"Who buys it?"

"Each crew boss buys it."

"How does he pay for it?" Cash raised his eyebrows.

"Well, they each have a debit card and – you don't suppose – NOOO! My people would never do that! Never!"

"Do they give you gas receipts?"

"Well… no. But I check the bank statements." Her voice trailed off, softening as her eyes widened. A flicker of guilt crossed her face, childlike and uncertain. "I guess I don't actually know how much gas we go through."

For the first time since he'd met her, Cash saw the steel in Sophia's demeanor falter—just slightly.

"Sophia, I grew up learning how to con people out of their hard-earned cash. That's what almost put me in jail long before I went into the Marines. I just didn't get caught."

"And here I've been trusting you," she said with a tone of sarcasm.

"Hey, I'm just giving you the benefit of my experience. From now on, tell the crews to look for the cheapest gas and to bring you receipts for the gas. Let's do some basic calculations and see how much gas you should be burning each week with the equipment and the trucks. Tell them we need to tighten up a bit on our efficiency or something like that. You need to talk to them. Tell them anything. Dangle pay raises in front of them. I don't think they'll listen to me."

Over the next three weeks, gas receipts started trickling in from stations off the beaten path, and they saw a gradual reduction over the previous months' spending. Cash could only wonder how much gas had been going into employees' cars. He also found alternate sources for replacement parts when the machines needed to be overhauled. Overhead costs began to slowly drop. Sophia reported to Christopher Hamm that she was more than happy with her Work Release trustee.

In fact, the Hamm family started using Argyle for their own yard and later managed to have the State pay Argyle for the upkeep of the grounds at the Work Release Center.

The days seemed to run together in one continuous stream of phone calls and wrench turning. The shop had started to feel like home. One late afternoon, Cash decided to clean out a neglected corner of the shop, neglected for a long time. Used parts, seemingly symbolic trophies of years gone by, were piled high in random order in case the need for them ever arose again. Cash had learned from his Marine Corps motor pool days to never throw away anything that still functioned, no matter how old. He came across a girly magazine hidden behind a workbench, away from Sophia's line of vision. Instinctively, he turned to the centerfold, and scrawled in the corner, he saw the name, 'Rusty.' It explained a lot.

Spring progressed into summer, keeping the mowing crews busy. Sophia's business was slowly growing, in part because of Cash's efforts and in part because of a sudden influx of new people into the area. Alexandria had been a city of static growth for decades, even a slight decline when England Air Force Base had been closed. But the city purchased the base property from the Department of Defense and built it into a retirement community of private citizens, people who needed their grass mowed and preferred not to do it themselves. Most of them opted to pay someone else to do it. Argyle Landscaping began offering chemical fertilizer and weed control for a nice markup.

Cash's church idea expanded, and Argyle began to gain more visibility and new customers. He and Sophia stopped in at the Community Church on MacArthur Drive, the first church he had called, to see if anything in their business plan needed adjusting or nurturing. She had told him to wear something decent so he could present a good image. They entered through the main doors and into the large narthex. From somewhere in the building, they heard a choir rehearsing with an organist. A momentary sense of awe came over him as he looked at the vaulted ceilings and majestic artwork. Cash excused himself for a moment and glanced through the sanctuary doors. He saw seating for three hundred at least.

Gladys Perkins emerged to greet them in the outer office. She was an attractive woman in her mid-thirties with dark, wavy, auburn hair, and almost as tall as Cash. She spoke as one with a strong personality, as Cash had imagined from their phone conversation.

"Hello, I'm Gladys Perkins. What can I do for you?"

"And I am Sophia Blessing. I own Argyle Landscaping. We take care of your church grounds. A few weeks ago, you spoke to my office manager…"

On que, Cash stepped forward and extended his hand. "Hi, I'm Cash Ratliff." He stopped and looked at Sophia sheepishly, realizing he had interrupted her. The two women looked at one another and smiled. Sophia continued.

"We were in the neighborhood, and we wanted to see how our service was working for you. We like to meet our clients in person when we can."

Gladys had a pencil in her hand that she buried behind her ear, and looked closely at Sophia, then at Cash. A few seconds went by, and she said, "Well, I'm happy with the service. But I guess there's always room for improvement. Hang on a second. Let me see if Bob's available." She turned and disappeared around a corner and emerged with a man holding a cup of coffee in his hand.

"Hi! I'm Pastor Bob Allen. Are you folks from Argyle? You're Mrs. Blessing, right? Can I get you folks a cup of coffee or something else?" His visitors politely declined.

Pastor Bob looked to be in his late thirties with a round face and kind eyes. He was close to Cash's height and fifty pounds heavier. His voice gave the impression of confidence, but not overpowering. He appeared honestly glad to see them. Cash looked at Sophia for a cue, and she nodded to give him a free rein in the conversation.

"Yes, sir, we're the keepers of the grass, you might say. We were in the neighborhood and just wanted to stop by and see how it was going. Just let us know if there's anything we need to improve on or do differently." He rocked on his feet as he spoke. His own smile was infectious, and he knew it.

The pastor looked at Gladys, who politely shrugged. Then he said, "No, I guess everything is fine. We appreciate what you're doing. And the price is well within our means, especially with that discount idea you gave us. I hope it's helping your business as well. Great idea, Mrs. Blessing."

Sophia put her hand in the crook of Cash's elbow, flashed a smile, and said, "Well, I don't mean to brag, but that was my grandson's idea! He's such a smart boy!" She patted Cash's shoulder with her free hand. Gladys had stepped back away from the conversation and watched with a look of cautious approval.

They took several business cards from the reception desk, promised to hand them out, said goodbye, and turned to leave. On the way out, when they reached the door, Cash leaned toward Sophia and whispered, "Grandson? What kind of bullshit was that?"

He winced as she secretly pinched his side and whispered back, "Hush, he'll hear you."

And Cash's time had dwindled down to just under four months remaining until freedom. Freedom?

Chapter 4

Friday afternoon, around 5:30, Cash was bringing Mr. Hamm up to date on his progress with Argyle Landscaping.

Upon hearing positive remarks from Cash, he gave a short nod and made a private confession. "You know, I didn't think this gig would be a good fit for you right at first. But we didn't have anything else on the horizon, so I gave it a shot, and it looks like it's working. Is it the job or is it working for Mrs. Blessing that makes it so good?"

"She's entertaining," Cash quipped. "Never a dull moment with her."

Hamm looked at him cautiously. "Okay, don't let me think you have any angles in mind to manipulate that poor woman in your favor. Just remember, she and I have a close line of conversation."

"Mr. Hamm, you have nothing to worry about. She's not as defenseless as you think."

When he turned to leave, the Director stopped him with a tone of voice that sounded totally different from his usual bulldozing demeanor. "By the way," he said almost meekly, "We're having a big gathering of friends and family at my house this weekend and I need some help to make it a real success. We want them to feel at home and comfortable. Think you could walk around with a tray of hors d'oeuvres and drinks for a couple of hours?" He finished with a broad smile.

"You mean like a waiter? I don't know. Never tried that before."

"Well, can you learn quick? Because I really need some help."

In Hamm's tone of voice, Cash quickly saw an angle he couldn't pass up. Help the man and he helps you. "You know, come to think of it, it doesn't sound that hard. Just a couple of hours? Am I the only one?"

"No. Rodney's going to be there, too. He's done it before. You just follow his lead."

Cash thought for a moment before asking with a slight grin, "So, what's the occasion for the gathering?"

Cash's question seemed almost too personal. Hamm returned to his usual bluntness and said, "You mean, why are we doing it? Not that it's any of your business, but my son just got accepted to medical school on a full scholarship, and we need to celebrate. Anything else you need to know?"

"No, sir. I'll be ready."

"Good, I'll have something for you to wear. Come by the house in the morning with Rodney and we'll give you the grand tour. Now, get outa' here."

When Saturday morning arrived, Cash and Rodney walked to Hamm's house near the front gate of Camp Beauregard. Cash was still trying to wrap his arms around the idea of acting like a waiter. When the post had been a National Guard installation a few years ago, the house had been the living quarters for the local commander and graciously embraced all the high-ranking social aspects of the job. The house was huge, expansive, with shiplap siding, painted multiple times over the past decade. It included six bedrooms, four baths, and a kitchen almost as big as Sophia's. A large bay window held watch over a regal breakfast nook, practically a room to itself. Four sofas and soft, overstuffed chairs gave the parlor a sense of comfort, accompanied by a wide fireplace that created a rustic but gentle atmosphere. The living room appeared updated with more modern décor, but it still begged to be a party house. If the walls could talk, they would tell of so many liaisons over the years where friendships and relationships germinated and died while conversations ranged from juicy gossip to world peace. Cash couldn't help wondering what part of the furnishings belonged to the Hamm family, and what came with the house. For certain, nothing cheap came within his line of sight. He looked out the back window and saw several men raking the yard and trimming shrubs. Cash had noticed a truck out front with a familiar logo on the door that read, 'Argyle Landscaping.' Sophia must have scheduled that herself. Small world.

Rodney pushed open the kitchen door with his hip to avoid touching the brass panel at the edge. Cash noticed and saw immediately that Rodney had done this before.

"Mr. and Mrs. Hamm like to have people over a lot. They don't do nothing halfway." He spoke with proud gestures like it was his own home. "Here, I need to show you where all the servin' stuff is."

In a large butler's pantry, he saw stacks of high ball glasses, champagne flutes, and stemware. The plates were ivory color with silver trim that matched the serving trays. Rodney gave Cash a quick tutorial on where to find things on the shelves and how to mingle with the crowd without stumbling or spilling.

If Christopher Hamm presided over the Work Release Center with absolute authority, Olivia Hamm ruled as the undisputed Queen of the Hamm household, and she fit the role perfectly. It was early Saturday morning, and she wore pearl earrings and a matching necklace. Tastefully applied eye makeup made her face look almost angelic. She had a knock-out figure that begged for plunging necklines. Pale gray Capri pants and a matching tank top brought out the best in her stunning appearance. If this was Mr. Hamm's better half, how could he possibly be so grouchy all the time? Cash couldn't wait to see what she would wear that evening. He guessed her age to be about fifty and he felt himself looking forward to whatever adventure the rest of the day held in store. He knew to restrain himself when outside the corral.

If Olivia could sing, it would have been soprano. "Rodney dear, do we have enough glasses for sixty-five shrimp cocktails?" Her eyelids fluttered in time with each syllable as she spoke.

"I think so, ma'am, but I'll go count them to be sure." He noticed Cash starring at her, grabbed him by the sleeve, and hissed, "C'mon, let's go count martini glasses!"

Silently, Olivia had followed the two men toward the pantry. When she spoke from behind them, it startled them both. "I haven't met you, have I?" Her voice had a musical lilt.

Cash turned around and the air in the small pantry space instantly filled with the aroma of Guerlain, maybe Jasmine, but he wasn't sure. It had been a long time since he had sensed such elegance. "No, ma'am, I haven't been here that long." He forced his eyes to stay locked on hers even though he knew the V-neck of her top floated just inches away, conjuring up a world of fantasy and arousal.

She stroked his shoulder and said smoothly, "You can't imagine how much we appreciate the help. You'll get to meet my son this evening!"

Rodney and Cash both nodded and smiled. When she left, Rodney looked at Cash and rolled his eyes. They both heard her speaking to a deliveryman about flower arrangements. Her manner of speech remained rich and smooth.

"Keep your mind where it belong," Rodney said to Cash. They both laughed quietly.

Later in the day and back at the Center, Hamm summoned the two men into his office. "Here's your duds for tonight." He held up two sets of clothes that looked like they came from the wait staff at Commander's Palace in New Orleans. What he handed them included black pants, a white tuxedo shirt with studs, a black bowtie, and a red vest. "My wife wants to put on the dog tonight, so this is what you wear. You both have black shoes, right?"

Cash whispered to Rodney, "I'm going to look like a friggin' bar tender from a Bourbon Street strip joint."

"I heard that," Hamm said. "But, if I have to wear a damn suit and bowtie, then you have to look like a flaming pimp. The rest of us will look like we just came from Easter Church Service, so quit your bitching."

Rodney remarked with a grin, "It won't be the first time, will it, sir?"

"No, it won't. Oh, I should mention, you can't change at the house because all the rooms are occupied with overnight guests, so you'll have to get dressed here by your bunks before you walk to the house."

Cash choked back a gasp and spoke up, "You mean, all the guys here will see us dressed like this?" He held up the clothes like someone had just asked him to strut down a runway in a skirt and high heels.

"You want to stay here? I can find someone else."

"No, sir. We'll be there on time."

Yes, they arrived on time. But not without the comments and catcalls from the rest of the group as they tried to get dressed discreetly in the sleeping quarters. Squirrel tried to straighten Cash's tie, mixed with motherly admonitions, only to have his hand slapped away and to be given a description of what would happen next if he tried that again. The hoots and friendly mockery continued as they exited the gate in the fence line and walked toward Hamm's house.

"Hey, waiter," someone shouted, "I need a refill on my Jim Beam! And some peanuts! Where's the other bartender? The one with the big knockers, where is she?"

Another one yelled out, "Hey, Cash, I didn't know Hamm needed a bouncer tonight! Bring me back some autographs!"

The front porch appeared well lit and decorated with enormous potted plants Cash had not seen earlier in the day. They could hear music coming from the front parlor.

He started to walk to the front door, but Rodney stopped him. "Hey man, we be the hired help tonight. We go in through the kitchen."

The overnight guests were already enjoying themselves, each with a drink in their hands, already mellow and ahead of those who were yet to arrive. The low hum of human conversation infiltrated every corner of the house and slowly escalated as each new guest arrived. Within an hour, the liquor flowed, and people politely shouted to be heard. A string quartet warmed up in one corner.

Cash caught onto his duties rather quickly. He knew how to use his charming smile that enticed others to respond in equal eloquence. Twice, as he emerged from the kitchen with requested drinks, only to have someone else snatch them off the tray before he could make delivery to the right person. Cash hesitated and felt his eyes dilate. The temptation to backhand the offender washed over him. But Rodney saw it happen and gave Cash a subtle shake of the head and a piercing frown that told him to go with the flow. He got the message and snaked his way back through the crowd and into the kitchen like a ballet dancer. "Stupid creep," he muttered.

He was coming back with an almost empty tray when he suddenly heard a voice from the kitchen that sent a shiver through his entire body like the first sip of fine whiskey from a freshly opened bottle. At first, he tried to ignore it, but the seemingly familiar musicality of it persisted. It floated and whispered like a cloud on a gentle breeze and settled in a secret place in his memory. The words did not sound fully audible, but the attached angelic laughter penetrated him like an arrow. He found the source, and as she turned around, his world imploded.

"Julie?" His next words never issued forth but hung in his throat.

"Cash? My goodness! What are you, I mean, why are you… I certainly wasn't expecting to see you here!"

Cash continued to stare at the most beautiful woman he had seen in a long time. She wore a long, dark grey sleeveless dress that hugged her figure like caressing hands. The tips of her red toenails showed barely visible from under the bottom seam. A loosely draped matching shawl lay wrapped around her shoulders. A touch of deep blue eyeshadow accented her dark brown eyes. His eyes went to her left hand and saw the wedding band he had secretly hoped would not be there.

When he finally found his voice, he said, "Ah - yes, I'm helping Mr. Hamm tonight." He cleared his throat and continued, "I was looking forward to meeting his son to congratulate him on his acceptance to medical school. Must be a big day for him."

Julie stammered at a momentary loss for words. She recovered quickly and said, "Yes, it is. He went through a lot to get where he is now."

Searching for the right words to keep the conversation going, he said, "Sounds like you know him. Is he around?"

Julie looked at him cautiously, and was about to answer, when her gaze shifted to a young man approaching from behind Cash.

"Hey, there you are," the man said, "I was wondering where you went." He walked around Cash and gave Julie a quick kiss on the cheek.

Julie never missed a beat. Without taking her eyes off Cash, she said, "Steve, this is Cash, one of your dad's helpers tonight. He was hoping to meet you."

"Hi, I'm Steve Hamm. Pleased to meet you. You two know each other?"

Cash looked down, shifted his feet, and before he could speak, a woman from the crowd barged into the room and blurted out, "Julie, or should I say, Mrs. Hamm, congratulations to both of you! Come with me, dear, I want you to meet someone from New Orleans. That's where the med school is, right?"

As she left, Cash processed what he had just heard.

Steve Hamm had politely stepped back out of the way, but when Julie left for the other room, he continued, "So, I assume you are one of my dad's trustees."

"Yeah, I haven't been here that long. Hopefully, not too much longer, either."

"Sure, I know you're looking forward to it. Did you say you knew my wife before?"

"Your wife, you mean Julie?" She's your – oh – uh, no, I never said that. I was just…"

Christopher Hamm's unmistakable voice cut through the air. "Steve! Steve! Where in the hell is that boy? Here you are! Come with me for a second." He started to escort his son back into the crowd, but turned and said to Cash, "Great job, Ratliff. You and Rodney are made for this. Thanks."

After a couple of hours, the party had progressed to a smooth glow. Conversation and laughter flowed from all directions. The string quartet had migrated into the living room and gave a classy touch to the ambience of the evening. Cash and Rodney had been on their feet for several hours, more than the two hours Mr. Hamm had promised. Looking around, everyone seemed happy for the moment, so they found a chance to sit in the kitchen for a few seconds and rest their feet. As Cash's thoughts retreated to his interrupted conversation with Julie, a tall, grey-haired gentleman appeared at the kitchen door.

"Excuse me, but may I trouble you fellows for a refill? Just something soft and bubbly, I'm driving tonight." As he waited, the man took a long look at Cash and then reached for the full glass Rodney handed him. "Wonderful night, huh?" He raised the glass a couple of inches in a polite gesture and said, "Thanks. Thank you very much."

"Any time, sir," Cash replied.

"So, both of you fellows are within six months of release, right?"

They both nodded.

"And where are you working?"

Rodney piped up immediately and said, "Taylor's Lumberyard! Good folks there."

He continued to study Rodney as though another hidden

message might surface. His stare then slowly shifted to Cash, who said sheepishly, "Argyle Landscaping."

"Oh, you work for Sophia Blessing! That should be interesting. How is she?"

As Cash was about to answer, Olivia Hamm entered and confronted them at the door and said, "Bob, darling, there you are! I was looking for you. Come tell me about your trip to Cancun!" As usual, her voice sounded thick as molasses and twice as sweet. She looked over her shoulder as they were leaving and said in a bubbly voice to Cash and Rodney, "My goodness, you two men could get jobs at the Hotel Bentley!"

Cash looked at Rodney, who rubbed his chin and kept his eyes on the older man as he walked out of the kitchen with his arm around Olivia's shoulders. Her pale green cocktail dress seemed to whisper to her legs as she walked. As soon as they walked out of earshot, Rodney quickly turned to Cash and hissed, "Man! Do you know who that was? That's Bob Preston, the head cop! It was his car you stole!"

Cash found himself beyond words. He sat down and rubbed his eyes, then looked through the kitchen door at the crowd of partygoers. "Do you think he recognized me? He sure gave me a long look."

For a moment, Cash felt surrounded like Custer at Little Big Horn. Would Chief Preston go out of his way to find a reason for Cash to return to Angola? The Chief probably remembers that Cash had been given a five-year sentence. It wouldn't take much for him to realize that the sentence had been shortened. In a rare moment, Cash let his imagination inflate a situation beyond the reality of the moment.

Moments later, the Chief appeared again right outside the

kitchen door with a woman clinging to his arm. Her martini was sloshing over her fingers and onto the floor, but she didn't seem to care. They both took short peeks into the kitchen, trying to do so unnoticed, but Cash didn't miss it. They left, whispering to each other.

Looking at the ceiling, he groaned, "Oh man, if that was his wife, my ass is grass right now!"

"Yeah, and you in the lawnmower business!" Rodney clutched his sides, laughing at his own words, and almost fell off the stool he sat on. Cash could only smile and shake his head.

With all his experience in dealing with tight spots, Cash could feel his capacity for calm control full to the rim that evening. First, Julie shows up in his life again, and now the Chief of Police from Alexandria just thanked him for a glass of ginger ale, and his wife is trying to recall her frightening joy ride that Cash gave her! What else could happen tonight? He looked at the clock on the wall and saw that there was plenty of party time still left. Without a further word between them, the two men both straightened their vests and went back to work.

Approaching midnight, Christopher Hamm tapped Cash on the shoulder. He had a look of stiff concern on his face.

"Ratliff, I need a favor and I can't ask anyone else to do this. One of our guests arrived late and now needs a ride home. She said she's not feeling well."

Cash's mind remained in a whirl, but he kept his cool. "Yes, sir, who is it?" The answer came quickly.

"Sophia Blessing. She says she trusts you to get her home."

How could he have missed her? Looking carefully around the room while he listened to the Director, he spotted her sitting in an overstuffed corner chair, looking like she was about to fall out of it. A pair of large potted plants had previously obscured her from Cash's line of vision. As observant as he was in other situations, he had simply overlooked her presence. She wore a beaded gold Lame' Bolero jacket and black crepe slacks. That was the extent of any elegance she might have had for the evening. Her eyes were half-closed.

"Mr. Hamm, I don't have a driver's license. They took that away from me a while ago."

"I can fix that. Let me talk to Chief Preston. If you get stopped, which is remote, he'll vouch for you."

"Sir, does he know who I am?"

"Yeah, he knows. That's why I think you'll be on your toes and not get stopped."

Cash swallowed hard. "Okay, but this all sounds a bit risky, don't you think? I mean…"

"Hey! I, uh, we need this done. I'll - I'll make it up to you." He smiled and patted Cash on the shoulder.

Cash took a long, deep breath and agreed.

The two men walked over to Sophia, gently roused her awake, and then guided her to the door. She willingly looked at them both, first one, then the other, like a compliant patient on a hospital ward. They walked her to her car and Hamm handed Cash the keys.

The drive to Sophia's house was uneventful. Fortunately, she managed to exit the car with minimal assistance but struggled to walk up to the front door. As he guided her down the hall to the bedroom, she stopped and turned toward the bathroom. "I gotta' go," she slurred. Carefully, he walked with her to the toilet and started to leave the room, but she bent over and almost fell headlong into the tub. Cash caught her in time and stood her back up.

"I need some help," she croaked.

"Okay, like what?"

"Hold me steady while I drop my drawers." Hearing her words, Cash froze like a statue. She tugged on his sleeve and half-shouted, "Don't just stand there, hang on to me!"

Obediently, he gripped one arm while trying to keep his field of view away from any indiscretion. From the corner of his eye, he saw her sit down. He then heard her sigh as a bawdy-sounding stream hit the bottom of the toilet. Suddenly, she reached for the small trash can near the toilet and retched an ear-piercing dry heave. Cash handed her a paper tissue, and she wiped her mouth.

"Okay, I'm okay," she said. "I can walk from here."

"You sure?"

"Probably. Let's give it a go. Help me up."

She pulled her pants up enough to cover any need of privacy, then slowly, they made their way to the bedroom where she shrugged off the jacket, kicked off her shoes, and peeled her top and pants off one arm and one leg at a time. Everything went on the floor. Her words still came out slurred. "That's enough. I can sleep like this. Thank you. You're a good one."

With that, she crawled into the bed, and he pulled the covers over her, then hung her jacket and pants in the closet.

Her bedroom centered around a queen-sized sleigh bed with a large mahogany headboard that looked like King Arthur himself had designed it. White sheer curtains covered the windows and matching tiebacks hung unused on each side. Her phone sat on a bedside table that boasted a dark cherry finish. A matching dresser and mirror stood to one side, holding a litany of cosmetics and facial treatment products. Around the room, he saw magazines scattered on furniture and the floor, most of which featured women's latest fashions. He saw no copies of Popular Mechanics or anything that a man would want to read.

Now what? Just leave her here by herself? He went into the kitchen and sat down at the breakfast table to consider his next move. Hamm had not told him what to do after he had delivered her home. He thought to himself, *Here I sit, a prison inmate, in an old woman's house in a waiter's garb, and she's undressed and passed out in the bedroom. This cannot have a good ending.*

The only thing he could think to do was call Hamm and ask for further orders. He reached for the kitchen phone on the wall next to the table and, after several rings, Rodney's voice sounded, "Hamm residence, Rodney speaking."

"Rodney, this is Cash. I need to speak to Mr. Hamm. Can you get him for me?"

"Cash! Where in the hell are you? I looked around and I couldn't find you nowhere! What's up with you?"

"It's okay. Just get Mr. Hamm for me."

After what seemed like an eternity, Christopher Hamm picked up the phone. "Cash, you get it done?"

"Yes, sir, I did, but this is kinda' awkward. Here I am in my waiter's clothes with an old, drunk widow passed out in her bedroom. What do you want me to do now?" His voice sounded almost pleading.

Hamm thought for a moment. "Just stay there. Sleep on the couch. Tomorrow's Sunday and I'll send a driver to pick you up. Just keep an eye on her. She's a sweet one, didn't I tell you?"

With the plan clearly communicated, Cash hung up and quietly walked down the hall to make sure she was okay. Surprisingly, he found her sitting in a rocking chair, wrapped in the bedspread, and clutching something swaddled in a pillowcase. Cash knelt on one knee in front of her and put his hands on hers. His eyes asked for an explanation.

She stared at the floor and said, "Saying goodbye is not supposed to go on this long," she said with a hiccup. "The last time I saw him when his thoughts were clear was two years before his last heart attack. We were drinking beer at the Oktoberfest in Rainer, Louisiana. But, every year, on this date, here we are again, the two of us. Maybe he can hear me clearly now."

"Sophia, who are you talking about?"

She slowly raised her head and, with bleary eyes, focused on Cash. "Today is the anniversary of the last day I saw Donald. I never told you about Donald, did I?" Her eyes seemed half closed. "He was – he was - my husband and the best f - friend I ever had. He died on this day, twenty years ago."

"What's in the pillowcase?"

"Hmm? Oh, Don was a Korean War vet, and this is his flag." She uncovered it and caressed it clumsily with her fingers. Her words came so softly, Cash had a hard time hearing her. "I always thought they could have folded it a little better, but that would look too artificial. It's better this way because human hands folded this flag." She gently stroked the seams. "Hands just like his." She stopped and buried her face in the fabric.

Cash stayed on his knees in front of her, amazed that anyone could harbor such feelings for so long. He tried to put his hand on her shoulder, but she gently pushed him away.

"There's nothing here you can fix, Cash. It's just my way of saying hello to Donald again and telling him how much I miss him. He was the peacemaker in the family. He always knew what to say when the kids got into some kinda' big argument. Nothing ever shook him."

Cash suddenly felt an enormous urging that rarely ever drove his thoughts. Her loneliness seemed so obvious. He wanted so much to do something, anything, for this wonderful woman who had been treating him like a son, or a grandson, for that matter. Watching her hug the flag and gently rocking side to side, made her sense of loss gradually begin to spill over on Cash, and he felt his own composure slipping. Never before had he cared for someone like this, at this moment, and he felt helpless. It wasn't romantic, certainly not with their age difference, but it was love, just the same. He knew how to use the gift of his voice. It always got him what he needed. Right now, he needed to be back in his own comfort zone if he planned to be of any help at all. He willed his imagination to kick in.

"Isn't it about time that you tell me something about Donald? I mean, I never even knew his name. What did he do in the service?"

Sophia raised her head up again and Cash handed her a tissue from the nightstand. She wiped her eyes and blew her nose. "Why - why do you want me to talk about him?"

He inched closer and said, "The best way to remember someone is to talk about them. Can't do that unless there's someone to listen. I'm right here."

She looked at him strangely, sat up straight and said, "He flew. He was a B-29 pilot. We met at MacDill Air Force Base in Florida, and I was a brand-new Second Lieutenant Air Force nurse, sir, working in the flight surgeon's office, sir. I got to meet all the pilots when they came in for physicals, sick call, that sort of thing." She waved her hand as she spoke. "I don't know why he caught my eye, but he stood out for some reason among all the others. Maybe it was because he was so tall. He was well over six feet tall. Every Friday after work, we had happy hour at the officers' club. All the swaggering, bragging flight crews would be there. Get a couple of drinks in them, and most acted like they could walk through fire and come through without even a singed mustache. Donald was different, though. He was quiet and shy when he wasn't drinking, but downright funny after a couple of drinks. He was simply a sweet man."

"I would like to have known him."

She showed a shallow grin and said, "There was a devilish side about him, though. I had had a couple of dates with his roommate. They lived in the bachelor officers' quarters, and he convinced his roommate to go on a double date with me and one of the other nurses. The four of us had a great time and he ended up asking me out after he convinced his roommate to start dating the other nurse. He knew how to work an angle, that's for sure."

"Didn't you think he was being a little devious?"

"No! I was glad to see he went to that much trouble to get closer to me. My earliest recollection was watching him take off in those monstrous, roaring airplanes. Squadrons of them would come thundering over the hospital, and I was convinced that every one of them belonged to him. Even inside the building, I could just feel the power, vibrating and pulsing on my insides. It made me want to cheer with happy tears." She waved her hands as she talked and almost dropped the folded flag.

"Like you're doing now? Remembering with happy tears?"

Cash could watch her eyes and could see her reliving the past as she spoke. "I was so happy and relieved when he came home from Korea." She gazed at Cash with a wistful look. "So many of them didn't come back. We got married right before he went over and never had a real honeymoon. When he got back, we made up for lost time and I got pregnant the first time we did the rodeo thing in the bedroom. That's what he called it. He was from San Antonio, and that, you know, that was what he liked to call it." Her voice seemed to fade.

Cash realized he was grinning. "How did he get into the lawn care business? He went from B-29s to lawn mowers?"

Sophia looked at him blankly, as though the question had never occurred to her. She rubbed her nose with the back of her hand and continued to stroke the flag in her lap.

"No, he tried truck driving for about three months. I rarely saw him when he had that job, so I took a nursing job at the Baptist Hospital. It was better than just sitting around here waiting for him to come home. Finally, I told him I had waited long enough while he was in Korea. Enough was enough. He admitted he didn't like it any more than I did. So, I kept on working while he figured out what to do." She began to nod off but jerked her head up to stay awake.

Cash started to suggest that she go back to sleep, but she wanted to continue.

"Green was his favorite color. Cut grass was his favorite smell. He hated the smell of an airplane hangar or exhaust fumes from those damn trucks, so the first chance he had, he got out of it. He was in line to make Major if he had stayed in the service, but he said it wasn't worth it. He could look at a tree and see how the shape told a story. He taught his mowers how to cut a pattern in the lawns of big properties so it looked like a checkerboard, or a bunch of swirls. He could do miracles with those machines. All his original employees are gone now. I didn't know how to teach them what he did. I still think of him every time I smell fresh-cut lawns." She stopped and wiped her eyes. "He was such a gentle soul. I couldn't ask him about flying in Korea because he'd start crying. He hated dropping bombs."

She looked at Cash and saw his eyes beginning to moisten. "So, what are you getting' weepy eyed about, boy? Huh? Maybe you're the one who needs consoling."

Feeling a bit embarrassed, he said, "It's been a long night for me, too."

Cash slept on the couch, but sleep meant waking every hour to check on Sophia. Finally, around 4 AM, he fell into a deep sleep only to have a hand shaking him awake at 8 AM.

"Hey, what the hell are you doing here on my couch? How did you get here?"

He sat up like explosions were going off inside his head. Dazed, he looked up at her for a moment and said, "Uh, yeah! Right! Mrs. Blessing, I brought you home last night in your car."

She looked at him with absolute disbelief. "Like hell you did! I drove myself home!"

Cash had to think fast. "Uh, sure, okay – yeah - well, if you did, where did you park your car?"

"In the driveway like I always do. What's with you?"

Cash knew he had easily backed her into a corner with no retreat, but he wanted to be careful. "Look in the driveway. What do you see?"

Sophia ambled to the window and her eye caught sight of her car near the front walk, not in the driveway. "How did it get there?"

"I just told you. I drove you home and I didn't have any way to get back."

"So, you just helped yourself to my couch, like you owned the place, huh? Do I need to count the silverware? And since when do you call me Mrs. Blessing? Some kind of guilty conscience?"

Cash found himself suddenly at a momentary loss for words. It would be hard to explain, even to a rational person. How could he make her know the truth? He could quote Mr. Hamm's instructions to her, but that seemed like a child's way out. The solution suddenly occurred to him.

"Have you ever thought about getting a nice wooden case to put Donald's flag in?"

Sophia stopped like a switch had been flipped. "What? Donald's flag? How did you know about Donald's flag?"

"You showed it to me last night. I put you to bed, called Mr. Hamm, and came back to check on you, and you were sitting in the rocking chair, holding it. I asked about it and you told me all about Donald. We talked for several minutes. Do you remember any of that?"

In her usual manner, she looked at him as though seeing him for the first time. Small fragments of memory started to creep into her consciousness. "Okay, it's coming back to me. You put me to bed? I wondered who hung up my clothes. They're not in the place where I usually hang them. What else do I need to know?"

"I was just doing what Mr. Hamm asked me to do. In case you're wondering, I was a perfect gentleman through the whole thing. And just so you know, the silverware is all there." They both silently looked at each other for a moment, listening to their own breath.

Cash finally spoke. "So, how did you enjoy the party last night?"

She scratched her head and lit a cigarette with no expression. "What parts I remember was really nice." She cut her eyes at him and said, "Perfect gentleman, huh? Well, that's no fun! Ha! Hell, I didn't even know you would be there. That was a lucky break for me. Too bad I don't remember parts of it."

"That's my other job. I'm Mr. Hamm's houseboy." Cash could feel the tightness in his neck beginning to loosen. He noticed that even without her hair combed and brushed, Sophia had a very soft-looking morning face. Her eyes did not have that scrutinizing look he noticed when they first met. She had obviously become more comfortable with the unusual situation they found themselves in that morning.

She reached over and squeezed his hand. "How much longer do you have at the, you know, at the place?"

"Let's see, less than four months, give or take a few days. Why?"

Before she could answer, a car horn from the front of the house interrupted their conversation. Cash looked out the window and saw a state car parked at the end of the walkway and a driver, one he had never seen before, standing beside it. The two of them emerged onto the front porch, Sophia still in her robe, and Cash in his red vest. He waved goodbye as he hopped down the steps and walked briskly along the walkway.

As he opened the car door, the driver leaned back toward him and said, "Looks like quite an old cougar you found there! You get some action outa' her last night?"

In a flash, Cash grabbed the man's collar and pulled him within inches of his own face. For several moments, he glared at the man until Sophia's voice rang out from the porch. "Cash, you forgot your bowtie! It's right here, come get it!"

Cash immediately released the man's collar and realized the good fortune of her timing as he trotted back to the porch and retrieved his bowtie. Her eyes were locked onto his as he approached. Just as he reached out, she stepped down to the sidewalk and stood almost toe to toe with him. Without hesitation, she cupped his face in her hands and planted a big, wet kiss on Cash's lips and said, "That'll give the neighbors something to talk about. Be sure to wipe the lipstick off before you get back."

As he walked slowly back to the car, he had the distinct feeling he was dreaming. When was the last time someone had kissed him? Whatever possessed her to do that? He could still feel the touch of her lips on his. Old, quivering lips that had kissed before when they were younger and knew how to do it with feeling. A feeling that carried a certain sincerity about her and made Cash feel uncomfortable, but only for a brief moment. What had she started?

As he climbed into the back seat of the car, the driver turned around and said, "What the hell was that all about? Wait, don't tell me! Ha!"

Cash could feel his face blushing until he saw the telltale smirk on the man's face. He felt his uneasiness turn to mild rage and said, "Never mind! Just drive! And listen to me, you sonofabitch, you didn't see anything back there, did you?"

Chapter 5

Cash made it to the breakfast line just before it closed. For a few hours that day, he dozed and caught up on sleep. He knew the adventure from this morning and the night before would stay in his memory for a long time. He knew he had crossed the line in several respects, but nothing that would endanger his status with the Department of Corrections. Or would it? After all, Mr. Hamm had put him in that precarious situation. He couldn't help but think there must be something within himself, buried since childhood, that made him do what he had done. All around him were people who trusted him. But could he trust himself? And then there was Sophia. Their relationship was now on a new level and Cash had no idea how to deal with it. Maybe it was just a fleeting moment. The whole thing gave him some sense of comfort and approval, even if it was of a bizarre sort. Fully rested, he got up, showered, and wondered what the remainder of the day would bring. As he let the cool water course over him, his thoughts went to Sophia. She probably had a lifetime of stories, joys, and sorrows locked up in her, memories she wasn't going to share with anyone. Why did her kids just up and move away? Had there been something she did or didn't do that drove them all away? Maybe it wasn't her fault. Who knows? Not that it should concern him anyway. Not that I could do anything about it, he thought. Still, the questions haunted him.

He dried off, dressed, and headed for the game room when Oscar appeared and said, "Hey, there's someone in the front office asking for you."

"What's her name?" he said with a slow grin.

"Wrong type. He's wearing a uniform. You better git on up there."

Cash felt an immediate stab in his gut. Uniform? From where? He had no relatives, no one in this area who knew him except Sophia and the guys there at the Center. Beads of perspiration formed on his forehead, and he was still guessing when he walked into the outer office and saw the familiar face. His apprehension melted away instantly.

"Stanley? What the hell – I never expected to see you again! How're you doing?"

The two shook hands like old friends that they were. Stanley replied with a big grin, "Big surprise, huh? I heard they were looking for more staff here, so I thought I would get out of that hellhole down there and try the real world for a while."

Cash searched for words and then said, "I can't believe you're here! Let me get you some coffee. We can sit and talk right here. It's really good to see you!"

Being Sunday morning, Hamm and his staff weren't around, so the two men sat in the outer office and enjoyed catching up on events in their lives with no fear of raising suspicions of impropriety or fraternization.

"What's it like here?" Stanley asked.

"Better than where I was, for sure. I got me a peach of a job."

"Doing what?"

"I'm the office manager for a lawn service company. The owner is an older woman who thinks I walk on water."

Stanley measured his next question closely. "Does she know why you're in here?"

"She knows. She probably knows more about me than you do."

"I doubt that. I've seen your record."

"Ha! Not everything is in my record. Say, have you met Mr. Hamm yet?"

"Only once, when he came down to Angola for a meeting. That's when I started thinking about a transfer. Tomorrow's Monday and I'm sure he'll take some time to get me up to speed."

Cash learned from Stanley that the Reverend Mr. Watchword had fallen into disfavor when someone caught him coming out of a house of ill repute in New Orleans. He had claimed he preached the gospel to sinners, but the picture in the paper clearly showed only half of his shirttail tucked in and a distressed look on his face. There had been a police raid looking for illegal substances and he happened to be in the wrong place at the wrong time.

"I knew he was a phony from the minute he opened his mouth," Cash declared. Stanley nodded in agreement.

"So, tell me about your job. Who's this woman you're working for?"

"Her name's Sophia Blessing. I have her convinced that I am a friggin' genius at running a business. She was skeptical right at first, but now she'll believe anything I tell her. So far, anything and everything I've done for her business has been an improvement."

"Sounds like you showed up just at the right time. What's her story? She got family? Husband? Kids?"

"She's a widow. Five grown kids all scattered to the four winds. I'm sure there's lots more to it than what she's told me."

They both heard footfall from the entrance and the soft murmur of voices in conversation. As Rodney and two other trustees appeared at the doorway, both men stood and tried to act nonchalant.

Cash spoke first. "Hey guys, this is Mr. Stanley Langston. Be nice to him. We need to break him in right."

Rodney spoke first. "Mr. Langston, I just came from Mr. Hamm's house. It's right up there by the main gate. You passed it on the way in. He wants to see you."

It had become clear since Cash's arrival that Rodney served as the eyes and ears for Mr. Hamm. No one seemed to mind. Who would have that job when he got out?

As Stanley walked back to his car, Cash caught up with him and said, "I'll ride up there with you. They might need some help cleaning up after last night." He quickly brought Stanley up to date on the highlights of last evening.

At Hamm's house, Cash heard activity in the kitchen and stepped in to investigate. He was surprised to see Julie and her husband, Steve Hamm, stacking plates and generally putting things back in order.

Steve spoke first. "Can I help you? You're – oh, yeah! We met last night. You're Cash, now I remember."

Cash looked at the floor and jammed his hands in his pockets. "I didn't know if the after-party cleanup crew needed some help."

Julie spoke next, clearly and calmly, "We missed you toward the end. Where did you go?"

"Uh, Mr. Hamm had something he wanted me to do. It took a while." She missed me, he thought to himself.

One of the overnight guests, a woman in her forties wearing jeans and a sweatshirt, wandered into the kitchen and exclaimed, "Hey, here you are! The soon-to-be new mommy and daddy!" She looked at Julie and continued, "When did you say you were due?"

This abrupt news about Julie hit Cash like a ton of reality. As he watched the others in the kitchen dive into a conversation about all the details of a new baby, he suddenly felt like a total stranger to Julie, like an old friend, simply left behind with nothing but vague memories and lost opportunities. He silently backed out of the room and walked back to his bunkhouse.

Monday morning, and Cash rose at the crack of dawn, ate breakfast, showered, shaved, and stood waiting at the curb when his driver arrived right on time. He opened the back door, and a voice stopped him in mid-stride.

"Come sit up here with me in the front seat," Stanley said in his unmistakable voice. "I'm your driver today. We need to finish talking."

For Cash, this would be the start of a good day.

As they turned the corner, approaching Sophia's house, Stanley still had questions. "So, you put her to bed Saturday night? That's got to be a classic. What did she say about it?"

"She said she didn't remember much. I guess I can believe it. She was eight sheets to the wind when I got her back home. But don't get the wrong idea; there's something really genuine about her."

The car came to a stop in front of the house. As Cash opened the car door, he said, "You want to meet her? She's a tiger, but she doesn't bite!"

"Maybe next time. I'll see you at the end of the day."

Cash turned and walked toward the front porch. He noticed a strange car parked in the driveway. As he got closer, he heard a man's voice from the interior of the house. It had a tone that put Cash's teeth on edge.

"Mama! What are you doing? You're letting those kinds of

people in your house? What else have you been doing, huh?"

He crossed the threshold of the front door and let the screen shut loudly to announce his presence. A tall, robust, middle-aged man looked around the corner of the kitchen door with an indignant expression and said, "Who are you?"

"Sorry, I didn't mean to intrude, I just -"

Sophia's raspy voice came from the kitchen like a faint whimper. "Cash? Come on in and meet my son!"

The man standing in the door gave Cash a piercing look of righteous indignation, but he stepped aside in deference to Sophia's wishes, for the moment.

"Cash, this is my son, John. He's the one I told you about from Atlanta. We were just having a morning cup of coffee. Care for some?"

Trying to be polite but not look intimidated, he answered, "Sure, if it's not too much trouble." John never took his eyes off Cash as he seemed to make himself at home in Sophia's kitchen. Cash offered his hand to John, who glanced at his mother and then shook it, reluctantly.

"I hear you work for a software company. How's that going these days?"

Cash couldn't tell if John's response was an answer or just a grunt. He sat down at the table, and John pulled up a chair and sat across the room. The man's persistent, glaring look began to irritate him.

Sophia brought two cups of coffee to the table and said, "Let me go for a minute and get out of this bathrobe. John likes me better when I'm fully dressed. He thinks his mother should know better."

Both men's eyes followed her as she left the room, and then John turned to Cash. Cash could see the man trying to form the words to say something, so Cash just let him smolder. The silent conflict lay clearly out in the open.

"Okay, look, my mother is getting up in years and sometimes she does some stupid things like -"

"Like hiring prison inmates to work for her? Is that your problem?"

"Yeah, that's my problem. She's in a very vulnerable state right now and I don't want anyone taking advantage of her in any way."

"You know, when I first met her, she didn't seem very vulnerable at all. In fact, she had me back on my heels from the first day."

"Yes, she can be a bit stubborn at times. We all grew up with it. But -"

"I wouldn't call it stubborn. I'd say she is well in charge and aware of what she's doing and doesn't want anyone trying to – what did you call it – take advantage? No, I'd say she's a woman of her own means who needs no protection or hovering from anyone."

John looked at him in disbelief. "So, I'm hovering, am I? I don't know who you think you are, but you don't come in here and start telling this family what our dynamics should be. As far as I'm concerned you can go back to your cage, for all I care. That's where they keep you at night, right? Maybe I'll have a talk with the Department of Corrections. I have connections to the Warden down there where you came from. What's his name – Fairman, Fairstaff, something like that. I called yesterday and they gave me a few tidbits of information that I bet my mother doesn't know. If that doesn't pan out, I know people in the Governor's office."

Cash could feel his blood pressure rising. How could this guy know anything about him? Was he just bluffing? Would the department give out personal information? Both men stood and looked at each other from across the room, just as Sophia came back into the kitchen. She looked at each of them and said, "John, I need to get to my appointment. Meet me at the car." John hesitated until she spoke firmly, "Now!"

John left the room and she turned to Cash. He could see a look of despair on her face.

"Sophia, I don't know what just happened. If you want me to leave, I can call and get a ride."

"You quitting? We were just getting started, pal. I'll see what's bothering John and then we'll talk this afternoon."

"You heard our conversation?"

"Part of it. But let's talk this afternoon." She turned and walked out the front door to John, who sat in the car, waiting.

Cash had no choice but to agree. He had a list of calls to make that day, and he could think of nothing to do about what he feared the most. It would be premature to call Mr. Hamm. John was right about one thing; he didn't know all the dynamics of this family. He had no idea how much influence Sophia's family had over her private affairs. He could only imagine the worst-case scenario in which a twisted, trumped-up report might find its way back to the Department of Corrections and the level of suspicion raised about his readiness to return to society. That's what the Corps taught him. Imagine the worst that could happen and be prepared to deal with it. But, in this case, too many unknown factors blurred his judgment. Maybe Mr. Hamm should know about the conversation with John Blessing. Should he? Cash faced a dilemma and felt like he was back in a foxhole in Afghanistan, helpless and not knowing what would come next. But he shook it off and picked up the phone. Stay busy today, he thought. This afternoon will tell.

His first call went to a residence in nearby Tioga. The housekeeper answered and said she didn't know when the lady of the house would return from shopping. No, she couldn't take a message. Call back later.

His second call was just as useless. A small child answered and said her mother was still in bed.

He paused for a moment, trying to steady the flurry of thoughts swirling in his head. The morning's conversation with John still hovered at the edge of his mind like a low, persistent hum, setting his nerves on edge. The problem John had created loomed large—an unsightly blob across the landscape of his conscience. It gnawed at him.

This wasn't how it used to be. There was a time he couldn't have cared less about anyone's opinion. Back then, he moved through life with a kind of reckless confidence, always landing on his feet, no matter how tight the corner. He'd faced down worse before and clawed his way out every time.

But Angola had changed him. Two and a half years in that place stripped him of the illusion of being unbreakable. He wasn't some untouchable kid anymore. He understood now—some battles can't be won with fists or bravado. Some losses carve deeper than scars.

And then there was Sophia. This extraordinary, gentle woman who had offered him something rare—a deliberate, genuine tenderness. Not out of pity, but from a place of quiet wisdom and grace. She'd opened a window to a life he'd never imagined—one with softness, with hope.

Now, he clung to the thought of freedom like a child waiting for Christmas morning. When that day came, he wanted to walk into the world with the lessons she'd given him cradled close to his heart.

How could he ever repay that kind of gift?

But now, John had said things that deflated all that and taken a big chunk of hope away from him in just a couple of minutes. No, maybe not. Was it just his imagination playing tricks on him? He was still here, working for Sophia, wasn't he? Should he consider his days in Sophia's house coming to a close? He felt like a child in a candy store who had been told he could smell the merchandise but couldn't touch it. Surprisingly, he felt his hands shaking. Try another phone call.

The next call turned out surprisingly pleasant. In it, there remained a few details to iron out and a cheerful, 'Have a nice day.' He started to feel better. Then, a call came in about a small accident involving one of the mowers that hit an underground sprinkler head. Cash promised to have the damage fixed, but the caller would not listen to reason. For ten minutes, he tried to smooth things over, but the customer heard none of his promising words. When he hung up, a cloud of uncontrollable, negative thoughts came to hover over him and discolor every image that came to mind. Without reason, Shauntae popped into his thoughts. Beautiful child. Beautiful personality. But then, beauty had no place in his life. Not today. In fact, gloom and despair displaced anything wonderful because he didn't deserve it. Nothing good and wonderful belonged to him. He thought of Julie and the way she looked the last time he saw her. But why wish for what was no longer available? Every thought, every wish, every upbeat word he could think of - the whole world was as tasteless as soured milk, like an unwanted bastard child. Hope and courage suddenly seemed like orphans to him. If only he could wake up from a dream and see a bright reality. Not a chance.

"Shit! Why is this happening?" He blinked and realized he was talking to the ceiling in loud tones. "Hey, you! You listening? Your buddy Watchword turned out to be a fake, didn't he? Listen to this! I'm no fake! I got stuff to do and lots more to live for! You gonna' take that away from me? Huh?" He looked down and felt something wet running down his cheeks.

"Damn you!" He got out of his chair and walked over to the window. He looked out at the gathering dark clouds on the distant horizon and mumbled under his breath, "C'mon, Cash, get your shit together."

He left his spot at the desk, went to the shop, and grabbed a broom. He made dust fly until the shop was clean, then he did it again. Then he cleaned and lined up every tool on the pegboard, displayed in descending size, then rearranged them again. Two hours later, and about to return to the house, he heard John Blessing's car pull up in front. John and Sophia emerged from the car and went inside. Cash felt it wise to just stay in the shop. Ten minutes later, John came out and strode quickly toward him.

"Hey, you, fella'! I'm telling you beyond any shadow of doubt, I'm calling the Warden, and you'll be out of here! We'll find someone reputable to help my mother!"

In his right hand, Cash held a large crescent wrench, and he suddenly had the urge to wrap it around John's neck. Instead, he just tapped it to his own forehead like a salute and said, "You have a pleasant drive home, John. Nice to meet you."

When John's car had disappeared around the corner, he went inside, not knowing what to expect from Sophia.

He saw her sitting on the couch and could tell she had been crying. He looked for a place to sit across the room from her, but she patted the cushion next to her and motioned for Cash to join her. She laced her fingers into his, cleared her throat, and began explaining.

"John is a very protective son. He's been that way ever since his father died. Of all my children, he gives me the most attention."

"Was there a reason for him to come to town this time? Just some random visit?"

"No, he and I had some personal business to take care of. But I had told him about you ahead of time, so he was loaded for bear when he got here. I thought he'd be more congenial and understanding. Now I know I should have warned you."

"What will he do next?"

Sophia turned directly toward Cash and said clearly, "If you're asking what he will do that affects you, he'll do nothing. Not if I have anything to say about it."

"And do you? Will he listen to you?"

"I think so. He's just mad right now. He promised to come back tomorrow and talk some more."

"I thought he would stay here with you for tonight, at least."

"He said he wouldn't as long as you were still here."

"My God! What is he thinking? I don't live here! In fact, there is my ride out front." With all that had happened, he welcomed the end of the day, but stopped at the door, turned, and said, "Sophia, would you like to meet a friend of mine? His name is Stanley. He's one of the staff at the Center and I met him down at Angola. Nice guy." He thought perhaps a distraction would take her mind off John's tirade.

Sophia shook her head. "Not now. This day has taken a lot out of me, and I need to lay down for a while."

Cash walked out to the waiting car with a jumble of thoughts creating a brain fog so foreign to him. Stanley put the car into gear without saying a word, just waiting for Cash to speak.

The two men had driven halfway back to Camp Beauregard while Cash described the day's events.

"So, this youngest of her grown children comes at me like I had kidnapped his firstborn, and Sophia's thoughts are on overload. She can't do anything with him. I've never seen her so helpless." He stopped talking and chewed on his lower lip.

Stanley had been listening with astonishment and disbelief upon hearing of John's threats and accusations.

"So, you really think he knows the Warden? How could someone from Atlanta know a warden in Louisiana?"

"You know, I can usually tell when someone is blowing smoke at me, but I just don't know about this guy. He could cause me a lot of pain. If nothing else, he'll stir things up."

"And that leads to a thread of suspicion, doesn't it?"

"Yeah, and I just – hang on! What's that up there? That car is head-on into that telephone pole!"

"Yeah! Just happened, too! Look! The cops aren't even here yet!"

"Stanley, step on it! I think that's John's car!"

"John? The one we were just talking about?"

"Go!"

Stanley brought the car to a screeching halt just beyond the accident. Smoke poured from under the crumpled hood, and Cash saw the first flicker of flames licking at the edges of the driver's door. They saw John slumped forward against the steering wheel, and blood covered his face.

"Get that door open!" yelled Stanley.

The car was leaning toward the driver's side, and the impact had jammed the hinges on the driver's door, but the two of them managed to pry it open with a groan of men and metal, while the doorframe grew hotter. Cash climbed in, reached through the growing intense heat and tried to unbuckle the seat belt. The airbag had not deployed, and Cash feared it might blow at any moment. In the distance, they could hear sirens.

"I can't reach the release button!" Cash yelled. The flames grew steadily. Stanley ran around to the passenger side and the door opened easily. A briefcase and a tote bag had emptied their contents throughout the interior of the car. He found the seatbelt button and pushed it. Nothing happened. Cash dug into his pocket and pulled out a rather large pocketknife and handed it across the seat to Stanley. The heat of the fire began to sting his face and neck. Five seconds later, the belt dangled loose and free. John was beginning to move his head as Cash wrapped an iron grip around the man's neck and shoulders. Together, they extracted him and carried him to a safe distance just as the fire truck arrived with police right behind. Surprisingly, Cash remembered noticing something in the back seat. He ran back to the car, opened a back door, and retrieved John's suitcase. Two seconds later, flames engulfed the car.

While they waited, Stanley asked Cash, "That knife you handed to me – where'd you get it?"

"I use it at the shop. That's where I found it. I guess I stuck it in my pocket out of habit."

"Does Hamm know you have it?"

"No. Come to think of it, you have it now."

"Yeah, and I'd better keep it until tomorrow when you go back to the shop. Make sure you leave it there."

Within minutes, the ambulance pulled away from the scene enroute to Rapides General Hospital while the two men spoke with the police. They had not seen the accident as it occurred, but others had and filled in the details. Twenty minutes later, they decided they should go back to Sophia's house and tell her the news. On the way, Stanley called Mr. Hamm and told him they would be late returning and why.

"Mr. Hamm says he needs to talk to you when we get back," Stanley said flatly.

"Did he say why?"

"No, but he sounded more concerned about talking to you than he was about hearing why we're late. Something's up, but I just can't figure it out."

Cash kept his eyes glued to the road ahead and thought, Now what? Is this day ever going to end?

They arrived at Sophia's house minutes later, explained the situation, and offered to take her to the hospital. She immediately declined and reached for her purse and car keys. They followed her car and parked outside the entrance to the ER. Once inside, Stanley flashed his badge and got Sophia quickly into the room where John lay, unconscious but breathing. Sophia clutched a Kleenex in one hand and spoke while never taking her eyes off John, still on a gurney.

"I can't thank you men enough," she murmured. "Most people wouldn't have taken the chance."

"Marine Corps attitude," Cash quipped. "Like riding a bicycle."

Stanley nodded in agreement, then reached for his cell phone. Cash hadn't heard it ring.

Stanley spoke in muted tones. "Yes, sir, we're at the hospital with her. We'd like to stay a while longer, we, uh – yessir, right away."

"Cash, Mr. Hamm just called and said we need to get back to his office. He's waiting to talk to you."

Cash looked at Sophia and said softly, "I'm sorry, Sophia. We need to leave. Are you okay?"

"Yeah, just worried about this one," she said as she held John's hand and never diverted her eyes from him.

"We'll come back tomorrow." He looked at Stanley and nodded, but Stanley backed away with an uncertain look on his face.

Christopher Hamm stood fuming in the office doorway when the two men arrived. He was chomping on a cigar as usual and said, "Both of you, get in here!"

Once in his office, Hamm turned to Cash and growled, "What's this I hear about you threatening Sophia's son with a crescent wrench?"

The accusation seemed to come from nowhere, and Cash stood motionless, shocked. He replied, "What? I – he – what? I mean - as he was leaving Sophia's house, I had a wrench in my hand, and I waved goodbye to him. That's all." He knew not to hide his thoughts. Hamm excelled at reading body language.

"You sure?"

"Absolutely! I'm not dumb enough to do something like that."

"No, but you're dumb enough to call one of my drivers a sonofabitch to his face."

The open office door behind them slowly swung closed, and from behind it sat the nameless driver Cash had encountered the day before.

Hamm continued, "Meet Eddy Maxwell. He told me about your amorous scene on Sophia's front porch. And now, John Blessing accuses you of threatening him. Mr. Blessing was right here in my office, bending my ear for twenty minutes! I hate to tell you this, but the fact is, I should call the Warden, and I know he's looking for any reason to recall you to Angola."

Cash was speechless. His nightmare was coming into focus. He looked at the faces of the other three men in the room and felt very much alone in the world.

Cash stood speechless, trying to gather his wits and find a last-ditch response. Hamm nervously shuffled stacks of papers on his desk. Finally, as the words came to him, Cash pointed to Eddy Maxwell and spat out, "First of all, you deserve to be called a sonofabitch for what you said about Mrs. Blessing. Secondly, she didn't have to kiss me. No one forced her." Then he turned to Mr. Hamm and said, "And last of all, Stanley and I just pulled John Blessing from a burning car before the EMT guys ever got there. If I'm such a wicked bastard, I could have just let him burn!" He pulled away his scorched shirt collar and exposed a patch of red skin.

Hamm waved his arms and shouted. "Wait, wait, hang on a minute!" He turned toward Eddy and asked with a growl, "What did you say about Mrs. Blessing?"

Eddy sat up straight and stammered, "I was just kidding, I didn't say much, but - you know, just guys talking."

Cash spoke up. "You called her a cougar, an old cougar, remember? Then you asked me if I had gotten any action out of her. I need to ask what you meant by that last part."

Hamm's face turned red. "This is my office, and I'll ask the damn questions! Maxwell, get out of here! Come back in two hours! And I don't want to see your face until then!" The man scrambled from the room like a rodeo bronc let out of a chute.

He then turned to Cash and asked, "You pulled him out of a burning car? The medics hadn't even arrived yet?"

Cash nodded. "We both did. I couldn't have done it by myself." He pointed to Stanley and said, "This guy is really cool in a tight situation. I'd hang on to him."

Hamm pursed his lips and thought for several seconds. Finally, he said, "Okay, you two go chill out somewhere. I have a phone call to make."

Once outside of Hamm's office, Stanley said quietly, "Eddy Maxwell is a distant nephew of the Warden. Be careful of anything you say within earshot of him. I've often heard him talking on the phone to folks at Angola. Even Mr. Hamm is careful what he says around him."

"Yeah, but Hamm didn't hesitate to toss him out of his office just now," Cash mumbled.

"Yeah, that's probably one of the reasons Mr. Hamm is making a call right now. He's covering his tracks before Eddy can call anyone."

The next morning, Cash and Stanley stopped by the hospital

and found Sophia next to John's bed. She wore the same clothes as the day before. A bedside table with uneaten food stood in the far corner.

They stood in the doorway to the room and knocked. Sophia looked up and immediately went to them and hugged them both.

"You guys deserve a medal. What angels you are! Come over here and speak to John. He's awake. John, look who's here!"

John Blessing was semi-dozing with a large bandage on his head. His left cheek had a wide abrasion, and his left eye was blue and swollen shut. When he saw them approaching, he tried to sit up, but Sophia put a hand on his shoulder, and he laid back down. He would not make eye contact with Cash, but just gazed at the ceiling.

Softly, he croaked, "I hear I owe you a favor."

"That's okay, just buy me a beer first chance you get. Mr. Langston was with me. He did as much as I did. Better make that two beers."

John paused as though gathering his thoughts. When he spoke, his words remained a little incoherent and choppy. "It seems I have some retractions to make. Sorry if I put you in a bind. Mom tried to tell me about all the things you did for her, and I guess I wasn't ready to listen."

Cash said nothing. This gave him his chance to rub it in, but he chose to remain quiet. Sophia broke the silence.

"His wife and daughter are coming tomorrow. They hope he'll be released in a day or two. He has a walloping concussion, and the doctor wants to watch him a little longer. When he gets out, the three of them will stay with me for a few days until it's safe to travel." She looked at Stanley and said, "We haven't met, have we?"

"No ma'am. I'm Stanley Langston. I'm a friend of – well – I work at the -"

"Stanley," she said. "Yes, Cash said he wanted to me to meet you." She shook his hand warmly.

Cash looked at John and saw he had dozed off again. "Sophia, I'll be at the shop. Just call if you need anything. In the meantime, we both need to get back to work."

Cash floated in a state of elation. He wanted to ask John if he had indeed called Angola, but he thought it wise to stay off that subject. Surely, this meant the Warden was not on his trail and that things would be back to the usual routine. In reality, he knew nothing could be routine anymore. There had been words spoken, feelings hurt and promises made. Nothing stays the same. Nevertheless, prayers answered, he thought. Hang on, did I just think that? Man, I'm getting soft!

He arrived at Sophia's house the next day just as she pulled out of the driveway. She waved from the car and Cash felt safe in assuming she was going to the hospital. He hoped she had rested somewhat after yesterday's drama.

In the shop, there were a few things requiring his attention before he put on his manager's hat. One machine needed a new drive belt and another needed new brake pads. He had just finished when he heard tires crunch on the gravel in front of the house. As the driver got out of the car, Cash shaded his eyes against the morning sun. He could tell by the figure it was female, but her face was in shadow.

"Hi, Cash. I hope I haven't caught you at a bad time."

"Jul – Julie? What the hell?"

She stopped at the sound of his remark. "Maybe not a good time?"

Cash's brain scrambled in a cascade of thoughts and images. He tried hard to hide his state of surprise, but he knew it appeared obvious. She stepped closer and she seemed more beautiful than he could remember.

"Julie! No – I mean, YES, this is a good time! Please don't leave." He wiped the grease from his hands and took a few steps toward her but stopped when he saw the look on her face.

"Cash, no one at the house knows I'm here. Please, don't make anything more of it. I just want to keep this between you and me. Promise?"

Cash realized his body language agreed with anything she said. They both stood in silence like slow motion, although they both knew it was only a few seconds.

"Would you like to sit down? We could go inside."

"No, I'm just here to give you what you need."

He shoved his hands in his pockets and squinted. "Yeah? What's that?" He felt the tension in his neck relax, and his imagination ran wild.

Julie crossed her arms, stared at the ground, and said without looking up, "I'm here to give you closure." She waited for it to sink in and finally looked up and continued, "I remembered at the party that you have feelings just like the rest of us, and we did have a thing going between the two of us at one time, even if it didn't last long. I want you to know that I did have feelings for you. I really did. I don't want you ever doubting yourself, especially because of me. You have so much charm and wit. You're a good-looking guy and I'm sure you'll find someone, eventually."

Cash felt like she had sent him soaring to the moon and now had dropped him in a free fall, a weightless feeling over a bottomless pit. How could he let himself imagine the impossible and then imagine it within reach?

"Closure? Closure? You came here to tell me that? Here, all secretive and hoping no one would see you? Are you that ashamed to be seen with me? What about all the charm and wit you just mentioned? Don't worry, I know exactly who I am. Thanks for rubbing it in."

Her voice trembled. "Cash, I'm sorry. I didn't mean to cause any hurt. I just wanted you to have a clean break with me, not like the one we had the night you were arrested." She paused and looked at him, waiting for a response. "Cash, I didn't have to come here like this. I took a real chance on how you would react and now I'm sorry I did."

She half-turned back toward her car when she heard Cash's voice.

He stammered, "Julie, wait. Just hang on a minute. You don't deserve to be spoken to like that. I have had a long time to think about you and where you were, what you were doing, all that stuff. It took guts for you to come here like this." His mouth groped for words, but nothing came forth. Finally, he said, "Thank you. I will always have a warm spot inside me where you used to be." He stopped and then continued, almost in a whisper, "Yeah, we did have a thing going. I screwed it up. Me and my jug."

"Is that still an issue?" she asked.

"No, I haven't had a drink since that night three years ago. Three years too late, I guess."

He saw Julie's face soften and melt. They both took a step

toward each other, but she held her hand up. "Stop. You are here," she whispered, "because my father paid for the attorney who handled your appeal. I asked him to do that. But the attorney apparently went further and spoke to the panel that allowed you to be here, which is more than my family paid for. Please don't read too much into that. It was like a runaway train. I had nothing to do with that decision, so bother thanking me or my father."

As if the weight of her own words had struck her just as hard as it had hit Cash, she clutched her hands over her mouth, shoulders trembling, eyes brimming with tears she couldn't hold back. When she finally turned and walked back to her car, Cash stood frozen, watching her disappear like the last fragile piece of a dream unraveling in slow, silent heartbreak.

Unable to concentrate, he went inside and sat at his desk, staring into empty space. On the desk, he found a note from Sophia informing him she would be at the hospital, where she would meet John's wife and daughter, then go out to lunch with them and come home. Could he please take any messages that might come in for her? She was expecting them.

He was in the middle of writing out invoices when the house phone rang. He wasn't sure if he should answer it; he had assumed she meant to watch the office phone closely. But didn't he do that anyway? No, she must have meant the house phone. On the fourth ring, he answered. A woman's voice came through the speaker.

"Is Sophia Blessing there, please?

"She's out right now. May I take a message?"

"Ah, are you family? This is Dr. Landry's office calling."

"Yeah, I can take the message. What is it?"

"Umm, okay. Just tell her that her appointment with Dr. Landry is confirmed for next Wednesday."

Cash tried to sound reassuring. "Right, next Wednesday with Dr. Landry." Think, think! "May I ask, does he have more than one office?"

"Yes, but this appointment is for the one right next to Cabrini Hospital. That's where her appointment is."

"Sure, thanks."

As soon as he hung up, he brought up Dr. Landry's website and saw him listed as an oncologist. He had to look that up on the internet to make sure he knew what it meant. Oncology, the study of cancer. It suddenly dawned on him what it meant. She's probably known for a while, told her family and that's why John came to be with her. He would tell her privately when she came home. Wednesday, that was a week away.

"This day has got to get better," he said out loud.

Mid-afternoon blossomed, and Cash found himself engrossed in gas tickets, invoices, and phone calls. He heard a car pull up in front, car doors opened and closed. Voices came up the walkway and into the living room. Voices, all female, three of them, one sounded a bit high-pitched, almost childlike. He recognized Sophia's raspy words, but he didn't recognize the other two. His office was not in the main part of the house, so he opted to wait until Sophia came to him instead of rushing out like a big, friendly dog. He tried to concentrate, but the trio made no attempt to maintain a quiet hush in the house, a solitude he had become accustomed to. Waves of laughter rolled in from the kitchen and then he heard Sophia's telltale cough coming down the hall.

"So, hard at work? Want some lunch or did you eat already?" Before he could answer, she continued, "Come to the kitchen. I want you to meet some folks."

He rose from his desk chair and followed her to the kitchen. He saw a middle-aged woman retrieving something from a shopping bag. She looked up when they entered the room. "Hi, you must be Cash," she said. "Heard so much about you."

"Thanks, nice to meet you, Mrs. Blessing."

"Please, it's Barbara." She shook Cash's hand firmly.

Then Sophia spoke up, "Where's Abigail?" In the background, he heard a toilet flush and the door to the powder room opened. "There she is! Abigail, meet Cash."

In Cash's life, women were available only for short-term flings until the newness wore off like an empty whiskey bottle. Commitment never entered his thoughts until he met Julie, and even then, it was a bust. Other women in his life had displayed a shallow attractiveness, bought and used for entertainment like a cheap novel, but this creature floating into the room hit him like a jolt of electricity, and his words hung in his throat.

As she shook his hand with both of hers, her cotton-soft palms matched the texture of her voice. "Hi, I'm Abigail Blessing. I hear my father owes you his life. I've never met a real-life hero before." She wore white Capri pants with a pink V-neck tee shirt and pink tennis shoes. Looking closely, he saw small, gold stud earrings and a faint wisp of lipstick. In front of him, he saw a lost, priceless treasure he had been searching for all his life, like a part of his life he didn't know was missing. From this moment forward, he could say he knew what an angel looked like.

After a split second, he stopped staring and quickly recovered. "Yeah - ah, hero? No, ah, I wouldn't say that. Heroes are just ordinary people who act quickly without thinking." He laughed gently and shrugged as he said it.

"Don't let him try to fool you," Sophia said with a serious look. "He's an ex-marine with two tours in Afghanistan. He knew exactly what he was doing."

As Sophia spoke, he realized he was still shaking Abigail's hands. He quickly regained his awareness and released them. "I'm just glad your dad's doing okay. He is, isn't he?"

Barbara spoke up and said, "The doctor wants to release him tomorrow, if he continues the way he is now. Call it lucky on several counts."

Mother and daughter were both cut from the same charming cloth. Abigail was simply a younger version of her mother. Both were about 5'5", dark brunette with shoulder-length hair that curled neatly at the tips, and flashing brown eyes. Abigail had a modest, well-proportioned figure and a flawless complexion with a hint of a dimple on each cheek. Her most attractive feature, however, shown in her sparkle. It wasn't just her eyes or her smile or the way her eyelids seemed to keep a subtle rhythm with the cadence of her words. It all came together with her energy and spoke a message of someone with both feet planted firmly on the ground and well aware of the world around her. Julie and his morning encounter with her suddenly seemed to be a distant acquaintance, a character out of a fairy tale, someone he had outgrown years ago.

Barbara and Sophia walked into the next room, leaving Cash and Abigail still talking.

Then he noticed the engagement ring on her left hand. It struck him as forbidden treasure as part of his punishment by society. Had he not been incarcerated, he might have met her first and that would be his ring, not someone else's. He felt no jealousy, but resignation that his lost years would always leave emotional scars representing all that he had missed.

"Nice ring," he said quietly. "Who's the lucky guy?"

Abigail's face seemed to come even more alive in response to Cash's question. "Oh, his name is Roger. I met him in college. He's in graduate school right now, almost finished getting his MBA."

"So, you're in college?"

"No, just graduated a couple of months ago. Looking for a job now."

"What college did you go to?"

"Roger and I both went to Emory. I got my degree in American Literature, and he got his a couple of years ago in Finance." Her voice had a bouncing, musical tone when she spoke of Roger.

Cash heard her words, but did not give them focused attention. The way she talked, the fluid motion of her hands, and the faintly visible twitch of her eyebrows all enveloped Cash in an enchanting and seductive daydream. Lost in his own world, he suddenly realized she had stopped talking and stood waiting for some kind of response from him. If there had been a question, he hadn't heard it. He recovered from his short mental journey and asked, "So, you want to write, teach, be an editor, or what?"

It was not what she expected to hear, but she answered at any rate, "Oh - I'm not sure. I'll know it when I see it."

"Must be hard searching when you don't know what you're looking for."

"That's the adventure of it all. Not knowing, but keeping everything on the high road. Good things happen to people who wait."

Her voice sounded silken, like a harp playing softly. Cash thought he could sit and listen to it all day.

She stopped and realized that he had kept her talking about herself, not paying much attention to his thoughts, if he had any. For some uncanny reason, she felt completely at ease talking to him.

He continued, "So, American literature. What do you like to read? Anything in particular?"

"I like family saga stories, especially around the Civil War time. I think the old South was a charming time."

"Yes, but a cruel time, don't you think?"

"Well, yes, it was. And there are stories on both sides of that cruelty line." She paused and continued, "And you know what? I don't know much about you. Tell me, how did you come to work for my grandmother?"

"How's your dad?"

"What? I asked about -"

"I know, but I want to know what your dad told you."

"About what?"

"About me."

For a moment, Cash felt like a cruel prankster who had led an unsuspecting prey into an embarrassing trap. He saw the telltale look of admission on her face as she shifted her eyes away from him, searching for the words of response.

"For someone with a degree in literature, you seem to be at a loss for words."

Cash's bluntness and candor caught her by surprise until she finally looked at him intently and said, "Yes, I know about you.

Daddy told me. He also told me today that he had misjudged you from the beginning. He was just worried about his mother, that's all."

"And he said I was in prison for doing – what?"

"That, I don't know. Do I need to?"

"That's up to you. I'll tell you this - in my flawed past, the only person I really jeopardized was myself." He didn't feel like mentioning the unsuspecting passenger in the back seat of his joyride.

Cash felt himself so drawn to this young woman, and yet, he knew she was off limits, already claimed by someone else. His imagination teased him, telling him how it might feel to kiss her, to dance close, to wrap his arms around her, to feel her warm breath in his ears.

Her words brought him back to reality. "Okay, now we're getting down to it. Tell me about yourself. I mean it, pal. I can be as stubborn as my grandmother, and I think you have already had a full dose of that. Okay?"

He had never known someone so easy to talk to. He felt as though he had known her all his life. Cash spent the next forty-five minutes giving her his life story in true candor, nothing withheld, nothing omitted. He slowly discovered she had a persuasive side and knew how to use it. She grimaced when he told her how Whip Langston had saved his life in their foxhole, but she didn't back away from hearing the rest of it.

"What a remarkable life!" Abigail sounded sincere when he finished.

"If you say so. You planned your life. I didn't plan any of mine. My life is just reacting to what's thrown at me."

Sophia and Barbara interrupted the conversation as they came back into the room. For a moment, Abigail and Cash stopped talking and looked up at them like two youngsters caught telling secrets.

Cash looked at his watch. "Oh, gee, look at the time! I still have stuff to do!" He stood and took a step toward the office, then stopped. "Oh, I almost forgot, Sophia, I have a message for you. Come to the office and I'll give it to you."

She followed him with a hint of curiosity until he handed her the note with the doctor's name on it and the confirmation of next Wednesday's appointment.

Sophia studied the note for a few seconds, then quietly asked, "Who else knows about this?"

"No one. That's why I brought you in here to tell you. If it's none of my business, just say so. But these other folks, your son and his family, what do they know?" He paused and looked at her more closely. "In a few days, they won't be here, but I will be. I'm here for whatever you need, Sophia. But it's hard to know what to do if I don't know what you're dealing with."

Sophia stood with her back to the open office door. She reached back and half-closed the door before speaking. Then she took both of his hands in hers, looked at him, and whispered softly, "I have had this hacking cough for months now. I blamed it on the cigarettes until John convinced me to have a chest x-ray." She stopped to clear her throat before continuing. "We saw my family doctor the first day John was here, and he immediately said I needed to see this other doctor." She stopped again and looked at him with fearful eyes and arched eyebrows. "It's time for me to stop pretending. Cash, I don't scare easily, but this -."

Cash had seen fear on the faces of others – men, women,

children. He knew he saw roaring fear in her eyes.

In the partially open doorway, out of Sophia's line of vision, stood Barbara and Abigail. Thinking they were alone, Sophia leaned her forehead against his shoulder. Cash gently gave her a squeeze and shook his head, almost imperceptibly, for the other two women to see, hoping they would get the message to say nothing. Then he leaned to one side and put a single fingertip to his lips. They understood and stepped back.

It had been one hell of a day.

Chapter 6

Two days passed, and John Blessing was discharged from the hospital. He came to occupy a bedroom in Sophia's house across the hall from the room where Barbara and Abigail slept. Try as he might, Cash could not keep his eyes off this 22-year-old jewel, especially when he arrived early one morning and caught all three women wearing bathrobes in the kitchen. They had invited him to join them, but he politely declined.

Everything about Abigail caused his thoughts to misfire and make no sense, smitten beyond rescue. She made him think he could hear music playing when he looked at her, music no one else could hear. She looked more beautiful each day, while Sophia looked more bedraggled each day. He knew his body language in Abigail's presence would be like a flag waving.

"Are you sleeping at all?" Cash asked Sophia when he could steal a private moment.

"Sleep? What's that? My mind is in a constant tumble. I can't seem to get my arms wrapped around the reality of all this crap."

"Can't the doctor give you something to help?"

"So, what's he going to do? Give me some junk to take so I can't see straight?

"Sophia, you're making assumptions that aren't helping you any. Call the doc."

"A couple more days and I'll see this new doc anyway at my scheduled appointment. What's his name? Oh yeah, Dr. Landry." She lit a cigarette and inhaled deeply.

"Have you ever considered giving up those things?"

"Why? At my age, what little else do I have left to enjoy?" She took a long draw and exhaled through her nose. "Besides, these are the filtered kind. Doesn't that help?" She finished with a mocking grin.

John drifted into the room, black-eyed and sleepy, and said, "No, Mama, I told you years ago to quit. It doesn't matter if they're filtered or not. Tell her, Cash. She listens to you."

John had done a complete turnaround in his mistrust of Cash. Too bad it took a near-fatal accident to bring that about. Regardless, it relieved Cash to see the change. Truth be told, John was a pleasant guy to talk to under less stressful conditions. His black eye improved gradually as the days went by. His headaches had become almost non-existent. The family even heard him laugh at Sophia's usual dose of blunt humor. She could tell you to go to hell and you'd still love her for it.

Wednesday arrived, and Barbara and Abigail took Sophia to her oncology appointment. While she was out, Cash took a break from his desk and struck up a conversation with John, who had stayed behind out of concern for his head injury, which was still healing.

"So, do you remember what caused the accident?"

"I never got to tell the whole story to the cops, but there were lots of witnesses. Apparently, someone changed lanes in front of me and I didn't see it until the last minute. I swerved to avoid the collision. That's all I remember."

"Yeah, and collided with a telephone pole. What about the car that caused it all?"

"Apparently, no one saw it stop. Just kept right on going. No one got a plate number and there were about six different descriptions of the car, so we'll probably never know. We're not even sure if it was a man or a woman driving." He stopped and looked toward the front door. "Say, when are they due back from Mom's appointment?"

"I don't know. I was busy and didn't see them leave. Did Abigail go with them?"

"Of course. She wouldn't let anything like this go by without her being right in the middle of it. Bundle of energy, that girl!"

"Have you met her fiancé?"

"No, I haven't and neither has Barbara. It all happened so suddenly." Cash noticed a hint of a frown on his face. Maybe a hint of fatherly concern.

"Have they set a date yet?"

"Haven't gotten that far. I heard some discussion about waiting until, ah, what's his name? Roger! That's right – until he finishes his graduate program next year. Abbie seems to be happy with the status quo right now."

Cash noticed the tone of endearment in John's voice when he called his daughter 'Abbie' instead of Abigail. He tried to imagine her as a small child. Daddy's girl, for sure. He couldn't remember anyone calling him anything except 'Cash.' Come to think of it, he couldn't imagine any affectionate form of his name.

As he let his thoughts drift for a moment, he found himself trying to remember what his mother's voice sounded like. He couldn't. She was someone he only heard about, some mysterious, mythical figure. Just as he turned to go back to his desk, the sound of Sophia's car penetrated the house from the driveway. He decided it was best if he remained in the background as they discussed family issues. Quietly, he returned to his office work and tried to listen through the walls. Nothing audible came through.

No amount of busy work could keep his mind away from the conversations going on in other parts of the house. Family dynamics had never been a matter of experience to him, only echoes of mental snapshots taken long ago and hidden between pages of the years. He knew he was not part of it. Checking his calendar and organizing his desk for the next day, he decided to slip out through the back door and wait for his ride. When the family came looking for him, he had already left.

The afternoon driver was Eddy Maxwell. Cash saw him behind the wheel and went for the back seat without a second thought. A familiar voice greeted him as he entered the car.

"Hey dude!" Oscar Kelly had been back on his meds for a while and now no one could shut him up. The transfer to Camp Beauregard had not been exactly seamless for him, and no one at the Center knew he needed medication of any kind until Rodney spoke up.

The surprise at seeing Oscar in the back seat took Cash's mind temporarily off the tension and drama back at Sophia's house. The short ride gave the two men time to talk and swap stories.

Cash asked, "So, where you been today?"

"I got me a job if you want to call it that. It's at that big Community Church over on MacArthur Drive, you know what I'm talking about?"

"Um, yeah, I think that's one of our lawn care clients. Come to think of it, I've been there. What do they have you doing? You preaching or taking up collection?"

"Naw, I just go around the place pushing a broom and emptying trash cans. I just try to look busy. They're nice folks.

They got a couple of single gals there in the office. Not bad lookin' ones."

"Did you meet Gladys?"

"Who?"

"Gladys Perkins. She's the office manager. Auburn hair?"

"Oh, yeah! Yeah, but I think she's out of my league."

"Why do you say that? I thought redheads attracted each other."

"Yeah? I dunno', maybe so."

"How many hours do you work there?"

"Not many. They can't afford too much." Oscar paused and continued, "You know anything about that trade school across town?"

"Yeah, I took some classes there right after high school. It's okay, I guess. It's been a while since I was there."

Oscar gazed out the window, then said, "So, tell me, I didn't know you had a grandmother in these parts."

The source of Oscar's false information quickly became apparent and brought a smile to Cash's face. "Yeah, sort of. But she's really not my grandmother. You're referring to the lady I work for. Sophia's a real character. Maybe next time you can meet her." He could see a look of confusion on Oscar's face, and he finally explained the highlights of the relationship, leaving out many details.

Eddy Maxwell listened to their conversation and, while waiting for a red traffic light to change, he half-turned and started to speak, "Yeah, she's a nice lady. I once knew…"

"Hey, the light's green. Let's go!" Cash reached across Oscar and spoke with a gentle bump on the back of the driver's seat. Oscar looked at him with a question on his face.

Minutes later, as they walked toward their bunkhouse, Oscar asked, "What's with you and that driver? He seemed nice to me."

"We've had words. He said some things that I didn't appreciate. I don't think he can be trusted. Right now, he's trying to act cool and get back on good terms with me. I wouldn't get too tight with him if I were you."

Supper brought on the usual boisterous time in the dining hall. Cash could hear a low-level hum of conversation throughout the place with random outbursts of laughter. Everyone sounded happy, but always a bit on edge. Right now, they all had a roof over their heads, clothes to wear, and free meals. They had a daily taste of freedom and more than just pocket change. Some had opened bank accounts and tried to save what little they could. One thing loomed over it all, however.

When their six months ended, assuming they had walked a clean mile, all would be free to go back out into the civilized neighborhoods with all the advantages and temptations that came with the territory. A small percentage, however, would probably find themselves back within the walls of Angola, but most would find a niche that fit.

One of the last things to happen before release was regaining their driver's license. When each trustee finally saw their name on the schedule for that event, they knew the end was within sight. And then their caution level went up tenfold. No one wanted to drop the baton on the final lap.

Cash and Oscar sat together during the evening meal. They were both content, for a while, to just listen and watch.

"So, tell me about Gladys," Cash asked.

"Gladys? She's nice, I guess."

"Do you ever talk to her?"

"Well, yeah, sort of."

"That's it? Just sort of?" Cash looked at him with raised eyebrows and pursed lips.

"Ah, no, not exactly. We, you know, we sat together in the break room yesterday and had a cup of coffee together."

"And? Nothing else?"

"She told me I'd look a lot more appealing – that's the word she used – if I got a haircut."

"And she told you that – because…..?"

Cash could see Oscar blushing. Maybe he had found something special.

Both men sat silently, staring into the depths of the groups gathered at different corners of the dining hall. Oscar finally asked Cash the burning question that every man in the place carried like a ball and chain.

"So, what brought you to a point of conflict with the wonderful State of Louisiana? Did you break into the governor's mansion?"

Cash grinned and collected his thoughts for a moment. "No, I just got drunk and stole the personal vehicle belonging to the Chief of Police."

"Wow! No shit? Where?"

"Across the river in Alexandria. Right over there!" He pointed and finished with a smile and a long slurp of his iced tea.

Oscar took a big bite of food and continued to talk with his mouth full. "Yeah, I knew there was something about you I liked.

I'm surprised they let you come here."

"Just dumb luck, I guess."

"Or providence. That's a word I learned at the church where I'm working. Gladys said it was providence that I came to work there. I have no idea what she meant."

Cash was amazed at the naivete of this man. "So, ask her. I don't think she was talking about a city in Rhode Island. On second thought, ask Pastor Bob."

"You ask him. He's coming here, you know."

"Who?"

Oscar stared at him wide-eyed. "Bob Allen, the preacher at the church where I push a mop, empty the trash, and have coffee with Gladys. What'd you think I meant?"

"When's he coming? Do you know?" Cash asked, trying to sound casual. "I knew a preacher when I was down in Angola. He used to come to AA meetings. The cops raided a strip joint in New Orleans and guess who they found in the back room?"

"You're kidding!"

"Nope. Not kidding. Just couldn't keep his zipper closed, I guess."

"Well, this guy's different, I think. Got a family and a houseful of kids. I've seen his wife. Good-looking hammer. I'm sure she keeps his home fires burning."

"Is she a redhead like Gladys?"

Oscar looked at him, puzzled.

Cash let him think for a few seconds and saw Rodney about to leave. He called out, "Hey, Rodney! C'mere a second. What do you know about a preacher named Bob Allen coming here?"

Rodney walked over to their table, proud to be the village voice of information. "Yeah, he's coming. Boss man's gonna' make an announcement tomorrow. He decided we need some spiritual uplift around here."

"When's he coming?"

"We'll find out tomorrow." With that, Rodney grinned, chewed on his toothpick, turned toward the door, and left.

Morning came and everyone checked the bulletin board, as usual, before starting their day outside the fenced area. Just as Rodney had said, Pastor Bob Allen would be in the dining room after supper the following day for a brief church service and discussion. This put a small damper on some of the residents because the dining area, the small game room, and the bunk room were the only three available places to lounge indoors after every evening meal.

Most of the men had developed a habit of using the dining area as a living room after supper. Their living space would now become a temporary chapel. Mr. Hamm believed they could give up an hour or so every two weeks.

Chapter 7

The two men walked to Hamm's office for privacy. "They want you to what?" Christopher Hamm could not hide the look of shock at what Cash explained to him. "That's the most cockeyed plan I have ever heard of. You don't know how to care for an aging woman with cancer!" He could feel the man's breath on his face.

"I know, I know. I had the same thought when they asked me. But it seems they have planned this through to the end. I'm going back and forth in my own mind, trying to decide what to do and I just…"

"You, of all people! That's the biggest pile of bullshit I have heard in a long time! You showed her a small morsel of attention when you took her home from my house and God knows what really happened on her front porch the next morning, and now they've practically adopted you into the family!" He walked toward the window and turned around and shook his finger at Cash.

"Can you imagine what the folks down at Angola would think of this? I'll give you an easy, undeniable answer! As long as you're here under my watch, you'll be there with her during the day and at no other time! Your job is with Argyle Landscaping, not Cash Ratliff's Guardian Angels! You got that?" Their noses were almost touching, and each man could feel the other breathing.

Cash remained calm, but he had never felt so torn as now between the compassion of his heart and the rules of the society he lived in. Never in his life had he felt so undecided about anything. But all that didn't matter. Mr. Hamm had just decided it for him. End of story. Cash turned without saying a word and left only to linger in the outer office as Hamm brushed past him on his way out. He still felt conflicted, however, between feeling relieved of an obligation or carrying a burden of guilt. Neither possibility gave him a warm, comfortable feeling of redemption. Neither one seemed – what was the missing word he needed? It just didn't seem right. What would he tell the Blessing family? How would he explain it? What amazed him most was Hamm's apparent self-contradiction. He acted very upset to hear of Sophia's illness, but he'd be damned if he'd let Cash help with her care. That didn't add up. He had nowhere else to turn. Or maybe…?

Pastor Bob had left him his home number. Seeing no one around in the immediate vicinity, he took a chance, dug in his wallet for the number, then went back into Hamm's office, glanced around again to be sure he was alone and picked up the phone.

Bob answered after two rings. "Pastor, this is Cash Ratliff. Remember me? Yeah, okay, I guess… Listen, I got this problem." He searched for words. "Uh, I told you about the Blessing family asking me to, you know, help take care of Sophia."

Bob answered carefully. "Yes, I remember. How's that working out?"

"Well, it's not. I just talked to Mr. Hamm, and he's got me doubting if I can do it."

"That you're not capable?"

"Well, yeah, that, too."

"You mean there's more? What else did he say?"

"A lot. In fact, he was really pissed – sorry. Yeah, he was upset, and I'm not sure why."

Bob sighed and said, "I hate to sound like a broken record, Cash, but what did I tell you to do the last time we talked about this?"

Cash felt perspiration forming on his forehead. He could take out a machinegun nest and never break a sweat, but he felt this decision testing his limits. "You said… you said…" Cash heard himself almost stuttering. "You amaze me, preacher. I come to you for answers and what I'm getting sounds like song lyrics. I tell you what, you talk to God for me, okay? You seem to have an open line to Him." With that, he hung up.

Leaving Hamm's office, he made a straight line for the bunkhouse with no deviations. In times like this, tunnel vision always kicked in. It always came as a reflex and it was all he had to get him through whatever threatened him. *No distractions, no sideways glances, just get me out of this!* He had always relied on his own judgement when big decisions landed at his feet. His enemy always showed itself.

Now he faced an adversary that defied definition, a feeling of indecision. This was one of the few times he found himself outside his comfort zone, in a strange land with no map, vulnerable to the guidance and opinion of other people instead of his own instinct. His confidence and self-esteem had never been rendered so fragile, a feeling as foreign as imagining he could speak Chinese.

Two men he had learned to respect, Christopher Hamm and Bob Allen, had left him in an emotional freefall with conflicting advice and direction.

Entering the door to the sleeping quarters, his bunk was at the opposite end of the room, and several men had to step out of his way as he shoved through the crowd milling around after supper. He sat on the side of the bed with his back to the others. They could tell something was on his mind, and they knew not to bother him. Twenty minutes went by. Finally, Oscar Kelly took a chance and sat down beside him, approaching him cautiously like he would a wounded, wild animal.

He waited almost a minute, sitting there, and finally said in a low tone, "Hey dude, what's up?"

Cash turned and stared at him with cold, hard eyes. His breathing came in short, labored gasps. He raised his eyes and looked up at the ceiling, still deep in thought. Finally, and while still looking upward, he said, "Does it ever seem like everything you want to do is stacked against you? Huh?"

Oscar moved an inch closer and continued to speak where no one else could hear. "Give me some details, pal."

"It's Hamm - who in the hell does he think he is? I've done everything he asked me to do and more. Now – now, he can't give me this one little bit of wiggle room! I needed advice and he gave me a butt chewin'! And that damn preacher was no help at all!"

Such words coming from Cash Ratliff boomed like a thunderstorm warning to those around him. He always gave the appearance that nothing rattled him. Oscar remained silent for a few seconds, then he whispered in a hushed tone to one of the men behind him, "Go see if Stanley has left for the day."

Oscar sat by him, not saying a word for about five minutes, just listening to Cash breathing. Stanley came in and saw the crowd of men standing around Cash with Oscar sitting beside him on the left side. He sat down next to Cash on the right side.

"I ought to wring that sonofabitch's neck! He gets me involved with people and then he doesn't let me do what I gotta' do, and then -"

Stanley finally spoke and asked, "Hey, can you tell me what's going on? They sending you back to the place?"

Cash looked first at Oscar and then at Stanley and then at the others who had gathered around. "You think that's what's happening? You think I'm going back to Angola? Hell no! That's the one thing that's NOT happening. My God, how could you be thinking that? Shit! If Hamm would just listen to me and try to understand what I'm going through, it would – he just – I don't know, I just don't know."

Stanley spoke in gentle, muted words. "I'm just trying to get some perspective on whatever is happening. Take your time. We have nowhere else to go tonight. Everyone here is on your side. Just tell us what the problem is."

Christopher Hamm arrived at home several minutes after his conversation with Cash. As he walked in the front door, his wife greeted him.

"You're working late tonight. What's up?"

Hamm rubbed his eyes, then massaged the back of his neck. "Oh, nothing important. Just had to do a little adjusting with one of the inmates."

"Who?"

He stared at the floor and answered, "Hmm? Oh, Cash Ratliff. He's got some crazy notion in his head that just won't work. I had to straighten him out. He'll be okay." Hamm went to the liquor cabinet and poured himself a drink. Olivia's eyes bore in on him.

"Must have been a deep discussion," she said.

He looked at the contents of his glass, then realized she had asked for an explanation. He responded, "Huh? Oh, nothing really. This woman he's working for -"

"Sophia? She's a piece of work. You can't help but love her."

"Yeah, that's what has Cash all wrapped around the axle about modifying his work agreement."

"Pour me one of those, too," Olivia said. "Modifying – like what?"

Hamm poured one for his wife and brought it to her. "Well, Sophia is a sick woman. I just found out today. Her family is here and they're making arrangements for her home care."

"So, what's the problem with Cash?"

Hamm took a long sip and said, "He's all twisted up inside about the Blessing family. They want him to be part of the caregiving team. I told him absolutely not! What a crazy idea!"

Olivia sat up straighter. For several seconds, her eyes explored the face of her husband, then she asked as though she hadn't heard it correctly, "They want him to be part of the care plan?"

Her piercing look did not escape Hamm's attention. "Yeah! A Work Release Trustee suddenly turned into a Florence Nightingale thing! Can you imagine that?"

Olivia sat her drink on the coffee table, cocked her head and looked straight at him. "Let me get this straight. You assigned him that job and for what purpose?"

"Honey, you know what my job is. We talked about it before we moved here." His voice became stern, and he gestured with his hands like an orchestra conductor. "Our purpose is to re-acquaint men in the system with the outside world so they can function when they get out."

She looked at him with a twinkle in her eye, a look her husband knew so well. "Is it working for Cash?" She paused to let it sink in. "Is he turning over that new leaf for you? Can he function in a normal environment?"

Christopher Hamm suddenly saw himself being gently and slowly backed into a corner. Olivia had a soft heart and frequently asked her husband to let the men do odd jobs around their house. She enjoyed their company and kept a mental list of those men due for release, which ones had family, which ones had personality quirks. Hamm knew he had to watch her closely to prevent too much emotional attachment. If these men had been puppies in an animal shelter, she would have rescued them all.

"Who took Sophia home after our house party?" she asked.

"Cash did, but he wasn't supposed to get caught up in anything else. Just give her a ride home, that's all I told him to do."

Olivia's voice remained quiet. "Like some kind of robot. Christopher, he's only human. You gave him a chance to see something outside of his usual rotten circle of experience, and now he's involved. You can't make him backtrack then just draw a line he can't cross and expect him to have no sense of loss or regret. You're giving him exactly what the system should be giving him. You can't take that away from him." Her voice was soothing and affectionate.

"But if the Department of Corrections finds out -"

Her eyes suddenly bulged, and she hissed through her teeth, "You know what to do! Screw the Department, Christopher!!"

In the sleeping quarters, several of the men decided to give Cash more space and went outside. He had brought certain details of his struggle out into the open, but his deepest feelings remained buried. He learned at a young age that showing one's inner thoughts suggested a sign of weakness. As the men left the room, they passed Christopher Hamm coming in through the door.

Hamm stopped when he saw the crowd. He waited by the entrance until, one by one, the remaining few men saw him standing there and began to disperse. Stanley and Oscar stood and quietly stepped back. Hamm knew the situation needed a private conversation and this was not the place for it. He closed half the distance to Cash's bunk and stopped before speaking.

"Hey, Ratliff, come walk with me. C'mon, really, let's talk." The remaining crowd finally broke up and Cash slowly stood and faced the man, but without taking a step. "I mean it," Hamm repeated, "Let's take a walk."

Once outside, Hamm spoke, almost in a stammering voice. Cash thought he caught a whiff of liquor on the man's breath. "Look, this has been a tough day. Ah, yeah." He stopped and rubbed his temples. "We all have tough days, and I have my share of them. Today was one of those days and I may have been a just a bit out of line with you a few minutes ago." As usual, he waved his hands as he talked.

Cash shot a cold glance at him. Only a slit of the evening sun shown, and the faces of both men melted into muted shadow. The heat from the walkway had not yet cooled down, so they walked on the grass and found a cooler spot under a large oak. Neither man made solid eye contact with the other.

"You, ah, you have met my wife, Olivia, haven't you?"

Cash folded his arms and answered sharply while looking at the distant tree line, "Yes, we've met."

The Director searched for the next thing to say and finally spoke. "Okay, I got home tonight right after we talked, and my wife, well, she's good at reading my face, and you know, she saw I was in deep thought about something. She has a way of pulling facts out of my head. Some women are just good at that, aren't they?" Cash kept his arms folded and turned his head to look at Hamm point blank but said nothing.

Hamm cleared his throat and continued with an apologetic tone, "I told her about our conversation, and she told me right away that my comments to you were the most cold-hearted thing she had heard today. And she's right! I have to make cold-hearted decisions in this job. I just didn't explain it well enough to you. Like I said, it's been a hell of a day!" He paused to let it sink in.

"So, you interrupted your evening at home to come back here and tell me that nothing has changed since we talked? So, why are we out here talking?"

Hamm threw his arms up in exasperation. "No! I'm trying to explain to you up front what today's been like, and I just wanted to tell you, well, I was wrong! Damn it, I was wrong, and we're out here because I didn't want to say it in front of the other men! I must have their absolute respect and, well, you know how it is. I just, I just can't let them see me give in to anybody. Not even you."

Cash stood perfectly still, not believing his ears. His whole world suddenly seemed in a reverse tumble. He felt a growing elation and euphoria that he had never thought possible. For a moment, he felt at a true loss for words, then disbelief tried to creep back in.

Hamm continued, "So, what do you think? Can you do it?"

Cash almost felt like kissing the man. He still couldn't totally restrain his enthusiasm. "Uh, yeah! You bet your ass I can do it! Oh, sorry! Yes sir!" He almost shouted his response, then wiped his eyes with bare fists.

The two of them turned and quietly started back toward the buildings. Cash had a thought and said eagerly, "Mr. Hamm, may I use your office phone for about half a minute?"

He walked into the director's office and dialed a number. It rang several times and went to voicemail. He left a message. "Pastor Bob, this is Cash. I'm calling to tell you…just to tell you…everything's better, it's like…oh, never mind."

The next morning, Cash was eager to bring his decision to the Blessing family. He found Eddy Maxwell behind the wheel again. Cash's cheerful mood perplexed Eddy so early in the day.

"Hey, Eddy, how's things with you? Beautiful day, isn't it?"

"Okay, I guess. What happened? Someone put happy juice in your coffee?"

"Naw, it's a great day and it's going to get even better!"

Eddy had a sparkle in his eyes. "Does that mean you heard about my news?"

"No, what's that?"

"I'm getting transferred back down to the big house. Big promotion for me."

Cash looked down to avoid eye contact so Eddy couldn't see the broad grin on his face. Christopher Hamm must have a magical way with words.

Eddy stopped the car in front of Sophia's house and Cash almost ran to the front door. Abigail sat in a rocker on the front porch, sipping a cup of coffee. Fully dressed, instead of lounging in her housecoat, she greeted him with a warm smile. He felt his heart skip at the sight of her. Her radiance never failed to grab his insides and make his pulse race.

"Come inside, I have some good news for you," he said with a cheery tone.

Reading his thoughts, Abigail wrapped her arms around his neck and kissed his cheek. They both stepped away from each other and their eyes locked on each other for a moment, just long enough for Cash to wonder what thoughts she held.

They walked into the living room just as Barbara and John emerged from the bedroom. Cash saw a look of anticipation on their faces.

He almost bounced as he spoke and didn't wait for them to sit down. "Okay, here's the deal. I had several crucial conversations with some folks last night," he began. "And it looks like we can do this – I mean – I can do this." He nodded positively and looked around the room at the Blessing family for their reaction.

Their beaming looks of gratitude told him this would be a full day, a special day. Cash thought John's face would split from the smile he wore. Barbara pranced across the floor and hugged him in a full embrace. He turned to Abigail, and she simply beamed with gladness but made no move toward him.

John announced, "So, in the next few hours, we need to do some planning. Is Mama awake yet? She needs to be in on this."

Barbara spoke in a more serious, focused tone, "We are going to be leaving tomorrow morning. Abigail is staying for another week, simply because she wants to be with her Granny, and there's nothing pressing back in Atlanta to make her rush back."

"I just want to spend more time with her," she said to Cash. "And you might get the chance to meet Roger!"

"Roger? Oh yeah, Roger. How will that happen?" His eyes spanned the room before looking toward her, and he felt a small stab in his gut.

Abigail saw the intensity of his stare, but slowly continued with a hint of uncertainty. "He's driving through on his way to Houston for something related to one of his classes. I'm not quite sure what. But anyway, he's going to stop off only for a couple of hours. He seems really anxious to get there."

John piped up and said, "It looks like we're avoiding our future son-in-law, but we just couldn't stay long enough to meet him. At least, not this time."

Barbara said, "Let's give Cash some time to organize his day, then we'll all sit down and talk. Sophia should be up by then."

Cash left the room, avoiding any more eye contact with Abigail. While he settled in the office, the Blessing family started breakfast. The smell of bacon frying penetrated through the house. He could hear their voices through the crack in the door. It sounded like Christmas morning, from what little he could remember of Christmas morning. Sophia's croaking laughter joined them after a few minutes.

As he approached a stopping point in his work, he heard the office door open behind him. Before he could turn, Sophia approached his chair from the rear and wrapped her arms around him. After a few seconds, she planted a quick kiss on the back of his neck and left the room without saying a word.

Cash thought to himself, *I think I remember, this is what family feels like.*

They had picked up the breakfast plates when Cash walked into the kitchen. Abigail stood by the sink and the others sat at the breakfast table. The unspoken atmosphere in the room spoke of both anticipation and dread. John had a pad of paper and a calendar in front of him. Twenty minutes later, he had outlined a clear picture of the family's tentative plans for Sophia. There would be an initial round of chemotherapy to buy some time.

For reasons known only to her doctors, radiation treatment had been ruled out. Then there would be follow-up appointments. Cash saw his role as pivotal in making it work. He had his driver's license now and he had nothing better to do than sit in doctors' offices waiting for Sophia to be seen.

Customers who might call could leave a message. In the recesses of his thoughts, he quietly looked forward to a week with Abigail. So what if she wore an engagement ring? He could still look, couldn't he? She reminded him of a fine museum piece planted there to feast one's eyes upon but not touch. Same difference. He just couldn't get enough of her. Nevertheless, he reminded himself, she's spoken for and furthermore, far out of his league.

When the discussion of plans ended, Sophia stood and said in her usual manner, "You folks excuse me, I got to go shake some dew off the lily. I'll be right back."

Cash saw John blush and Barbara shake her head in silent laughter.

Abigail spoke up, "That's my Granny." She noticed a perplexed look on Cash's face. "Never mind," she said, "I'll explain it later." They all heard the bathroom door close shut.

With Sophia out of the room, Cash brought up an additional point to consider. "You know, all this planning is based on our best guess of timing. We can't ignore the fact that her condition is not predictable, and this may all go out the window and make us re-think and start over."

"And we cross that bridge when we come to it," John said. "Right now, we have a plan that makes sense."

The next morning, Cash arrived and found Abigail talking to someone on the phone. Sophia had not roused up for the morning yet. She had been sleeping later and later each day as her energy levels slowly drained. John and Barbara had already left.

The insurance company paid for a rental car while the final facts of the accident report fell into place. Cash went straight to the office and turned on the computer. He heard Abigail saying good-bye and hanging up the phone. She came into the office with a glorious, beaming smile and a bounce in her step.

"Roger just called from Monroe. He stopped there for the night, and he will be here today around lunchtime. You'll like him. He can't stay long, but he's eager to get here. I can't wait to see him again!" She clapped her hands like a child as she spoke.

Cash looked up from his desk and smiled weakly. He felt like a detached, invisible outsider when Abigail talked about Roger. She had no idea of the hunger and yearning growing in him, and he could imagine a scene where he could only watch the two of them from some isolated vantage point where his feelings had no impact, no connection, no value. It was someone else's joy, not his. And now, Sophia, the one person he had grown to love in a special way, faced her remaining days with rare strength and courage that he had never witnessed before outside of the Marine Corps. He saw newly found treasures in his life, sadly slipping away before he could savor the full taste of them.

Roger arrived mid-afternoon in a dark green Mustang. Cash watched through the window as Abigail ran out to the car and wrapped herself around him in a seemingly endless embrace even before he could completely exit the car and stand on his feet. He looked young and slender, about mid-twenties, wearing sunglasses, tight-fitting white shorts, a pale green plaid shirt open at the top three buttons and the shirttail flapping in the breeze.

A gold chain hung loosely around his neck. On his feet he wore penny loafers and no socks. On his left arm, Cash saw a large, ornate, gold wristwatch that seemed to reflect the daylight like tiny searchlights, in addition to a matching ring on his other hand. He had a tanned complexion and wavy, dark hair that covered the tops of his ears.

She paused to smother him with more kisses and then led him by the hand toward the house. He had stopped briefly to grab a briefcase from the front seat of his car. Cash went back into the office and heard them talking in hushed tones in the living room. He forced himself to give them their moment until she heard Abigail's voice calling him.

"Cash, can you come out here? I want you to meet someone!"

He took a deep breath and rose from his desk chair. When he walked into the living room, the two of them stood loosely arm in arm and both looked in his direction with bright faces and smiles. Cash saw Roger give Abigail a quick squeeze as Cash extended his hand.

"Hi, I'm Cash Ratliff. I'm Mrs. Blessing's office manager."

"Roger Fitzpatrick, pleased to meet you." He shook Cash's hand vigorously. "Heard good things about the way you're running the grass clipping business. Deep turf stuff!" He stopped to grin for a moment and continued, "But, a dollar's a dollar, right?"

The remark gave Cash a moment of hesitation, but he decided to ignore the condescension. Abigail didn't seem to hear it. He noticed how Roger meticulously ran his fingers through his hair and tossed his head to one side ever so slightly as he spoke.

Abigail stroked Roger's arm, looked at him, and asked, "Are you hungry?" He nodded and whispered something inaudible in her ear. She giggled and walked toward the kitchen. Abruptly, she stopped and turned to Cash. "I'm sorry, do you want something to eat, too?" He nodded and thanked her.

Sophia was napping when Roger arrived, and she now stepped into the room with the two men. "Hi, do I know you? I'm Sophia Blessing, Abigail's grandmother. You must be Roger."

Roger spoke as smooth as fresh cream from a dairy parlor as he greeted Sophia with a gentle handshake, a toothy grin, and a slight tilt of his head. He commented on his drive from Atlanta and how glad he was to finally meet some of Abigail's family. The whole time he talked, he stroked Sophia's hand like she was royalty. *More like stroking a lapdog,* Cash thought. Cash stood back and watched. Sophia gave Roger the same close look she gave Cash at their first meeting.

Abigail came back into the room and remarked, "Hi, Granny! Oh, good, you've met my guy." She glided up next to him and wrapped her arm around his waist. "Come on into the kitchen everyone, I've got a plateful of sandwiches made."

The four of them sat around the table, with Roger doing most of the talking. Ironically, he grew up in Alexandria and had graduated locally from Bolton High School. He seemed rather proud of the fact that he had attended Emory and frequently referred to it as 'The Harvard of the South.'

Within only a few minutes, he told them all about his future plans, why he planned to be the first multi-millionaire in his family, and how he intended to spend it. The more he talked, the more his head tilted upwards.

At one point, Cash was almost looking inside the man's nostrils and he turned his face away to hide a chuckle. He reminded Cash of a coonhound sniffing the air.

Roger continued like he was his own biggest fan, "I have an

economics professor who says this country will someday abandon the almighty dollar and come up with a different currency and a program of shifting funds between various investment instruments with such seamless effort we'll all be doing it in our sleep someday. I plan to be the first one to show what it does."

Abigail sat, mesmerized and in total belief of everything he said. Sophia and Cash seemed at a loss for words. Then Abigail proudly reminded them that Roger had majored in Finance.

"Yes, in simple terms, I majored in finance," Roger said with an eye-rolling look. "Actually, my project was a population algorithm based on global stock index of large and small cap mutual funds. For the time being, that's where the money is." He finished with a lukewarm condescending look that made Cash want to rub the guy's face on the sidewalk.

Cash finally got a word in. "Finance? Okay, I get it. So, like – you majored in money?" He finished with a cheshire cat smile. He could not tell if Roger saw the veiled sarcasm. Abigail certainly did and gave him a frown.

Finally, Sophia spoke up. "So, why don't you look at the bookkeeping template our accountant showed us and tell us what you think of it?"

"Ah! That would be my pleasure. You see, CPAs these days are still in the dark ages. My professors at Emory have a new way of doing things and they -"

"What do they call it?" Cash interrupted.

"Well, they haven't settled on a name yet. In fact, there's still a lot of details to iron out and -"

"Let's go in the office then and you show me." Cash's voice had a hint of blunt firmness that broke into Roger's rhythm.

Roger stopped, glanced at Abigail and said, "Sure, won't take but a second."

Sophia stood and said, "You two go talk shop while Abigail and I straighten up the kitchen."

"Don't be long," Abigail chirped.

Cash led his new acquaintance into the office and stood by the desk chair. More than anything, he wanted to take Roger away from his audience and see through what appeared to be a façade portrayed for Abigail's benefit and approval. He shut the door behind them as soon as Roger was in.

Roger wasted no time. He quickly pulled out the desk chair to sit before Cash could offer it to him. He looked at the notebook on the desk and blurted out, "Why isn't this on the computer? You guys are still in the dark ages!"

Cash took the comment in stride and said in a calm, unwavering voice, "That's the system Sophia feels comfortable with. She owns the business, and I work for her. Does that answer your question?"

Roger shrugged, cradled his briefcase in one arm and reached inside it for his laptop with the other. In his eagerness, the briefcase shifted, and parts of the contents spilled on the floor. He bent down to scoop up the accident and his shirttail inched upward. Cash joined in to help him, and in his direct line of vision, he saw the outline of two condoms packets in Roger's hip pocket. Something didn't add up.

Cash raised up and measured his next words carefully. "So, how was your drive from Atlanta? What time did you leave?"

"Oh, yesterday, about mid-morning. Why?"

"Abigail said you stopped in Monroe for the night."

Roger continued rummaging through his briefcase. "Yeah, and I had a few phone calls to make." Cash saw a brief shifting of the other man's eyes, almost a nervous twitch.

"I've never been to Monroe, but I hear it's not too far from here, right?"

"No, not far. Why do you ask?" He paused and then continued, "So, this new accounting system -"

Cash interrupted him, "How long are you staying in Houston?"

The question caught Roger off guard. "Just a few days, why?"

"Or maybe just long enough?"

"That's an odd way to put it. What do you mean?" Roger looked at him with the innocence of a spring lamb.

"You must have gotten dressed in a hurry this morning."

"Huh?"

"I noticed you came prepared. You should find a better spot for those things besides your back pocket."

Cash's remark hit Roger's blind side. With two off guard questions from Cash, Roger's demeanor began to shift. After a few seconds, he recovered and responded with a sheepish grin, "Ah, that! Yeah, I suppose you're right." Several seconds of silence passed. "Let's just keep it between you and me." He finished with a squint that wrinkled his nose.

Cash pressed further, "That might be hard to do. Was it a quick phone call in Monroe?"

Roger now regarded him with more suspicious eyes.

Cash now spoke almost in a whisper, "If you were staying here overnight, I might understand coming prepared, but it seems you spent some unexplained time in Monroe and now you're in a hell of a hurry to get to Houston."

Roger gave Cash a perplexed look and then finished with a forced chuckle, but never took his eyes off the glare from Cash.

Moments passed and Cash finally said, "What's her name?"

Roger answered nervously, "Who?"

"Is there more than one?"

"Look, I'm going to meet some folks at a company headquarters in Houston for an interview. I don't recall all their names off the top of my head."

"Actually, I was thinking first of someone in Monroe." Cash gave him a second to form an answer. "Am I getting warm?"

"Monroe? What do you mean?"

"You said Monroe's not far from here. You must have left, oh - about, 10 this morning? Actually, my memory is coming back to me. As I recall, Monroe is only a couple of hours from here. Good chance to sleep late. And to think Abigail's been so eager to see you."

"Yeah, like I said, I had phone calls to make."

"Or maybe a personal interview?" He waited a few seconds and continued, "Harvard of the South, huh?"

Roger's jaw tightened, and he replied through clenched teeth, "What do you care?"

Cash could feel the veins in his own neck bulging. "We have a name for this where I come from."

"Now, look here…."

"Actually, Abigail's grandmother has a better name for it. But I doubt if you would want to know what she calls it."

Roger rose from his chair and the two men stood inches away

from each other. Cash opened the office door and spoke loud enough to be heard in the next room, but never taking his eyes off the other man.

"Okay, Roger. That's an interesting way to manage the books. I'll give it a try." With that, he left Roger standing in the office, wondering what had just happened.

Two hours later, Roger walked toward his car with his arm around Abigail. They stopped at the end of the walkway and exchanged a long goodbye kiss. Cash watched from the living room window.

A familiar voice behind him said, "Okay, something's eating at you. I can tell."

He turned to Sophia and said flatly, "I don't think he's Abigail's type. I just hope she's not going into this with blinders on."

"What makes you say that?"

"Just a feeling."

"Care to share? She's my granddaughter."

"What if I'm wrong? I've misjudged people before."

Cash had learned to read Sophia's face. She had a certain look when she knew he wasn't telling her everything.

"What are you worried about?" she said. "What's it to you, anyway?"

The two of them shared a pregnant pause. Cash finally broke the silence and said, "I wonder how well she really knows him. He just seems too wrapped up in himself. Can he really shift his focus and care about someone else?"

"Yeah.... I saw it, too. Anything else?"

He was about to answer further, but Abigail came back in the front door. They could hear Roger's car pulling away.

"Cash, Roger says he wishes you the best of luck with your job. He said to make sure I told you that. Isn't he the sweetest guy?" When she looked back toward the window, Sophia and Cash glanced at each other. Cash sank deep in thought and Sophia took a long draw on her cigarette.

The next morning started with a small crisis. One of the mowing crews called and said their utility trailer had a flat tire, and they didn't have a spare. They had just started mowing the grounds of a small, old, cottage-type motel on the far side of town.

Cash remembered it from his time in Alexandria before he went to Angola. *Pelican Cottages* was the name. He informed Sophia of the problem and she suggested he drive the pickup truck and take a spare tire to the scene of the problem. Before he left, he made a phone call.

"Mr. Hamm? This is Cash. I need to go to the other side of town to change a tire on one of our trailers. I'd like some help. Do you mind if I stop by and pick up Oscar? It's his day off, I think. We won't be long."

Hamm agreed, and Cash pulled out of the driveway for the short trip to the Work Center.

When he arrived, Oscar waited at the gate, eager to do something different for a change of pace. He noticed that Oscar sported a fresh, clean-cut, short haircut parted on one side, and his beard neatly trimmed. Beside him stood Stanley in his official uniform.

"You have room for two of us, I hope," Stanley said. "You're in legal status because you're on an assignment, but he isn't," he explained while pointing to Oscar. "The policy says someone from the department has to go with him. You okay with that?"

"Like old times," Cash heckled. All three men were larger than medium size and when they all crowded onto the single bench seat of the old truck, Cash had to drive with his elbows almost touching.

"Everyone use their deodorant this morning?" Oscar quipped. "Looks like we'll get to know each other really well by the time we get there."

"No problem," said Stanley. "Just roll the windows down. My God, Oscar! What did you put on your face after you shaved?"

"Yeah, I decided to change my appearance. Certain people seem to like it." He looked at Stan with a pinched nose. "By the way, Officer Stan, what did you eat for breakfast?" The old truck seemed to hiccup as Cash changed gears.

Pelican Cottages had been built in the early 50's and by some miracle, not only still standing, but still in business. Cash remembered hearing rumors about how they rented cottages by the week, the day, and the hour. It consisted of eight small cabins of about 300 square feet each, just enough room for two twin beds, a couple of chairs, and a refrigerator.

The outside of the cabins had not been painted in over a decade and the peeling white paint revealed pale grey pine clapboard siding, cracked and warped in places. But Argyle Landscaping had kept the grounds looking nice. They paid their bills promptly, although their business that day seemed a bit sparse. *Don't ask how they do it because then you have to live with the answer,* Cash thought.

Cash pulled into the entrance driveway, composed of crushed

oyster shells, and he saw one car parked by the office and two cars at the far end of the lane in front of the last cabin. There was no exit except by way of the entrance. Cars came and went by way of the same dusty pathway. No one could leave without passing by the office on the way out. They saw the disabled trailer in front of the third cabin, and the mowing crew looked busy completing the job.

Changing the tire presented no problem for the three of them. When they had almost finished, Oscar stood up and said, "Now that guy knows how to live." Cash and Stanley stopped and looked where he was pointing.

At the last cabin, about one hundred yards away where Cash had noticed the two parked cars, a man and a woman stood in the doorway, wrapped in an embrace and a kiss that a crowbar wouldn't open. She had her hands around his waist and massaged his back. His hands were cupped behind her at the bottom of her shorts while she stood on her tiptoes.

All three men stood motionless, watching. Finally, Stanley said candidly, "They've got to come up for air at some point!" The three of them laughed quietly and returned to their task.

But Cash remembered something. He stopped, stood upright again from where the other two still knelt, and looked closely at the two cars. One was an old, rusted Chevy Impala and the other a dark green Mustang, partly hidden behind the Chevy. He watched the two lovers separate, kiss again and again, and then walk to their cars. The woman wore pale green shorts and a white halter top that barely covered anything. She got into the Chevy and the man leaned into the open window and kissed her again. Then he casually walked to the Mustang and got in. The woman's car roared past them, kicking up dust. Before the dust could settle, the

Mustang approached the group of men, passed by them, and stopped at the office. The man emerged from the car, entered the building and Cash could see he wore white shorts, a wrinkled pale green plaid shirt and a gold chain around his neck.

"I'll be damned," he murmured to himself.

In less than a minute, the man reappeared and walked toward his car. Cash couldn't pass up the opportunity. He gave a shrill whistle and waved as Roger looked up. Cash saw him stop and, even from a distance, could read the indecision on the man's face. After a moment of hesitation, he got back in the Mustang and left.

"You know him?" Oscar asked.

Cash chuckled and said, "Yeah, I know him." He also knew this was not the last he would see of Roger Fitzpatrick. He now had a decision to make. Or maybe not.

The rest of the week passed without significant incident. Sophia had two medical appointments, which Abigail drove her to. Sophia could drive herself, but she wanted someone else to hear what the doctor said in case she needed her memory reinforced later. Her first round of chemotherapy would start the following week. Sophia had already told them it would be the last one. Abigail would be back in Atlanta by then to meet several job interviews she had pending.

The day of Abigail's departure finally arrived. All three stood by the car with silent conversation passing between them. It was an overcast day and a tinge of gloom hovered over them as they each searched for the right words to say goodbye.

"You understand I'll be back as soon as I can," she said, breaking the silence.

"Even if I have to fly, Cash can pick me up at the airport,

right?" She looked at him with eyes wide open, and he thought his heart would burst.

"I'll miss you," he said.

She looked at him again with tears in her eyes and touched her teeth to her lower lip. She did a loud sniff and reached for a tissue from her backpack.

"Damn it, I said I wasn't going to cry! Look, you've both got my cell phone number. Call me if anything comes up. I mean it! Call me!" She turned to Sophia and hugged her like a little girl hugging her granny. Cash could see the enormous love in this family, and it made him feel even more like an outsider.

Abigail reached to open the car door, but turned to Cash and wrapped her arms around his neck for only a moment. She quickly backed away and looked at him with her hands clasped together. Their eyes met, and he was poised and ready for whatever came next, but she simply turned, got into the car, and started the engine. The two waved to her as she drove away, leaving him standing there looking wistfully as her car disappeared around the corner.

Sophia squinted, studied him closely and said, "Come on inside, Cash. Let's get drunk!"

An hour later, Cash had finished off a bottle of ginger ale and Sophia was on her second scotch. He looked at the calendar on the wall. He had only two months left.

Christopher Hamm had a certain amount of latitude in granting furloughs to trustees. Giving Cash limited furloughs to stay at Sophia's home over night and on weekends had extended his hospitality almost to the point it might become noticeable, and word might filter back to the Department of Corrections. He wanted to help as much as possible, but not beyond his own safety zone. Sophia's low energy levels and physical encumbrance kept her from driving and Cash used her car, an ancient Dodge, to go back and forth between her house and the Center. It relieved Hamm from using a driver for him. There had been an agreement among the family that Sophia should have a sitter at night and on weekends when Cash couldn't be there. As expected, she had something to say about it after the first week. Monday morning, she was leaning against the office doorframe in her pajamas talking to Cash with an unlit cigarette in her hand.

"You'd think they could find someone who spoke English without such a heavy accent! With a name like Mildred, I didn't expect someone from Jamaica."

"So, do you have to talk to her?"

She lit her cigarette and said, "Nah, I'll just use smoke signals."

Cash stopped and asked, "You hungry? I'll fix you something." He had been learning to cook basic things for Sophia. Her appetite mimicked a bird pecking at a piece of bread.

Sophia stared at the floor and said, "My stomach's not right this morning. Thanks anyway."

A few minutes later, Cash could hear her making a retching sound in the bathroom. She had left the door open in her rush to reach the toilet. He walked down the hall and stood outside the door, just out of her line of sight. He could hear her softly cursing and coughing, then the water in the sink gurgled, telling him she was washing her face, like she always did. He quickly returned to his desk. It had become a common occurrence.

Sophia had developed the habit of taking several naps during the day. This gave Cash the chance to check all her medications, and he discovered that several of them were needed refilling, each designed to give her some relief from diarrhea, nausea, headaches, and whatever else seemed to invade her peace and calm. He called the pharmacy and had a promise that refills would be available later that same day.

Sophia had dirty clothes scattered all over her room. Each time he picked them up to be washed and re-folded, it seemed only hours before more of the same appeared. But he said nothing to her about it.

The next time she was up and awake, he'd change the sheets on her bed. The last time he did, he'd noticed a small spot of blood on her pillow. He had promised to keep John and Barbara updated. Today seemed like a good time to do that.

As he hung up from talking to John, he heard someone on the front porch. The living room door uttered a faint squeak and Cash knew someone had entered the house. Quickly, he crept down the hall and saw a tall, stately looking gentleman standing in the living room, going through some of Sophia's mail.

"I don't know who in the hell you are, but you better have an explanation for being in this house without an invitation!"

"And who in the hell are you?" the man yelled.

Cash could feel an old familiar adrenalin rush. "I'm the one who's supposed to be here. Answer my question!"

"I'm Trevor Blessing from California. And you?"

The name threw a curve ball at Cash for a moment. He finally collected his thoughts and said, "Okay, I know that name. I just got off the phone with your brother, John."

The two men stood looking at each other for what seemed an eternity.

"Well?" Trevor asked.

Cash folded his arms and said, "My name is Cash Ratliff. I'm Sophia's caretaker during the day. I also help run her landscaping business."

"Mama doesn't need any help. If she did, she would have asked one of us."

"And you would have just come running, I suppose. Something tells me she asked for me out of desperation."

"How would you know? How in the hell did you get here? What agency did you come from? Houseboys for hire?"

Cash rubbed his hands together and restrained himself from following his instincts.

Trevor continued going through the stack of mail and spoke without looking up. "Well, we can relieve you of your duties as of today and let you get back to whatever you were doing before."

"Like hell you will!" Sophia's voice thundered throughout the house in a way Cash had never heard. "Twenty years hasn't changed you much. You still think you can barge in here and have the last word in other people's lives, don't you? What the hell are you doing here? Put that mail down!"

Trevor was just as shocked as Cash at the visceral response coming from this withering old woman. "Good to see you, too, Mama." He stopped and gathered his thoughts. "I talked to John, and he told me you weren't doing well. So, I came to see for myself. He didn't tell me about this one," he said as he pointed to Cash. "It was a long flight. Mind if I sit down before you throw me out?"

"I just got off the phone with John, only minutes before you came in," Cash remarked. "He didn't mention talking to you."

Trevor stood again and looked at Cash. "You calling me a liar?"

Both men took a step toward each other, and Sophia spoke up and said, "Okay, okay. So, maybe John did tell you. Trevor, you should have called first."

"It's good to know you're glad to see me."

"Yeah, and still sarcastic, I can see," Sophia quipped and shook her head. "Trevor, this is Cash. He's here because I want him here. That's my final word – he stays!"

The next hour involved talking about plans Sophia had made with the help of John and Barbara. While they talked, Cash slipped into his office and dialed John's number.

"Hey John, this is Cash. Say, look, we have a visitor. Your brother Trevor is here. Just popped in unannounced. You know anything about this?"

"What? He's – I mean, oh my God. Now I remember. Yes, I called him when we first suspected Mom was having a medical problem. That car accident really rattled my memory."

Cash did a quick calculation in his head. According to what John said, Trevor had known about his mother's condition for a few weeks and had just now found the time to see her. "Okay, I'll go back in the living room and try to soften things up a bit. I got to tell you, your brother really knows how to push hard."

"Yeah, that's Trevor. He's the oldest, you know. Oh, by the way, will you be able to travel in about three months? Abigail and Roger are zeroing in on a wedding date. We finally met the guy. Seems nice enough."

Cash gripped the phone even tighter. "Yeah, I'll do my best to be there. It depends on how your mother is doing." Both men said goodbye and hung up. Cash sat there a few seconds looking at the phone like it was a live spirit with an ability to take sides and tell lies.

He re-entered the living room to find that the atmosphere had calmed down significantly. He heard Sophia finishing her update.

"And so, Cash and this other fellow pulled your brother out of the car just before the whole thing went up in flames."

Trevor saw Cash in the doorway and said, "You seem to have been at the right place at the right time. I'm sure my brother thinks so." He finished with a weak smile. "So, how did you come to be here in the first place? I feel like I'm getting the middle of a story without knowing how it started."

Cash glanced at Sophia, who showed no expression of concern. It became obvious she had left out some key facts. "That's a long story," he said. "Maybe some other time. I need to get back to the office."

The next morning, Cash walked in and found Trevor and Sophia in a heated conversation that, at first, did not make sense.

"I can't believe you did that to me!" Trevor's voice boomed.

"Well, you had it coming. Next time, act a little more hospitable in my house and I'll be a little kinder."

"Mama, I wasted an hour last night trying to figure out how to get some sleep."

"Well, if you had turned the lights on, you would have seen it immediately."

"And give you the satisfaction of knowing I was in the bedroom trying to undo whatever you did? Never!" With that, Trevor walked out of the room, waving his arms.

Cash waited a full minute and asked, "What was that all about?"

Sophia chuckled and said, "I got his goat last night. Even as a kid, we had to pop his balloon every so often." She let out a weak giggle as she continued, "I short-sheeted his bed so bad, he couldn't straighten it out until this morning." She walked to the hall door and yelled in the direction Trevor had gone, "You never could take a joke, could you? Don't get your drawers all twisted! Lighten up, kiddo!"

Trevor stayed one more night and went back home, still with many unanswered questions. He had witnessed Sophia's nightly trips to the bathroom but ignored any questions or comments it might have brought about to someone else. Cash avoided him as much as possible. Throughout that short time, Cash heard him on the phone talking to various people at length about Sophia and the latest events in her house.

As she watched from the window while her oldest son departed for the airport, Cash heard her mumble, "His daddy always liked him best, I think. But I'll be damned if I'm going to let him jump back into my life at the last moment." She turned to Cash and said, "You look worried. Don't be. He knows all about you. I told him in bits and pieces. He'll connect the dots eventually. Don't lose any sleep over it."

"Okay, good advice," he said. If he had been honest, his thoughts were actually on Abigail, but he said nothing else.

The next day was a rainy Saturday, and Cash looked forward to sleeping in and just listening to the rain outside. Sophia's nurse was supposed to be with her today. He was the last one in the breakfast line and the last one out of the dining hall. After he had stacked his plate in the dirty pile and stood waiting for a break in the showers to let him go back to the bunk house, Oscar's voice rang out.

"Cash! Cash! Mr. Hamm wants to see you."

"Aw, c'mon man, it's Saturday," he muttered. "Is he going to screw up my day?"

Christopher Hamm met him at the dining hall door with car keys in his hand, like he was anxious to go somewhere. "Your boss called, and she wondered if you could come over today for a while." He stopped and looked at Cash, expecting an immediate response. "Your boss, Sophia Blessing – she wants you…"

A look of both recognition and confusion came over Cash's face. "Oh, yeah! What does she want?"

"I told you. She wants you over there."

"Mr. Hamm, it's the weekend and I had planned to -"

"Do what? You got somewhere else to go? Somewhere I don't know about?"

Cash reached in his pocket for his keys to Sophia's car, but Hamm stopped him.

"C'mon, I'll drive you over there. I'm going over in that direction, anyhow."

Reluctantly, Cash climbed into Hamm's car and within a few minutes, they arrived in front of Sophia's house. The rain appeared to have stopped for the moment. Waiting on the front porch, dressed in starched jeans, Shauntae hopped on one foot and clapped when she saw Cash open the car door.

"Who is that?" Hamm asked.

Cash quickly sized up the scene and realized this would not be an idle Saturday, with loads of free time. He turned to Hamm and said, "Her parents work on one of the mowing crews. I met her once before and she really took a shine to me. Don't ask me why." Cash felt a touch of guilt when he said that. It was a small lie, and he knew it.

"Well, go see what she wants," Hamm said flatly. "Call the

Center when you're ready to come back."

The rain had stopped, and Cash was halfway up the front walk and waved to Shauntae. His gesture came like a signal to explode out of a starting gate. She raced down the steps, stomped through rain puddles, and leaped into his outstretched arms. She said nothing, but her bright grin voiced a thousand words. He half-carried her back to the steps and put her down on her own two feet. Sophia stepped out onto the porch from the living room and had watched the encounter with a broad smile.

"Good morning," he said. "What's up?"

"Her," Sophia said plainly.

"What do you mean?"

"Her parents dropped her off while they went shopping and she said she wanted to see you."

"You mean, I came all the way over here and -"

"I brought my coloring books," Shauntae announced with authority. "I have new ones. And new Crayons. They're 96 colors of nontoxic, ecofriendly product." She finished with a bright smile.

Sophia looked down at her and said, "Go on ahead into the kitchen with your coloring, Shauntae. We'll be right there."

As she left the porch, Cash looked at Sophia and said, "What am I supposed to do with her for the next, ah, how long did they say they would be shopping?"

"Hey look, you found something for her to do the last time she was here."

"I hadn't planned on working in the shop today, not on Saturday."

"So, go color with her. You didn't do that last time."

"Well, yeah, and for good reason! I never liked coloring! Look, I flunked coloring! I can't stay inside the lines!" He realized he was looking at her with a glare on his face.

Without warning, Sophia burst out laughing. "Aw, what's the matter? Does the little fellow not like to color?"

Unable to restrain himself, Cash chuckled at his own words and went into the kitchen. Sophia could hear him talking in gentle tones. *Not bad for a substitute family*, she thought, and left the two of them together to decide what to do with this new friendship.

Shauntae wasted no time getting organized. From her stack, she pulled out two coloring books and gave one to Cash.

"Start with the green color," she said firmly. "Green's my favorite."

"Why is that your favorite?"

"It just is. I don't know why. I look at it and I hear music, far away music."

"You do?" Cash had obediently picked up the dark green crayon and started slowly tracing the lines of a tree with grass around it. "What kind of music?"

"I don't know. It's like those things that make tinkle sounds when the wind blows."

"Wind chimes? You see green color and you hear windchimes?"

"Can't you hear them?"

Cash just shook his head and could not take his eyes off this precious child, so focused on her page.

Suddenly, she stopped and stared intently at Cash. "Are you married?"

The question coming from a child her age hit like a shot to his blindside.

"No, I'm not. Why do you ask?"

"Why aren't you married?"

"I haven't met the right one yet."

She looked back at her page, thought for a few seconds, and said, "Okay, in a few more years, I'll be old enough to marry. Will you marry me when I'm old enough?"

Cash suddenly felt very conspicuous, as though he feared someone would be listening. How could he answer such a question? Although a child's question, no doubt, it came dripping with sincerity. How could he have known that her thoughts were drifting into such innocent territory? His own thoughts were interrupted by her next words.

"No, maybe not," she said. "That would be a long time. You probably couldn't wait that long."

He felt a crumb of relief but wanted to pick her five-year-old brain a bit more. "So, when you do get married, how old will you be?"

"I don't know. Maybe ten – or seventeen. I don't know. But I already know about the bedroom stuff."

Cash stopped coloring and just looked at the far wall. His thoughts were paralyzed, and he knew that anything he said could be repeated at the wrong time and the wrong place.

Shauntae had also stopped her coloring and looked at him closely. "You know what I mean, don't you?"

Cash slowly turned his head and saw a deadpan, serious look on the child's face. Finally, he used the only outlet he could imagine and said, "Oh, there's not much to it, is there?"

"Mama says she knows how Papa likes it."

Cash felt totally helpless. He needed to change the subject quickly.

"Shaun…"

"You're right, there's not much to it, not really. Just change the sheets once a week and fluff up the pillows. Mama says that's her job and has been since she got married. She said Papa likes it that way."

Cash gave sigh of relief and tried to keep it subtle.

An hour later, Shauntae's family returned to take her home. She gave Cash a big hug and a kiss on her way out the door. He stepped onto the front porch, and she turned around to wave from the driveway. A child's love – something he had never felt before.

Cash turned and went back inside. Pondering Shauntae's childish freedom of thoughts, he turned down the hall to check on Sophia. He found her back in her bedroom, already in bed, facing away from the door, most likely having a different set of her own thoughts. Cash could see her labored breathing from the rise and fall of the bedcovers, like a clock ticking the moments away.

He called Mr. Hamm and asked if he could stay a bit longer. With Hamm's approval, he returned to the room, pulled up a chair next to Sophia's bed and sat quietly.

Chapter 8

The next day was Sunday, and Cash casually updated Mr. Hamm of the events of the previous week. The retelling of his time with Shauntae brought a brief smile to the man's face. Cash remarked how Sophia's candor and bluntness seemed to have passed on to her oldest son. He had decided against telling the story of her practical joke with the bedsheets.

Hamm said smugly, "Don't let that California dude get in the way of State business. You're working at Argyle Landscaping because I put you there. Next time he starts complaining, give him my number. Hell, tell him to call the friggin' Governor!"

"I've only got a month left. What do I do after that?"

"You're on your own after that, my boy. But I know you'll come up with something. Just stay out of trouble."

"Yes sir, I've got to start making some real plans. But first, Sophia's asked me to do something I may need some help with."

"What's that?"

"She's got this bucket list. Well, that's what she calls it. Ever heard of that?"

"Go on."

"When I get my release papers, she wants to go to New Orleans. In all these years of living in Louisiana, she's never been there."

Hamm could not hide his surprise. "She - she what? With you? Man, this beats all! That woman sees the world her own way and to hell with what anyone else thinks. You gotta' love it! Are you going to do it?"

"More uncharted territory, sir. It's what I do best."

"I assume she's paying for it."

"That's the only way it could happen. But she's not telling her family until the day we leave. She doesn't want any debate from them, especially from Trevor."

"Trevor? Oh yeah, the California dude. You're right, from what you've told me, he would probably blow a gasket if she told him ahead of time!"

"She's going to tell John and that's it."

Hamm had difficulty keeping all the names straight. "John, that's the youngest, right? He's the one who had the wreck."

"Yes sir, lives in Atlanta."

"You said you needed some help."

"Have you ever been to New Orleans, sir?"

"Well, sure - several times."

"I need suggestions about where to take her, what to see, and how to manage this whole thing."

"Manage? Wait a minute, what's there to manage?"

"I can't leave her in a room by herself, not at this stage of the game. She depends more and more on the sitter that stays with her at night. Have you seen her lately? She needs help getting around, like, at night, after bedtime – and so forth."

"You'd be sharing a room with her?" Hamm's eyes were wide open when he spoke.

"I can't think of any other way. One room. Couple of single beds."

"Can't you take the sitter?"

"She won't hear any of that. I'm sort of in a corner here. I've got to just go with the flow." Cash waited for Hamm to say something.

Hamm just rolled his eyes. "Hmm, I see what you mean. Now, this is after your release, right? Yeah, you gotta' do what she wants. She probably doesn't have much longer, anyway." He saw an immediate change of expression on Cash's face. "Aw crap, that was an impersonal thing for me to say. I'm sorry." He paused and looked closely at Cash. "You've grown really close to her, haven't you?"

Cash just nodded.

"Maybe my wife could help. You okay with that?"

In the past few weeks, he had noticed how the Hamm family had grown closer to him as his release date grew nearer. He had become a familiar face around their house on weekends and some evenings, doing odd jobs and favors.

The other men also noticed but said nothing. They all played their cards carefully and quietly until they could get out and go home to whatever home they had waiting for them. Cash had nothing waiting for him. Just Sophia.

Later that same day, Cash and Olivia Hamm had a long conversation and made a few phone calls. He came away from it feeling a little more comfortable. She had suggested a small, historic hotel on Decatur Street in the French Quarter. It had an airport shuttle and complimentary wheelchairs for their guests. It also presented only a short walking distance to restaurants and some civilized night spots. Cash wasn't sure what she could tolerate, so they planned modestly.

Sophia could not contain her jubilant enthusiasm when she heard of the plans Cash had in mind. They called the hotel and the airline and made reservations for the day after his release. It would be one short travel day each way with two nights and a day in the middle.

Olivia had suggested that was probably all Sophia could handle, considering her lack of energy reserve. They spent hours talking about the trip and each segment of it, including the ride to the airport in Alexandria, the flying time to New Orleans, the private limo taking them to and from the hotel and all the spots they planned to visit.

Cash noticed a hint of bloom on Sophia's face each time they talked about it. The bloom was always followed by near exhaustion, so Cash watched to serve the plans in small bites.

As his day of release approached, preparation for the trip to New Orleans distracted him, but he still found time to ponder on what freedom meant to him personally. When Cash allowed himself time to let his imagination roll, he found the process of a new life a little frightening, because he wasn't sure if he could trust his own judgement. Sometimes he felt the need to pinch himself to make sure he wasn't dreaming. Graduation didn't seem like the right word, more of relief from a prolonged time of feeling judged by society and wondering if he would feel any indelible change in how he looked at himself. He wondered about his own ability to maintain the straight and narrow without someone standing over him all the time. What aspects of normal life had he missed or forgotten while being cooped up in a cell in Angola? How would he make up for lost time?

The Work Release Center had freed him and many others from the hazards of an abrupt change to freedom and allowed him time to deal with a litany of mixed feelings during the transition to normal life. But could life ever be normal again after prolonged incarceration? He, and others like him, could not rely on memory to plan a future because the past remained so tainted. What previous pattern of living was there to follow? Even his life before Angola was not a Norman Rockwell picture. He would have to make his own.

The day came for Cash's freedom and Sophia had already laid out clothes to be packed. One would think they planned to be away for six months by looking at the various changes she wanted to take. It didn't matter. He packed whatever she asked.

That night, he overheard her end of the conversation with John. She sounded like a teenager headed off to Walt Disney World. "Yes, that is what we're doing. Your father and I had always planned to do this, but we just had too much to tend to. Don't worry, the mowing crews will be fine for a few days. They know what to do. John, John - I didn't call to ask your permission. We'll be fine. Oh, my God, no! Don't call your brother! Yes, we're leaving tomorrow. That's right, you KNOW why I waited to tell you. I'll call you from the hotel, okay?"

The drive to the Alexandria airport the next morning was uneventful until they got to the main terminal. Cash stopped at the entrance and went inside to find a wheelchair. When he came out, he found Sophia giving a security officer a piece of her mind over the fact that their car occupied a no-parking zone. Cash convinced the man they were in the process of departure and then talked him into pushing Sophia's wheelchair into the terminal while he parked the car.

A few minutes later, when he arrived out of breath at a fast trot from the parking lot to the main building, he heard her telling the young man behind the counter how inefficient their customer service was. They finally had their boarding passes and luggage checked and had stopped to wait by the gate. Sophia seemed to squirm in her chair.

"Where's the ladies' room? Have we got time?"

"It's right over there. Can you manage?"

"I don't know. Can you come with me?" Sometimes Cash had the feeling that she purposely put him in awkward situations just to see how far he would take it.

"Sophia, I can't go beyond the door. You know that." Cash felt panic slowly rising into his usual stoic consciousness. They hadn't even boarded the plane and she already had a minor crisis.

"So, take me in the men's room."

Cash had a look of astonishment. "The men's room?"

"C'mon, or you're going to have a mess to clean up right here in this airport! Let's go! It'll be fun. Think of it as an adventure. I'm not going to see anything I haven't seen before!"

They reached the door to the men's room and a young man was just coming out. He stopped, looked at Sophia and then Cash, then proceeded to hold the door open.

"Over there," she said. "Take me to that handicap stall. Yeah, now open the door and wheel me inside."

Cash parked her wheelchair next to the toilet and waited.

"That's good enough. Just step back out through the door and hold it shut. Go on, just do what I tell you."

Cash stood by the door of the stall, hoping that no one else would come in. What was taking her so long? He was about to peek under the door when he heard the toilet flush. He could feel a sense of relief, but his relief deflated when he saw two middle-aged men come through the entrance.

A voice rang out, "Okay, open up. I'm done."

Cash opened the door and found her seated in the wheelchair with an angelic look on her face. "I feel better now," she said.

The two men each stood in front of a urinal as Cash tried to quietly progress toward the exit. Sophia stopped him and said, "I need to wash my hands. Go over there by the sink."

By now, the two men were fully engaged in their own relief efforts and tried to pretend they weren't seeing or hearing something unthinkable that was happening just a few feet away. Cash parked Sophia at the sink and as she leaned forward to reach the water, she turned and looked at them and said, "How're you fellas doing? Big travel plans?"

Cash could feel his face turning red. Both men finished their task quickly, zipped up, and made a fast pace to the door.

"Not very friendly, were they? Oh well, hand me a paper towel."

Cash did as she had asked and swiftly headed for the exit. He turned his back to the door to back the chair out when the door suddenly opened, seemingly on its own. Holding the door stood a large male security guard who looked just as astonished as the two men they had encountered inside. He held the door open for Cash and Sophia and she simply waved a hand in a gesture of thanks.

"That wasn't so hard, was it?"

They almost made it back to their gate when the public announcement speaker crackled to life, and they heard their flight number broadcasted. As luck would have it, the two men they had met in the restroom were waiting for the same flight. As was the custom, wheelchair passengers boarded first. As they entered the jetway, Sophia turned in her chair and blew a kiss to them, then gave a double fist-pump as they disappeared down the ramp.

Halfway down the jetway, Sophia looked over her shoulder at Cash and said, "How does it feel to be a free man? What a way to celebrate!"

He wasn't sure how to answer. A year ago, he could never have imagined his first day out of the joint would unfold like this one.

The brief flight to New Orleans was less than an hour. Sophia slept through most of it. Cash couldn't help wondering if this whole trip was asking more than she could handle. Their limo driver stood waiting in the baggage claim area with a sign that said 'Blessing.' He made them feel like visiting dignitaries on the drive to the hotel.

The scenery unfolded in layers of time as they drove on a modern highway, then residential neighborhoods, and into turn-of-century avenues with streetcar tracks. The French Quarter beckoned like an old movie.

Sophia had a million questions about the city and the driver seemed to have a limitless repertoire of answers. Cash felt content to just listen. During one of the few quiet moments, she called John to tell him they had survived the flight.

There was plenty of daylight left when they arrived at their hotel. The concierge made dinner reservations for them at Tujague's, just one block away from the hotel and said to be the second oldest dining place in the city. They ate a quick lunch at an oyster bar and spent the remaining time before dinner strolling through the French Quarter, looking in shop windows and watching street performers.

People would get older and show their age, but the Crescent City never aged. Sophia marveled at the vast number of little shops, eating places, bars, and exotic looking entertainments, all seemingly jammed into one small neighborhood in history, timeless history. At one point, they crossed Bourbon Street and Sophia decided against going that way. 'Maybe tomorrow' was her decision.

At one point, they both became gradually aware of a distant rhythmic thumping sound surrounded by the clanging of cheap cymbals and bawdy brass notes. Cash parked Sophia's wheelchair on the curb where she could see the event as it came closer. A throng of people surrounded a procession of old men in tattered suits and tuxedoes, marching in rough tempo with their music. Their clothes were adorned with colorful plumes and flowers that looked like they had endured the spirit of countless parades in years gone by. The leader wore a wrinkled derby hat.

Cash asked a man next to him what the celebration was for, but his response sounded muffled by the band and the crowd noise. Onlookers joined in and circled around the musicians, dancing and singing.

Cash thought he heard someone mention a funeral procession, but he wasn't sure. It didn't matter; Sophia clapped her hands in time with the band and yelled like a cheerleader. It was life at its fullest for her. When it was over, she looked exhausted, but determined.

About the time Cash's arms began to ache from pushing the wheelchair, Sophia said, "Is that our restaurant over there? Over there, across the street! C'mon Cash, I'm hungry!"

They were seated at a small table for two in a far corner. The lighting was dim, but intimate. Parts of the building showed its age. One wall next to their table was ancient brick that looked almost antebellum. By contrast, most of the remaining interior was accented by elaborate floral bouquets, white tablecloths, and delicate candles on each table. Their waiter came wearing formal attire. Cash almost felt underdressed. Dinner arrived in five courses. By the time they had eaten their way to the entrees, they were both stuffed and Sophia was getting tired. Still, she wanted to talk more. Sophia's ability to still act almost normal amazed Cash, but at closer look, he could tell she was pushing her limit. She seemed to have an endless litany of questions. It was as though there were details about Cash that she always wanted to know, but never asked.

"What did your dad do? Can you remember?" she asked.

"He was a construction supervisor. He had an engineering degree from Texas A&M.

"What was his name?"

"Marvin. That was his dad's middle name. All his relatives were from Midland, Texas."

"Nothing but oil fields out there. Have you been there? Did you like it?"

"Midland? Miles and miles of open prairie, if that's what you like."

"I asked if you liked it. Did you?"

"I'd prefer living in Houston. I was twelve when they both died, but I remember Houston fairly well."

"But you grew up in Colfax. What was that like?"

"Coming from Houston, it was hard to fit in with small town folks. It's hard to believe there were other towns in that Parish that were even smaller. My grandparents had forgotten how to establish boundaries for a growing boy. Maybe they never knew. They just let me run wherever I wanted. I guess I got mixed up with some of the wrong people."

"So...."

"So, I'm trying to put all that behind me. Sometimes it's hard, because there's reminders everywhere, reminding me where I screwed up. I'm twenty-eight years old and I'm just now getting a decent grasp on what kind of person I am."

She wiped her mouth on her dinner napkin, folded it beside her plate, and looked at him with piercing eyes that Cash had learned to recognize as a signal she had something profound to tell him.

He returned her stare and said quietly, "What?"

Sophia leaned toward him and whispered, "I raised five kids. Each one was different. You may not know who you are, but I do, and I can't wait to see how you turn out." Her eyes were riveted onto his. She reached across the table and squeezed his hand. "I'm not very good at detective work, but I know people who are. Someone I know at LSU searched some newspaper archives for me and found the article about your parents' traffic accident." She stopped and let it that bit of news soak in. She squeezed his hand again and spoke even softer, "I left it in my desk at home. It's there for you to read when we get back."

"Why did you do that?" He couldn't hide his discomfort from what she had said.

"I wanted to give you whatever information I could find to let you know more about yourself. You deserve it."

Cash was momentarily silent, searching for words. He decided that a change of subject made the best defense at that moment.

"We need to get you back to the hotel," he said discreetly. "We don't want to wear you out on the first day."

Sophia looked at him through half-closed eyes and finally agreed. Before Cash could summon the waiter, she called out loudly and all heads in the place turned to look. Their waiter came immediately.

Her voice had grown raspy, but was still projecting. "Yes, we need to get going. This young stud here says he's going to put me to bed!" Sophia looked at Cash to see what reaction she had created.

She paid the waiter, and Cash felt himself blush. Glancing up, he saw smiles throughout the dining room as they made their way out to the sidewalk.

As soon as they arrived at the hotel, Sophia managed to change into night clothes by herself. Respecting her need for privacy, Cash excused himself to the restroom until she told him to come out. With Sophia in bed, he found a magazine and settled in a chair across the room with a small lamp turned on beside him.

In the semi-darkness of the room, Sophia said, "Not many young men would do what you're doing for me, Cash. I won't forget it."

He peered into the darkness and wondered the same thing. "Good night," he finally answered. When he felt his own eyes getting heavy, he peeled off his clothes down to his boxer shorts and climbed into the other bed.

Around midnight, he heard a muffled voice coming from Sophia's side of the room. He realized she was sitting on the side of the bed and gently blowing her nose.

"You okay?" he asked.

She didn't answer. Listening closer, he could hear her crying. Carefully, he crossed the room and knelt beside her.

He repeated, "Are you okay? Is your stomach bothering you?"

In the dim light, he could barely see her face. Her voice

sounded weak and garbled. "I had a dream," she blubbered softly.

"Bad dream?"

"No, it wasn't. I just wish it hadn't been a dream. I didn't want to wake up, but I did."

"Tell me. What was it?"

Her words came in gentle sobs and muffled hiccups. "He - he was walking toward me, all dressed up in his flight suit with that silly cow - cowboy hat he always wore. He had the sides turned up and he always took it with him when he was flying. His hair was sticking out in the front. He had blonde, curly hair, just like you." She stopped for a second as though catching her breath, then continued, "He called it his 'Go to Hell Hat.' That's what he called it."

"Who?"

"D - Donald. My Donald. The father of my children. It felt so real, like he was here, alive, calling me. He had a laugh like no other and I could hear it in my dream. He seemed so happy." She gulped for a full breath. "He was saying to me, 'Why are you crying? This is a beautiful place!' I could feel the way he used to hug me."

Cash held her hands as she spoke. He reached up to her face and could feel the dampness of her tears. "What can I do to make you feel better?"

"You can't. I know I'm going to see him, and it gets closer every day."

Cash pulled the corner of the sheet to her face and dried her tears. He noticed she had begun to shiver.

"Cash, I'm cold. What's with the air conditioner in this place? Are there more blankets?"

In the closet, he found two blankets that he spread over her and tucked in around her body. Cash couldn't understand why she felt cold. The thermostat registered a comfortable 73 degrees. He waited a short while and asked, "Is that better?"

"No, I'm still cold." She struggled a bit with the blanket and hesitated before posing a delicate question. She turned her head toward him and almost begged, "Cash - would it be okay if I asked you to lay down next to me and warm me up? Please help me. This chill feels like death to me."

Without saying a word, he gently rolled onto the bed, slid under the covers, and wrapped his arms around her. He held his chest to her back and her whole, frail body felt like a block of ice. Within minutes, she fell asleep. He waited a while longer to be sure, then slowly climbed out of her bed and into his own. Before he closed his eyes, he wondered what Trevor would think if he knew. For a moment, he wasn't sure if he was being used or loved.

The next morning, Cash called room service around 9:30 and had toast and coffee delivered. Sophia remained asleep when it arrived, but she rose to the smell of the French Market elixir. She shuffled her way into the bathroom and emerged looking slightly more refreshed. "What's the plan for today?" she asked through half-closed eyes.

Two hours later, Cash thought he would have blisters on his hands from pushing the wheelchair before they could even get to lunch. Sophia spotted a small hole-in-the-wall restaurant where she asked to see a muffuletta sandwich. The size of it amazed them both and they decided to split one.

Even after finishing, they had a healthy portion left over and Sophia insisted on taking it back to the room. They stopped at almost every shop on Royal Street and loaded up on gifts to send to each member of her family.

Every sale item, every trinket seemed to fascinate her. She had a million questions for the shop owners and wanted to talk to anyone who would listen. They both saw the city's beauty in its blend of different cultures, and they knew they could see only a small fraction of it in the short time they would be there. But it carried a taste that they both would savor and remember.

"Wait until they all hear that I was in New Orleans! And with a good-looking young fella' taking care of me! We'll hear the uproar until the day I pass on! Talk about scandal! HA!"

Cash stood amazed at the implied admission of mortality and in awe of the courage she projected. He knew she had pushed her body to the limit, but she refused to admit it. As soon as they returned to the room, she opted for a much-needed nap.

That night, after a supper of shrimp creole in the room, a jazz band played in the street below their second-story window. They had been wondering about their evening plans, and Sophia finally admitted she was tired.

"Why go anywhere? Throw some change down to them and ask them to stay and play more! Here, let me give you some money." She handed Cash a one-hundred-dollar bill.

Cash found a hotel envelope, stuffed the bill in it, added some coins to give it weight and tossed it down. When the clarinet player picked it up and opened it, his broad smile guaranteed an evening of New Orleans best jazz.

But the jam session stopped momentarily while a group of three college-aged young women came wandering down the street toward them with tall drinks in their hands and singing at the top of their lungs. They stopped at the sight of the jazz band, urged them on, and got in rhythm, dancing to whatever tune they heard playing. It was clearly obvious this was a threesome of happy drunks.

At the end of the number, Cash and Sophia heard a man's voice yell from the window next door to them. He and a group of others were waving at the three women and dangling Mardi Gras beads out the windows.

"What are they doing?" she asked.

"I'm not sure, Cash answered. "I think they want to get those gals' attention about something."

Just as Cash finished speaking, all three women jerked up their tank tops and gave everyone a bare-breasted view for about five seconds. The men threw the beads down to them.

"Did you see that?" Sophia looked both astonished and delighted. "Look! They're doing it again! Look at that!"

All Cash could do was grin and shake his head.

"Cash, didn't we buy some beads today? We did! Go get them! Hurry up before they leave!"

Cash returned to the window in only a few seconds. Sophia grabbed the beads from his hands and yelled out the window, "Hey, you, sweetie! Here's some more!"

To the amazement of both, all three young women turned around, dropped their shorts, and mooned the entire array of hotel windows. Hoots and catcalls came from all three floors. Looking for more adventure, the trio resumed their original direction of walking, drinking, and singing as the jazz band remained and played on. Sophia laughed to the point of coughing until her face turned blue.

They stayed at the window for an hour. Exhausted from all the day's events, <u>Cash knew</u> Sophia would have no trouble sleeping that night. Before he turned away from the window, he stopped and noticed a young couple half a block away. They walked arm in arm down the middle of the street, looking at each other as two people very much in love. Even from this distance, he could see she wore maternity clothes. She – Julie? He couldn't help but stand there, immobile and transfixed by what appeared to be a dream. What were the odds of her walking under his hotel window at this exact moment? They lived in New Orleans, didn't they? He started to wave but decided against it. She seemed so happy. As they strolled closer, the man said something in her ear, and she laughed in a clear, audible voice that was not hers, not Julie's. It wasn't her.

As they got closer, he felt foolish, wishing for something that couldn't be, a fairytale wish. He gave a long sigh, then reminded himself that he had less pleasant responsibilities inside that hotel room. For a moment, a split-second, he wanted to escape, to break away from those obligations. His life seemed to be developing into a string of morbid disappointments, one after another.

The next morning heralded room service again for breakfast and a wheelchair trek to the French Market. Fortunately, the wait for a table at Café Du Monde was short. The Delta Queen riverboat had docked within sight of the café and the boat's steam whistle startled all the customers.

After coffee and beignets, they slowly wandered toward Jackson Square. Sophia sat and looked, astonished at seeing St. Louis Cathedral with the bells chiming, something she had previously only heard about or seen in pictures.

Sidewalk artists had begun to find their favorite corners for a new day. New Orleans had not disappointed her with its mixture of beauty and brashness side by side, a stark contrast within a city that would not be the same without it. Cash could see the look of satisfaction on her pallid face.

"We can go home now," she finally said with a note of

fulfillment and sadness.

Traffic interrupted the ride to the airport, but their driver found an alternate route that avoided huge delays. Sophia tipped him another hundred as Cash stood by trying to look nonchalant. She seemed to be in a daze until the gate agent announced their flight number. When they landed in Alexandria, they were surprised and amazed to see Abigail and Roger waiting at the baggage claim area.

"What on earth are you doing here?" Sophia gasped.

Abigail rushed up to her grandmother and said, "We were just worried about you, traveling and all that! Roger and I thought we should be here in case you needed help." She shot a glance at Cash who stood behind her wheelchair.

"Worried? Worried? About what? I had Cash with me! We had a great time. Look, when the bags get here, I can show you all the shopping we did and souvenirs we bought for the family. It's – what? What's the problem? You came all the way from Atlanta?"

Abigail continued, "I just wanted to be here when you got home. It was actually Roger's idea, and so we drove all the way, non-stop, to be here. And just so you know, Daddy doesn't know we're here. He thinks we've escaped to make wedding plans."

That's when Cash noticed Roger had retreated a distance behind Abigail and began dialing his cell phone. Within minutes, as the baggage claim carousel began bringing the checked baggage into view, three Alexandria Police Officers appeared, one holding handcuffs. Roger made a subtle gesture and nodded his head toward Cash. Cash could feel his blood run cold when one of the officers reached for him.

"Cash Ratliff, you're under arrest. You have the right to remain-"

Sophia responded like lightning. "Hang on a minute! Arrested for what, you little shit? Get away from him! Hey, I'm talking to you! I mean it! Explain yourself!"

The second officer spoke up and said, "He's charged with petty theft, ma'am. He pulled a document from his shirt pocket and continued, "He's taken money out of an account belonging to, ah, Sophia Blessing. Do you know her?"

"That's me, you ignoramus! How could he steal money from me?"

"There have been two ATM withdrawals from your account for $500 each. They both happened about four or five days ago. A security camera caught his picture, and his face didn't match the name on the card, so we contacted the family."

"The family? Who?"

"Ah, you were not available, obviously. The bank told us that John Blessing is listed as co-owner of your checking account, so we called the number in Atlanta."

"You talked to John?"

"I don't know who they talked to, ma'am. I just know we're supposed to arrest this man and bring him in."

The two officers began forcefully leading Cash toward the door. He looked back over his shoulder and tried to shout to Sophia over the noise in the airport, "Don't you remember? You sent me to the bank to make a withdrawal before we left."

"What?" Sophia shouted back in her croaking voice. "I couldn't hear what he said. Shit! Bring him back here!" With Cash firmly in their grasp, the policemen continued toward the door, then hesitated.

The third officer approached Sophia. "Ma'am, our records

show that this man is a prison inmate.

"Not anymore! You hang on a minute. Don't you take another step until I call Bob Preston." Sophia dug in her purse for her cell phone. The Chief's secretary answered after five rings and put her on hold. Within seconds, a man's voice answered.

"Good afternoon, this is Captain Reilly."

"I wanted to talk to Bob Preston!"

"Chief Preston is on vacation, ma'am. How can I help you?"

For one of the few times in her life, Sophia seemed at a loss for words. She finally stammered, "Well, this is one hell of a situation! Your officers are here at the airport trying to arrest my office manager, Cash Ratliff, for stealing money out of my checking account and… I can't see how that could have happened. I know what goes on with my money. I trust him completely! None of it is missing!"

Captain Reilly tried to be understanding. "Hang on. Put one of them on the phone."

She handed her phone to the older-looking officer and put it on speaker as she did.

"Captain? We have a warrant for this man. The precinct issued it based on a conversation with someone at the home of John Blessing in Atlanta. Everything seems in order."

"Does the warrant say who was on the phone? Who took the call in Atlanta?"

"No sir, it only says what I just told you."

"Okay, bring him on in, and we'll straighten it out here at the station." The three officers directed Cash toward the door with Sophia's voice echoing throughout the airport.

Outside, they loaded Cash into one of the waiting patrol cars with his hands cuffed behind his back. Abigail tried to get Sophia's attention with little success. "Granny, how could Cash do this? You trusted him so much. I just can't believe it!"

Sophia turned to Abigail, shaking her finger, and said, "Don't go jumping to conclusions, young lady! Something's not right here and we're damn sure going to figure it out! Are you coming with me? I'm going to the police station, and they better not ruffle one hair on that man's head!"

It took several minutes for their luggage to arrive and for Abigail to find Sophia's car where Cash had left it three days before. By the time they left the parking lot, Sophia and Abigail in one car and Roger in his Mustang, Cash was already booked, fingerprinted, and in a holding cell downtown.

As they drove into town, Sophia dialed a number on her phone. A voice answered after three rings.

"Barbara? Hey, is John there? He is? Can you interrupt him?" Moments later, she continued, "John, did you receive a call from the Alexandria Police about four days ago? No? Did Barbara? Okay, I'll call you back later. No, we're trying to clear up a little mix-up here. New Orleans? Fabulous! I'm so glad I went. Me? A little tired now and I can't wait to get home and get my robe and slippers on. I'll call you back later."

Seconds after she hung up, her phone rang. Abigail heard her say, "Yes, Captain Reilly. Do you have any new information? Who?" She turned her eyes toward her granddaughter who sat behind the wheel and said slowly, "Yes, we know that name. This explains a lot. Don't worry, we'll be there in ten minutes." She hung up, gave Abigail a hard look and said, "Step on it, girl."

When they arrived at the station, an officer escorted them to Captain Reilly's office. Cash was nowhere to be seen. Reilly spoke first.

"Is he here?"

Sophia answered quietly and firmly, "He'll be here in a minute."

Abigail appeared dumbfounded. She whispered to Sophia, "Who are we waiting for?" As if on cue, Roger appeared in the doorway.

Sophia pointed to him and said calmly, "That's who we're waiting for."

Captain Reilly played his role perfectly. "Does anyone here know Roger Fitzpatrick?"

All eyes turned to Roger who tried to look innocent. He said finally, "Yeah, that's me. What about it?"

Captain Reilly asked, "Did you take a call at John Blessing's house at the time in question?"

Abigail quipped, "You were at Mom and Dad's house a few days ago, right?"

Roger shrugged and said, "I don't really remember any phone calls then. I could have."

Sophia's voice became audible throughout the station. "You have a damn degree in Finance! If you took a call about someone's checkbook, you would certainly remember! It's not like it's a damn foreign language to you!"

"Roger?" Abigail's voice sounded pleading.

"I probably took a call, maybe. Why is that important?"

Captain Reilly shoved the notes he held under Roger's nose and pointed to the hand-written name, 'Roger Fitzpatrick.'

Reilly's voice echoed forceful and authoritative. "Do you think our team here just makes up names?"

Roger stepped back and shifted his eyes among all the faces staring at him. "Okay, yeah, I remember now. They asked me if I knew someone named Cash Ratliff and I said yes. I told them he was Sophia's office manager. I didn't know it would lead to this. I don't think they mentioned anything about a checking account. Just wanted to check on the name, that's all."

Sophia spoke up and said, "That's all? That's all? It didn't occur to you to ask the police why they were calling, did it?"

Captain Reilly looked at Sophia and asked, "Were you aware of the withdrawals?"

"Of course I was aware of it! I told him to get a thousand from my checking account at the ATM. We would need it for our trip to New Orleans. I didn't know it would take two withdrawals to do it. Doesn't matter how he did it, I trusted him to get it done somehow and he did." She looked across the room at Roger, who slowly seemed to step back into the hallway, and yelled, "Hey, you! Come back here!"

Roger sheepishly ambled over toward Sophia but kept his distance. "I'm sorry," he said, "if I caused any trouble. I meant no harm, really."

She responded, "No harm? Where are your brains, you dumbshit? You sittin' on them? How did the police know when we were coming back? At the airport, no less?"

Reilly interrupted, "From the phone notes, someone called back from Atlanta and gave us the flight number for today. Sorry, I can't read the handwriting. Can't tell you who called back."

Abigail looked first at Sophia, then at Roger like her head was on a swivel. Finally, she just stepped away and wrung her hands.

A shuffle of feet became audible from the hallway. Cash, now free of hand restraints, had stopped and was listening in the doorway. He stood next to Roger, then took a step closer and spoke so only Roger could hear, "Is that who you were calling when we first saw you today at the airport? Huh?" His voice spoke now a whisper. "Mr. Harvard of the South? I told you we have a name for that where I come from. Now get out of my sight, dumbass. Oh, by the way, how was Pelican Cottages?"

Roger's face turned almost crimson.

There remained a few papers to sign, then reassuring comments came from all directions, and the group shuffled out onto the sidewalk. Roger hurried ahead and sat in his car.

Cash drove Sophia home and she went straight to bed. The whole emotional encounter at the airport and the police station had drained what little reserve she had left. She asked for a small waste can be near the bed in case a wave of nausea developed. Cash heard a car pull into the driveway and saw Abigail walking toward the house. As she got closer, he saw her tear-streaked face when she met him on the porch.

"Where's Roger?" Cash asked.

"He's in the car. He'd rather not get out. Cash, I'm so sorry all this happened. He's really a good man, he just made an error in judgement, that's all. He thought you were trying to take advantage of Granny. Cash, he sounded so convincing!"

He stood there, scratching his nose. "If that's what you want to think."

Her tears began to flow again. Cash could only stand and watch.

"I don't know what to think, right now," she said. "We're

making our wedding plans and honeymoon plans. I don't want to lose him. Help me, please! Please come out to the car and talk to him." She gave his forearm a gentle touch and he backed away.

"And say what? Have a nice day? Abigail, you better go into this with your eyes wide open. Have a good look as to what you're getting into."

"Why? What am I missing? Tell me!"

"He wanted me out of the picture. Ask him why. Why he would want to discredit anything I might say. Ask him. That's all I can tell you."

"No, you ask him. I can't get a sensible word out of him. Cash, I'm asking you to help me!"

Slowly, Cash strolled down the driveway and stopped at the driver's window. He leaned down and said, "What's on your mind, Roger?"

Roger just shrugged and muttered, "I don't know. You tell me."

"You playing the innocent victim? Is that the best you can do? The stuff at the airport, what was that all about?"

Roger looked off in the distance and shrugged again.

Cash leaned into the driver's window, inches away from Roger's face, just out of Abigail's earshot and half-whispered, "You know exactly what it was all about. You were trying to make me look like some old lady's molester or some gold digger trying to get my hands in her pocketbook. And I know why. It's all about your stopover in Monroe and your eagerness to get to Houston. I'm the only one who's figured it out and you want to destroy any trust this family has for me in case I decide to tell them all about you. So, hear me straight, asshole – you do one thing to embarrass or hurt anyone in this family and I will find you and I will permanently change your shit-eatin' face. I can't make it any plainer."

Roger nervously hit the window switch, and the glass closed shut. Cash turned to Abigail who had approached the car and said apologetically, "A little misunderstanding, that's all. He's fine. Have a nice trip." He walked back to the front porch while Abigail stood on the walkway with her jaw dropped.

He heard the car door open and shut and looked around to see Abigail talking to Roger as they sat in the car. She apparently was trying to pry information from him about his conversation with Cash and was getting nowhere in her efforts. Finally, she sat back in the seat and Cash could read her lips through the car windshield saying *Just go! Just go!*

He watched as the car back out of the driveway. As he turned back toward the door, he thought, *Why didn't I tell her? What am I avoiding? What am I afraid of? Why did Roger let her come back here?*

It suddenly dawned on him that Roger wanted a confrontation to impress her, and Cash had spoiled that plan. The reality suddenly hit him, and he raced out to the street shouting, "Abigail! Wait!"

Roger's car sped away from the house and Cash's voice faded, lost in the breeze.

Chapter 9

August drew to a close. The routine of taking care of Sophia had started to wear on him, but each day Cash took a deep breath and forged ahead with her needs, which were becoming more frequent and more demanding. The days were hard enough, but the nights sapped his own strength.

At least twice each night, he heard Sophia stumble out of bed and head for the bathroom. Her gagging and coughing were a nightly occurrence, clearly audible in spite of the closed door. Once, he tried to enter the room to offer help, but she motioned him out, telling him there was nothing he could do. It left him feeling helpless. His days were no different from the nights. Unfinished work in the shop accumulated while he looked in on her almost every hour, and the mowing crews still required his presence at the beginning and end of each day.

Evenings, while he tried to relax and control his thoughts after supper, old familiar cravings in his palate began anew with increasing regularity. On those occasions, he would check on Sophia and stay busy, anything for a distraction, so the liquor cabinet stayed closed.

September arrived, as always, and years of memories reminded everyone that autumn waited just around the corner. The temperatures in Louisiana still smoldered in the middle of the day, although heatwaves on the roads had become barely visible. But something in the air foretold the change of seasons. Could it be the sight of tractors and wagons in cotton fields, harvesting what would become next year's bedsheets and t-shirts? Maybe the abundance of school buses and children, or the stadium glow of

Friday night football games carried the message. Along with all these changes came swirling weather formations in the Atlantic off the west coast of Africa. Formations that could meander across the wideness of the ocean and find their way into the Gulf of Mexico, where they gained strength and put costal residents on edge.

Weather forecasters had so many models to use as examples that people tended to ignore the early warning signs. Many residents of Louisiana had withstood storms and hurricanes before with the sacred rationale that they must stay to protect their property. Like history repeating itself, Mother Nature proved time and again beyond any doubt that she packed a punch beyond any protection mortal humans could provide.

Sophia Blessing possessed the demeanor of those who spit in the face of bad weather and never allowed it to intimidate her, even in her weakened state. Sitting in her favorite chair and wrapped in a floral quilt, her voice had a wheezing drawl, but with a determined message for Cash.

"Hell no!" she croaked. "We're staying right here, Cash. Right now, it's just a little tropical storm out in the Gulf. It's so small, they haven't even given it a name yet. Just cool your jets, man. We're going nowhere!"

Cash had been watching the weather forecasts for the past three weeks and this developed into the first tropical depression that looked like it may come inland toward Rapides Parish. He could imagine a disaster if Sophia suddenly had a special need at the same moment they lost electrical power. Her frail condition had become an obsession for Cash, although he knew that professional help could be found only a call away. But what about downed trees that might block roadways or knock out telephone lines?

For the past three days, he caught himself falling into needless pits of worry, something totally foreign to him. The Marines trained him to look after his friends in situations where a mortal enemy constantly threatened him, and he knew he could depend on them to watch over each other. But here in the home of Sophia Blessing, where he had control over very little, he felt out of his element, helpless.

"Cash, would you please sit down and stop pacing the floor over this little silly-ass storm in the Gulf? Even if it does finally get this far inland, it won't be more than a few hard gusts of wind and it'll be over. Let's just watch the weather forecasts and see what happens. Folks will be calling us to come clean up their yards. Concentrate on the business and stop worrying about me."

Cash complied, but his thoughts continued to bounce back to Sophia's needs. Tomorrow, while she napped, he would make sure he had not overlooked any loose items in the yard that might become flying projectiles if the wind turned worrisome. Thirty minutes after supper, the phone rang, and Sophia answered.

She said 'hello' then coughed softly and cleared her throat. "Trevor, how nice of you to call your mother! What is it now, once every six months?" Cash could hear Trevor's voice from across the room but could not make out his exact words. Soon, it became clear that he had been watching the news and called to find out if the storm preparations impacted his mother.

"Tell him I've got every contingency covered," Cash said in a loud voice from across the room.

Sophia listened to Cash and then said to her son, "Trevor, did you hear that? Really? Well, get on a plane, come over here and see for yourself." She paused and listened.

"Well, I didn't think you would, so I felt safe saying it." The conversation continued another five minutes, and both parties said carefully measured goodbyes.

Cash sat still and studied her face as she flipped through the TV channels. Her stoic attitude remained a mystery to him. The only things that rattled her were her children, her five grown children. Suddenly, it all distilled into one thought in Cash's mind.

"Sophia, are you afraid of anything? Anything at all?"

"Would it help if I said I was? Of course, I am. I just don't have time to show it. If I talked about it, would anyone listen?"

"I've seen guys hide their feelings, but I can always see through it. They hold up this fake image of bravery, but it's always so transparent. It's not bravery, it's denial."

"You think I'm in denial?"

"No, I don't think so. That's what baffles me. I just want to know how you stay so - I don't know - just above it all, knowing what you know about yourself?"

Cash was suddenly struck by the full weight of what he had just asked her. The words hung in the air, heavy and irreversible, and a cold rush of awareness swept over him as he grasped the enormity of his question.

Sophia sat motionless on the couch with her eyes fixed first on the carpet, then on the ceiling. Almost a minute went by with nothing said between them. Cash was a breath away from trying to soften his remarks when she looked at him with sadden eyes.

"You're not talking about the weather, are you?"

"No, I'm not."

"Why are you doing this to me?" she said softly.

"Doing what?"

"Making me face what I fear the most. Why are you doing it?"

"That's not what I was asking. Sophia, I have never known anyone like you. You don't let anything bother you. Not relatives, policemen, hurricanes, checking accounts -"

"Death? Is that what you're leading up to?"

He glanced around the room nervously and finally said, "Yeah, I think so."

"Yeah, you know so. You want to know how I face what I know is going to happen. I'm going to die, Cash. And so are you, someday. I don't have any brave words for you, so don't go looking for any. I just hope and pray it happens in my sleep. My fear is that it won't happen that way."

"Hope and pray? Do you pray?"

"Yeah, I guess. Not enough, probably. Maybe I'm not sure how to do it."

"Pastor Bob says we most likely do it without knowing."

Sophia snorted a small chuckle. "Yeah, I heard somewhere that God was a mind-reader. You think that's true?"

"I hope so," he said.

"You know, I should be asking you these questions. Tough Marine, you've probably seen more death than most people. How do you get through it?"

Cash thought for a few seconds before answering. "They train us to tell ourselves we're already dead, so don't worry about it."

"You're kidding."

"Well, not in so many words, but, yes, that's what we end up thinking. That is, until we get home, and then it all comes unraveled."

"Maybe I should be glad I didn't talk to you about it first."

Cash responded gently, "And yet here you are with enough spunk left in you to throw my own critical questions back in my lap. Just so you know, I finished unraveling a long time ago. I'm as normal as the next guy. But I have a long memory."

She smiled weakly and said, "You know, for a damn convict, you turned out pretty good. Come over here on the couch and sit with me."

Cash rose from his seat, sat next to Sophia, and draped his arm around her shoulders. She leaned her head against him and in a matter of minutes, fell fast asleep. He slowly turned toward her, picked up her withered frame and carried her to the bedroom. He covered her and then leaned down and kissed her forehead.

"Please God," he whispered. "Let it happen in her sleep."

The storm in the Gulf never reached them.

Chapter 10

Five days after Trevor's phone call, Cash had finally settled back into a steady routine between the office and the shop, but not for long. He was greeting the mowing crews as they arrived when a small familiar voice piped up behind him.

"Hi, Mister Cash!" Shauntae's shrill voice took him by surprise. He turned and saw her running toward him as her parents were still closing car doors behind them. When she reached him, she wrapped her arms around his waist and looked up at him. Her eyes carried a message of worship, a message Cash had never asked for.

Her father followed her to Cash and remarked, "Grandma finally got her driver's license. She's dropping us off and taking this little one to school. But Shauntae wanted to say hi to you while she had the chance."

"Thanks for bringing her. I always enjoy seeing her. You're my sparkplug changer, aren't you?" He looked down at the child and winked. Shauntae's face beamed.

"Okay, time to go. You can talk to Mister Cash some other time." Her father's voice sounded rich and deep.

In the midst of people milling around and the sound of Shauntae's grandmother shouting matronly instructions to her family as she pulled out of the driveway, another voice grabbed his attention like a vise.

"Looks like you have a fan club of one." Cash whirled around to see Abigail Blessing casually walking toward him. She wore white capri pants and a pale blue long sleeve, V-neck blouse and a thin gold chain around her neck. Her eyes carried a touch of makeup.

"Wha.. what are you doing here? How did you, I mean, I didn't know you were…"

"And good morning to you as well!" Abigail spoke with a firm, cautious look on her face, knowing she had caught Cash by surprise.

"Uh, yeah, good morning. Sorry, I wasn't expecting to see you. Did you drive here?" He looked over her shoulder and said, "Is that the car you came in? I don't remember it."

"I flew in this morning. Caught an early flight out of Atlanta and picked up a rental car at the airport."

"I would have picked you up. We had that agreement the last time you were here."

Abigail looked down and poked the toe of her shoe in the gravel on the driveway. "I know, but that was then. I guess I knew you would be busy this morning." She paused and said, "Anyway, Granny doesn't know I'm here. I wanted to surprise her. Is she awake?"

"No, she sleeps later each day. She'll be up in an hour or so." He stood looking at her with a momentary loss of words. "Have you eaten? I can fix you something."

Abigail turned slowly toward the house and responded over her shoulder, "Never mind. I know my way around this house. I'll take care of myself."

Cash watched her walk to the porch and enter the house without looking back. Burned in his memory was the scene at the airport, Roger trying to squirm out of a tight situation, and Abigail's livid anger when she and Roger drove away. And yet, here she was, unabashed, at least willing to say good morning. He knew she was forbidden treasure, but something stirred inside him, something that wanted to see her infectious smile again, the one that always melted his heart and warmed his insides. But why did he care what she thought of him?

Get over it! he told himself. *You're just looking at something that isn't for you. She never was. While the rest of the world lived their lives with hope and clarity, you put yourself in Angola, willing to accept a raincheck on all the things you missed.*

"Yeah, press on, brother," he mumbled.

An hour later, he was walking back from the shop to the house and heard Sophia's voice floating through the open kitchen door, weak and trembling like a forced whisper.

"Abby! What a wonderful surprise! What are you doing here?" She ended with a gurgle and a sputtering cough.

Cash could not hear Abigail's response and decided he wasn't needed in the house at that moment, so he quickly turned and trotted back to the shop. For the next two hours, he tried to occupy his mind with menial tasks that really didn't require his full attention; tasks that only served as a diversion, but with dismal results. His thoughts seemed trapped by the image of knowing that Abigail was just a few yards away, probably sitting in the comfort of the living room with her legs crossed and her voice sounding like soothing melodies, not just sentences. It was then he realized that she had come with no luggage. Okay, a short visit and then gone. Good. One less thing.

Around noon, the melody spoke from the door of the shop. "Cash, Granny wants you to come inside and have some lunch with us. We'll wait for you to clean up first."

He turned to answer, but she had already left before he could say anything.

Sophia sat at the kitchen table, struggling to look alert and awake. She ate sparingly and pushed her plate away. Abigail sat across from Cash.

Sophia croaked, "Wasn't this a wonderful surprise, Cash? I wasn't expecting to see Abby here today."

Cash cleared his throat and answered with a quiet voice, "Yes, today was full of surprises." His gaze seemed drawn to Abigail like a magnet.

Abigail broke the spell and asked, "Cash, who was that little girl I saw you with this morning?"

Sophia sat straight up and asked, "What? Who?"

Cash felt the muscles in his neck relax as he said, "Oh, Shauntae was here. Her grandmother is driving now and was taking her to school. I saw her only for a second while her parents were being dropped off."

Abigail commented, "She seemed to like you fairly well. How did you get so popular with her?"

Sophia interrupted, "Cash is...." She stopped and caught her breath.

"Cash is popular with a lot of folks." She looked at Abigail intently. "That shouldn't surprise you."

"Sorry, I didn't mean he was unpopular, I just wondered because she's just a child and - "

Seeing Abigail talking her way into an awkward corner, he quickly commented, "That little girl has the mind of a genius. Anyone would be amazed at her talents. She's very artistic, plays the keyboard, has a vocabulary like a, like a – well..."

"Like a well-educated adult," Sophia said almost with a

bragging tone. "She adores Cash because he paid attention to her. She probably has trouble relating to other kids."

Abigail sat listening, and Cash caught a faint smile that slowly formed on her lips. A warm flush crept up his neck, but he quickly looked away, pretending he hadn't noticed.

Sophia rose slowly and said, "I'm going back to bed. You two sit and talk. Just let me make my own way back to my room."

Cash stood quickly and said, "C'mon, I'll help you. We're not going to break our routine. Here, take my hand."

Abigail sat and watched Cash slowly and tenderly guide her grandmother down the hall. As they stopped at the bedroom door, she saw Sophia say something to Cash and glance back toward the kitchen.

Within a minute Cash was back in the kitchen and headed for the back door. Abigail stopped him.

"Cash, come sit for a minute, would you?"

He paused and looked at her with reluctance. Without saying a word, he pulled up a chair and sat.

"What was Granny saying to you as you took her back to bed?"

Cash rubbed his eyes and stared at the ceiling. He finally looked down at the table in front of him and said without making eye contact with her, "She asked when you and I were going to call a truce between us."

"A truce? Did she explain what she meant?"

"You have to ask? Abigail, she may be sick, but she still notices things. Are you going to deny that conversations between you and me are like fingernails on a blackboard?"

Abigail sat up straighter and squirmed in her chair. She cleared her throat but said nothing for a full minute. Finally, she stammered, "I suppose she's right. There was this business with Roger at the airport and…"

Cash quickly interrupted and said, "We don't have to go into that. No need to dig up the past."

"The last time we talked, I knew there was something on your mind about Roger, and you wouldn't tell me. Has that changed?"

Cash just shook his head.

"Well, so much for making a truce."

"Are you looking for a truce or for information?"

All she could do was give him a blank stare.

Cash rose and said softly, "I need to get back to work."

At the end of the day, Cash was honing a mower blade on the grindstone when he glanced toward the house and saw Abigail on the front porch talking to Sophia and holding car keys in her hand. He forced himself to concentrate on the machinery in front of him and didn't notice her approaching the door of the shop. The room grew quiet when he turned off the grinder. Her voice penetrated the quiet and startled him.

"Cash? Cash, I'm leaving for the airport."

He saw her standing in the door with the sunlight behind her, making her gorgeous figure look like a shadowy silhouette of everything that Cash wanted and needed at that precise moment. He looked at her with his lips pursed and his eyebrows arched. He nodded and said, "Okay, it was good to see you." His imagination was bursting with urges and arousal. An image popped into his head of her enveloped in his arms in permanent, perpetual ecstasy.

Reality reclaimed his thoughts as she walked directly to him, put her hands on his shoulders and gently kissed him on the cheek. "That was for Granny." Without saying another word, she turned and left.

Cash couldn't help wondering if she was teasing him by giving him a taste of what he couldn't have. *How could anyone be that cruel?*

Chapter 11

The next few days seemed to drag by. Summer had become a memory, and autumn temperatures prevailed. Mowing for Argyle's clients had progressed with the change of season from once per week to once every ten days.

Cash had started an advertising campaign for leaf removal, especially in older neighborhoods with massive trees. The company now had two crews skilled in performing tree service. Their ability to drop a tree in pieces without damaging anything on the property always amazed him.

Cash discovered that Shauntae's father had a hidden talent for that task. Not only that, but he also knew how to supervise a work crew and developed into Cash's right-hand man in communicating schedules to any of the work crews.

Sophia seemed to be no worse, but no better. Cash felt a little surprised at his own energy level as he found himself managing the household, caring for Sophia, and running a business. She had dismissed the sitter as soon as they returned from New Orleans and given Cash a room of his own.

Late one morning, he was surprised to hear Sophia's weak, stammering voice, speaking to someone on the bedroom phone extension. "Wednesday? Did you say Wednesday? Okay then, ten O'clock. I'll be ready."

She emerged from the bedroom with a slightly staggering gait, closing her robe and fumbling with the waistband. She managed a faint smile when she saw Cash.

"That was my attorney on the phone just now. He's coming here to discuss some things in a couple of days. You'll like him."

She reached for a cigarette, then changed her mind. "I have an appointment with my doctor this afternoon. You okay with driving me there?"

Later, after they had finished lunch, Sophia walked to her bedroom. A few minutes later, Cash could hear her faintly calling him.

"Cash, come help me with this damn blouse! I can't make my fingers work."

For her own reasons, Sophia had chosen to wear a pink blouse that buttoned down the back. She was trying to reach behind herself, fumbling with the buttons when Cash walked in. Without hesitation, he slowly and gently fastened the buttons, one by one, as though each one meant a token of appreciation for all she had done for him. He noticed again how frail her body appeared. Her ribs and shoulder blades protruded like a Halloween skeleton. She no longer had a need for a bra and wasn't wearing one.

The change was seemingly noticeable from day to day. With the last button fastened, he silently turned and left the room, lost in his own thoughts. He had seen starvation among people in Afghanistan, but never had his hands on such an emaciated body. Why could life be so cruel to some and apparently blessed and abundant to others. It didn't seem fair that a woman who had such a zest for life to be – what? Cursed? Ignored by whatever God there was? She didn't deserve this. With five kids and a herd of grandchildren, she should be basking in a pool of overflowing love and affection. But what did he know? He had nothing to compare this to. How would he know what fair even meant? When she walked out of the bedroom, he looked at her gaunt face and felt a boulder in the pit of his stomach.

"Are you ready?" she asked quietly.

They drove in silence to the doctor's office. Only a few people sat waiting in the reception area. A nurse called her name within less than five minutes. Cash rose from his seat to follow, and the nurse spoke.

"Why don't you wait here, sir. This won't take long."

Sophia slowly turned to the nurse and said in a low voice, "Where I go, he goes. I need him with me."

The doctor came into the exam room almost immediately. Wasting no time, he said, almost apologetically, "Mrs. Blessing, we need to change your medication. Your PET scan shows the tumors have progressed and begun to spread even further. Are you feeling numbness in your fingers? It's in multiple organs, including the brain, the spinal column, and several bones. We're recommending a six-week regimen of -"

"No, you won't," she said with quiet confidence. "It won't be six weeks of anything. I'm not doing it."

"I understand your concern, Sophia. But you must understand, this is a small cell carcinoma, and it is one of the deadliest lung tumors we know of. With treatment, we can buy more time while you get things in order."

"My things are in order. I would like to spend my last days doing something besides puking my guts up every thirty minutes. Understand?"

Wednesday arrived as it always does, and Sophia's attorney arrived right on time. He spent two hours with her in the living room and left without any dramatic fanfare. From his vantage point in the kitchen, Cash could see she was struggling to stay focused on the man's words.

When they finished, he watched her get out of her chair and

slowly totter down the hall toward the bathroom. Thirty minutes went by, and he felt powerless and helpless. He had no idea why the attorney had been there, but he knew it had not been a social visit.

He followed to check on her, and she came out of the bathroom with her hands on the door frame to steady herself. She had a shadowed look on her face. "Cash, this may be hard for you to do, but I need you to see something. Go look in the toilet."

She had not flushed it yet. Her urine was as dark as coffee. A morbid stillness filled the room, punctuated by a faint, rancid odor. "I'm a nurse. I know what it means," she gasped. "My liver is failing. Call John. Tell him I'm ready for Hospice."

The next few hours became a flurry of activity involving hospice employees and the delivery of a hospital bed, a bedside commode, an oxygen tank, and various monitors. Sophia quietly objected to the way her bedroom began to look like a nursing home. Cash tried to help but found himself feeling like a background shadow. John promised to be there in two days with Barbara, and Cash was more than a little relieved to hear this but did not want to admit it.

Throughout the entire set-up process with Hospice, and despite her cachexic state, Sophia's disapproval of minor details hung in the air like a fog and gave spice to any conversation.

She sounded weak but her words still had venom. "Cash, tell these people I'm a dying woman, not a damn astronaut! What's all this stuff for? I just want peace and quiet."

"Okay, sounds like this is not what you were expecting. Just let them get everything set up, and it'll be quiet as a church on Monday morning. They're just making sure you're comfortable."

Her voice was a whisper but still had a commanding presence. "Comfort, hell! I can't even turn over with all these damn wires I'm hooked up to. What are they for?"

Cash searched his imagination for a response. "They're just keeping track of things like your heartbeat and your breathing. You know, that sort of thing."

"Why? If I don't feel like breathing, that's my business. Are they almost done? Cash, get these people out of my house."

The supervisor of the hospice workers was a quiet man named Dan who looked to be about 40. He was leaving as Sophia continued her grumbling. He stopped at the door, winked at Cash, and handed him a card with contact information. "Don't worry about us," he said. "We're used to a daily dose of verbal abuse. She has no reason to be in a good mood."

"They're gone, Sophia," Cash said as he closed the front door. "John and Barbara should be here day after tomorrow."

Sophia held a tissue to her mouth and coughed. A faint rattling sound escaped each time she inhaled. "So, what am I supposed to do now? Just lay here and wait for God knows what?" She drew the bedsheets up close to her chin.

Cash reached for a brush on the dresser, pulled up a chair and sat close to the bed. Ignoring her steady stream of loaded questions, he began to slowly brush her hair. She pushed him away at first, but he persisted gently, and she finally calmed down and closed her eyes.

He spoke softly as he brushed. "We had a good time in New Orleans, didn't we?" His words seemed to bring her to a relaxed state of mind. "We'll have to go again someday."

She opened her eyes momentarily and quietly whispered, "You

are so full of crap."

That's when he noticed a yellow tinge in the whites of her eyes. She dozed off and slept with a faint snore. Like small bellows, her cheeks puffed out each time she exhaled. Cash leaned forward and laid his head down next to her.

He stayed with her until hospice came that evening to check on the equipment. Dan told him her oxygen saturation was beginning to drop. Both men tried to fasten an oxygen tube under her nose, but she slowly pulled it away after each attempt without opening her eyes. They both knew what that meant. Dan folded up the tubing and took it away.

Cash had brought in a recliner to sit in and maybe catch a nap if he had the chance. But every little movement of her arms or legs caught his attention and kept him awake. Finally, about midnight, he fell asleep.

At six the next morning, Sophia coughed loudly and woke him. An odor that defied description filled the whole room. He checked the bedsheets and saw the source. In seconds, he had hospice on the phone, and they promised someone would be there shortly to clean up the problem.

Dan and a nurse arrived thirty minutes later. The nurse told Cash, "She probably has nothing more in her system, so that should be the last of any more bathroom accidents like this. I can't believe you slept in here all night."

Cash was gazing at Sophia the whole time the nurse spoke. "If you knew how special she is to me, you'd understand," he said without taking his eyes off her.

"Let me guess, Grandmother?"

"You could say that, yeah."

Cash walked with them to the front door and Dan stopped to say something before leaving. "It won't be long now. Oh, I meant to give this to you." He reached into his satchel and brought out a small bible. "If you're going to sit with her, you may as well have something decent to read. Don't be surprised. We're a faith-based organization. We give these out to everyone."

Cash thanked him and watched Dan's car drive away. He returned to Sophia's room and found her asleep. He sat in the recliner and opened the bible. It flipped open to Psalm 46, and he remembered that Pastor Bob had told him to read that part.

He read out loud to himself, "God is our refuge and our strength. An ever-present help in trouble. Therefore, we will not fear…". He closed the book and shut his eyes tightly. The tears still came through.

Two hours later, he reached for the phone. Pastor Bob Allen answered on the third ring. An hour later, he heard a knock on the front door. He greeted the minister warmly and led him into Sophia's room.

"Can she hear me?" he asked Cash.

A weak voice spoke from the bed. "I can hear you. Who's there?"

The two men moved toward the bed and Cash said, "Sophia, Pastor Bob is here. Remember him?"

She remained silent, but both men saw a slight nod of her head. Cash offered the bedside chair to the pastor.

Cash broke the silence and said, "I was reading something in this bible, and it reminded me of our conversation a while back. So, I called you. I hope that was okay."

"I'm glad you did," Bob said. He reached forward and gently

brushed Sophia's hair out of her eyes. She remained motionless. Her breathing became shallower. "Get some water and a cotton ball. We need to moisten her lips a little bit."

Cash stood and watched this gentle man of God caress Sophia's forehead with his fingertips as though she was the most beautiful woman in the world. Her breathing stopped for several seconds, then she took several rapid breaths and then another few seconds of nothing. The whole cycle began to repeat itself.

Bob looked at Cash and said softly, "I'm glad you called me when you did. I've seen this breathing pattern before in others like her. I'm not a doctor, but I think she'll be with God before the day is over."

Cash moved closer and remarked, "She never talked about going to church. I don't know what she really believed."

The pastor looked closely at Cash and said, "At this point, that's not for us to decide. God knows what's in our hearts better than we do. We just need to listen for His voice and do what he tells us."

"I've never heard it. I wouldn't recognize it."

Bob pursed his lips and looked intently at Cash. "You left me a voicemail message a few months back. Remember that?"

Cash searched his memory, and it came to him. He had called Bob when he found out he would be allowed to be Sophia's caretaker. His eyes widened as he realized what the man meant.

"Maybe I have heard it."

Bob smiled and directed his attention back to Sophia. He then bowed his head for a few seconds.

They both heard the front door open and voices in the hallway. John and Barbara appeared in the bedroom door. They had driven nonstop from Atlanta. Cash and Bob stood and stepped away from the bed without saying a word. The Pastor motioned to Cash, and they went into the living room.

"Family, I assume?" Bob asked.

"Her youngest son and his wife. They're from Atlanta."

Bob spoke in a hushed tone, "I must go. I'll leave you to fill these folks in on the details. Call me later, okay?"

Cash opened the front door for Bob and saw Abigail coming up the walkway. She had arrived with her parents but stayed in the car to compose herself. On his way out, Bob nodded politely as he crossed paths with her on the front porch and she continued into the house. She looked at Cash with cold eyes and kept walking into Sophia's bedroom. He sat in the living room, listening to faint voices from Sophia's bedside.

Abigail reappeared, wiping her eyes, and headed down the hallway. Cash picked up the living room phone and called Hospice again, waited another minute, and walked outside.

In the shop, he sat on Sophia's favorite lawn chair, looked toward the ceiling, and half-shouted, "This isn't fair! You give me someone to love like I never had before and then you take her away! What kind of cruel joke is that? Damn it, why?" Not since childhood had he felt such desolation and grief. It seemed like the floodgates that held back tears he had stored up since his parents died had now burst opened beyond his control. He buried his face in his hands and heard a sound, a scream, a roar, a moan, all mixed together like a wounded animal. He took a breath and realized the sound of agony was his own voice. He got up and walked around behind the shop, leaned against a large oak tree, and let the tears flow freely, without any pride or inhibition.

Minutes later, he heard the hospice car pull into the driveway. He didn't bother to greet them or meet them in front. Let John and Barbara talk to them. Minutes passed and footsteps sounded behind him. He grabbed a handkerchief from his pocket and wiped his eyes before turning around.

Expecting to see John or Barbara, he was startled to see Abigail staring at him from about ten feet away. Her eyes looked red and damp. She clutched a Kleenex tissue in one hand.

"The folks inside need to talk to you," she mumbled. She turned sharply and went back toward the house.

Dan from Hospice stood waiting in the living room. "Cash, I'm so sorry about this. It went faster than we expected. She was just fighting that oxygen tube so much."

"Then, she's -?"

"Yeah, just as we got here. She's gone."

"But just a couple of hours ago, she… she spoke."

"The tumors were in her brain. Massive strokes are not uncommon in cases like hers. Things can happen quickly." He kindly waited a few moments before continuing.

"Do you know where all her medications are? We need to account for all of them, especially any pain meds she might have had."

Cash realized his thoughts were in turmoil as Dan spoke to him. A kaleidoscope of pictures, confusion, and memories tumbled through his consciousness. What now? Where do I go? Regaining his awareness, he said, "Sure, I can show you." He led Dan to the medicine cabinet in the bathroom and then went back into the living room.

Barbara suddenly appeared, wiping her eyes, and sat down

beside him. Attempting to remain calm and practical, she said, "Tell me," she asked, "How was New Orleans? Unfortunately, we didn't get to talk much after you got back. You cannot imagine how much this family appreciates the time and care you gave to Sophia. I hope you know that."

"Do they? Really? All the others besides you and John? Abigail told me a lot about her family, and I can't help but wonder."

"Don't open that box," Barbara warned. "I'm talking about John and me. The rest of them are like a smoldering coal that needs to go out. Sophia wouldn't want you to fan that flame."

Finally, he rose and said, "Well, I guess I should get my stuff out of here. I've got some money put away and I'll have me an apartment by tomorrow."

John had appeared and his voice came across the room in clear diction. "You'll do no such thing. You are staying right here in this house until we can figure something out. After all you did for Mama, there's no way we're kicking you out. Your room is still your room. No debate about it."

Cash saw Abigail standing behind her father with her arms folded. Her face was still tear-streaked, but without expression.

John and Barbara spent the rest of the day and into the evening talking to the funeral home and calling relatives. Cash mentioned that Sophia had a lawyer, and Abigail found a folder in a kitchen drawer with the attorney's name, address, and phone number. The paperwork in it made no sense.

In a matter of three days, the house overflowed with all five grown children and herds of grandchildren. Some had to find room in a nearby hotel in Pineville. Cash overheard occasional whispers among the family members about hm taking up a whole bedroom, but John put his foot down and Cash stayed.

Pastor Bob was more than glad to officiate the memorial service and graveside committal. Cash was glad and surprised to see Oscar and Gladys together in the crowd. Oscar had apparently gone to the barbershop that day and Cash almost didn't recognize him. The Pastor suggested that perhaps Cash should sit with the family rather than stand among the visitors, but Cash thought this would not be the time to start raising eyebrows. Behind the people gathered there in the cemetery, he saw little Shauntae and her parents standing at a distance, and the child saw him as well. She left her parents and stealthily crept around the crowd and maneuvered her way to stand beside him. When he looked down, she reached her arms upward toward him. He saw a look of approval from her parents, so he picked her up and she wrapped her arms and legs around him, burying her face in his neck. He pulled out his handkerchief and wiped the tears from the child's face. The gesture did not escape Abigail as she sat with her family beside the grave and casket.

Gazing across the group of family and friends, he saw Christopher and Olivia Hamm, and beside them stood Julie! Her baby bump had become definitely prominent, and her face had a rich glow. Even from a distance, Cash made eye contact with her, and she smiled, ever so briefly.

When the ceremony ended, he tried to find Julie in the crowd, but it seemed she had vanished like a morning fog. He felt tempted to ask Mr. Hamm where she was, but that would prompt too many questions and require too many explanations. Where was Steve? Then he remembered that school had started, and he was probably still in New Orleans.

The family extended dinner invitations to all present and the crowd met at the Hotel Bentley in Alexandria. Cash found a seat in a corner among strangers. Trevor rose to thank everyone for coming and to say how much it meant to the family.

Cash couldn't help but remember what heartache the distance and neglect within the family had done to Sophia. The hypocrisy in Trevor's flowery words became acutely emblazoned in his mind. He wanted to say something but didn't. Some assumed he might be a distant relative, and no one asked for details.

The following day, Sophia's five grown children went to the attorney's office around mid-morning, while the rest of the crowd passed the time commiserating with each other. Cash stayed in the office and tried to immerse himself in the business of lawn care and landscaping. He had expected the five to return before lunch, but noon came and went with no one in sight. Finally, around 3 PM, he heard chatter out front and car doors opening and shutting. Voices in deep discussion approached the front door of the house and spilled into the living room and kitchen, where they joined the others. He could hear what sounded like an argument at times, as well as moments of laughter and jocularity.

Trevor's voice carried like a bulldozer. "John, I can't believe this is what you want!"

"It's what Mama wanted," he said calmly but with obvious trepidation. "I'm following what she said clearly in her final papers."

Barbara chimed in, "That attorney isn't going to let us do anything different."

Another voice spoke up. "Just watch me!" Cash couldn't identify the voice.

"Yeah, we've seen you in action," said Trevor to the owner of the voice, probably a relative Cash had not met. "Just sit down," he barked.

The conversation died down in volume and tone. Cash could hear feet shuffling and muffled conversations. He walked to the door of the office and caught Barbara's eye. She smiled and continued talking amongst the crowd. A few passed by him in the hall on their way in and out of the kitchen, faces he was not familiar with. They politely said 'hello' and kept walking. He decided to return to pressing issues in the office. An hour later, Trevor knocked on the office door with a coffee cup in his hand. Cash invited him to come in.

"Looks like your lucky day, kid." He leaned against the doorframe and took a long slurp from the cup. "Mama was really good to you."

Cash could not hide his look of confusion. "What are you talking about?"

"You'll see. I don't know what you did to impress her so much, but it seems you did. Maybe I should have stayed longer the last time I was here."

"Maybe so," Cash replied. "Maybe you would have found out what a wonderful woman she was."

"I knew my mother."

"No, you didn't. You missed the best parts of her. All of you did. Well, almost all of you."

"What do you mean, *almost* all of us?"

Cash hadn't answered when John poked his head into the office.

"Hey there, come have a cup of coffee with us. We don't mean to be ignoring you. Just a lot of, you know, family crap to deal with."

Trevor looked at his younger brother as though he had interrupted a crucial conversation. Crucial or not, Cash appreciated the interruption.

Cash rose from his chair, stretched a moment, and started to follow John. Still blocking the doorway with his intimidating size, Trevor looked at Cash for a few seconds over the rim of his cup, then stepped back slowly only a few inches to let him pass through the door. In the kitchen, all eyes focused on him as he came into view. He tried not to act embarrassed, but he felt conspicuous, nonetheless. The room became suddenly quiet.

Barbara spoke up first. "Cash, how do you like your coffee? Cream and sugar?"

Cash nodded in agreement. He looked around the room of blank, staring faces for a few moments and finally said, "It has been so good to meet all of you as a family. I haven't met each one of you individually, but I hope to. I have not had the chance to tell you what Sophia meant to me."

He cleared his throat and continued, "I didn't have much family during my younger years. I always thought I was some sort of tough guy and she saw right through it. I've never met anyone quite like her. I know I'm a better person for having known her. She spoke of you often. All of you. She missed her children and…"

He started to say more, but he saw Barbara frown and give a faint shake of her head.

Trevor then slowly stood, inhaled deeply, shot a glance at John, and then spoke, trying to hide his own disbelief in what he had been appointed to say.

"Okay, so, now that you brought that up, Cash, we had some surprises waiting for us at the attorney's office." He stopped for a moment. "Did Mama tell you anything about her estate?"

Cash saw that as a loaded question coming from Trevor, so he tried to play innocent. "Estate? She had an estate?"

"In a manner of speaking, yes. You know, the house, the business, checking accounts, that sort of thing. She never discussed any details of that with you?"

Cash shook his head and looked puzzled. John gestured to Trevor, asking him to cut to the chase.

"Well, the house is being divided among the five children. I guess that means we all have to buy chainsaws!" Everyone in the room laughed.

"We're still trying to decide what brand to use! But we each have the option to buy each other out, so there could be just one owner, eventually. And that's still up in the air." Cash could hear quiet murmurings and shuffling feet among the group.

Babara spoke and said, "Trevor, I'm probably speaking out of turn, but I know Cash is on pins and needles right now. Let's not complicate things."

His mind tumbled in a somersault. He felt the gathering of faces still looking at him. What was he missing?

John piped up. "My oldest brother always takes the long way around to tell something and get to the point. The point is, Cash, she left 51% of the business to you. There was a ton of discussion at the attorney's office, and we all came away in agreement. And so the five of us will each own just under 10 % and the rest is yours. Are you okay with that?"

Cash felt trapped inside a tunnel, but now he saw the reason for Trevor's dark mood. Faces and voices seemed all directed at him, and he didn't know how to respond. Finally, he spoke and said, "Looks like she's still full of surprises. I don't know what to say. I mean, really, I'm not family -"

"Mama thought you were," interjected John. "She talked about you all the time. She said you were a blessing, no pun intended."

The group erupted in laughter. Cash smiled, but he remained still perplexed. He cautiously looked around the room and noticed Abigail had covered her mouth with both hands and gazed at the ceiling with moist eyes.

Trevor just looked at the floor and shook his head.

Then John continued, "Cash, who in this room is better equipped to run this business than you? Certainly not me, not any of the others. Look how much it has grown since you started. What would we do with it? Hire someone to run it? And who would keep watch on that person to check his work? No, we all decided that you are made for this. If you agree, the attorney will draw up the papers later this week and contact you."

"Or, maybe you don't agree," Trevor shot back. "Maybe this is just too much for him."

John rose from his chair and responded, "Trevor, being the oldest doesn't mean you have the last word. So, stop trying to make it that way." John looked at Cash and spoke gently, "Cash, take you time. Tell us tomorrow."

Trevor glared at his brother.

They also offered to allow Cash to stay in the house at a rent rate of one dollar per month, payable to John, if he decided to take their offer.

Cash finally began to grasp the weight of the decision. His

feelings felt so mixed, almost beyond comprehension. He didn't know if he should laugh, smile, cry, or say thank you. Above all else, he missed Sophia. The house would seem empty without her. The pathway ahead of him suddenly seemed so clear.

"It'll be lonely around here without her, but I see no reason why this business she tried so hard to preserve should wither and die. Yes, I'll do it."

Trevor jingled car keys in his pocket.

The next day, the crowd began to thin out as the five branches of the Blessing family tree went home in different directions. When the last of them left, the house seemed so empty, so vast, so much – Sophia. Each room held reminders of her presence and yet, many reminders were missing. He found himself expecting to hear her voice echoing down the hallway, telling him that lunch was ready. He saw no clothes to pick up and wash, no slippers, and no robe to hang in the closet. This house embraced so much of himself, even after just a short time.

Some could see it as only a few months in the big picture of time and space. But for him, those months were packed with a richness he could only have dreamed about. Was it over now? Is this when he wakes up and faces some kind of new reality? Looking back over the last year, he knew he had become a different person. He had found feelings and emotions he never knew he had. But now, that's all he had, feelings and emotions, sitting here in this empty house. Everyone around him had found their pot of gold and were out of his life, counting their blessings. Was that a cruel pun? He had never felt so lonely as he sat and pondered his next move.

All that night, he sat in the living room in the same chair that Sophia always occupied, dozing and rousing awake as though his brain couldn't decide which way to go. When his thoughts finally distilled into a clear picture by the next morning, he reached for the phone and dialed. He left a message at the Work Release Center and the phone rang minutes later.

"Cash, my man! What's up, dude?"

"Oscar, you want a real job when you get out?"

Oscar had continued his part-time job as custodian at the Community Church and, as it turns out, still had time on his hands. Cash needed a part-time maintenance person and found out, along the way, that Oscar had learned small engine repair at the local trade school, the same one Cash had been to years before. It appeared as a perfect fit, and the timing of Oscar's release could not have been better. He called John Blessing and asked if Oscar could rent a room in the Blessing house, to which John agreed. Since John and Cash had developed a close relationship while Sophia still lived, the family agreed that he would be Cash's point of contact on questions of propriety that needed a quick answer.

A month passed and the rhythm of running the business had seemed to settle into a steady routine. Stores and neighborhoods began decorating for Christmas. Cash had a continual stream of bills to pay, a handful of phone calls to return, and no time nor inclination to decorate for the holiday. It was his first Christmas season on the outside and Holiday joy felt like a foreign emotion, one he could not recognize, but he knew he was missing something.

As he sifted through the pile of papers in a lower desk drawer, he found an envelope bearing his name written in Sophia's unmistakable handwriting. In it were several newspaper clippings from Houston. He remembered she had told him while they were in New Orleans that she had information on his parents' death.

Somehow, he couldn't bring himself to peel open the flap, so he shoved it further back into the drawer he had taken it from. After a moment's hesitation, he retrieved it again and threw it in the trash, telling himself it was old news and didn't change anything in his life, such as it was. He almost closed the drawer when he spied a stamped envelope addressed to Abigail. He assumed it came from Sophia because it looked like her handwriting.

Apparently, she had meant to mail it and failed to do so during the eventful and emotional conclusion of her last days. He made a mental note to put it in the mailbox next time he went in that direction. In the meantime, the envelope found a home in his shirt pocket.

As bedtime approached, he remembered the envelope. He paused to wonder again what the letter might contain. His imagination soared, tempting him to open it, but that would be a harsh violation of trust. Most likely, it contained a private conversation between grandmother and granddaughter. He knew that whatever it entailed, it was genuine, just like their relationship had been. He saw clearly that the people in his life all seemed to be following their own path. In his bathrobe and barefoot, he slipped out to the mailbox, put it in place, and raised the flag. Looking again, he saw a small envelope that had somehow been pushed to the back of the box. He pulled it out and saw the return address belonging to Barbara and John in Atlanta. He opened it and saw an elegant invitation that caused him to utter a small gasp. He saw the words, *cordially invited to the wedding of*, and he could read no further.

As he walked back to the front porch, he wondered why did he always find himself on the outside of everyone else's dreams. Where were his dreams? Did he have any? Any at all? What fate awaited him? Oscar had developed a growing friendship with Gladys Perkins who worked in the church office. It explained his newly discovered style of haircut.

Stanley had met a young lady named Melissa at the driver's license office. She had relatives in Morgan City, and they connected immediately. For a fleeting moment, Cash felt not only alone, but abandoned, like his life had stopped moving and everyone else was finding new happiness. As he pondered, an old urge suddenly re-awakened.

Back inside, his eyes darted around until his attention focused on a small cabinet in Sophia's kitchen, one that he had never opened. Without hesitation, he looked in and found her cache of liquor. Most of the bottles sat almost empty.

Faint images of treasured moments from the past, lost in an ethanol fog, floated through his thoughts like mystical characters. It would be so natural to reach in, grab one, and pull the cork. He remembered the sweet, reassuring sound of ice cubes hitting the bottom of a tumbler and the gurgling of smooth, calming liquid dribbling across their surfaces. It beckoned to him like an old friend, one that had not abandoned him, rather, just waiting for him to come home and renew the intimacy. Instinctively, he looked around to see if anyone was watching and immediately felt foolish.

"To hell with it all!" he muttered and took a long slug of Johnny Walker, straight from the bottle. The liquid softly burned a track down his throat, and he felt it hit his stomach. Within seconds, a warm glow crept up from somewhere deep inside that made him feel loved in a way he had not felt in years. He looked at the wedding invitation again. How can a man return to a liquid mistress that requires nothing of him but a glass of ice and a moment alone, when all that was holy told him that he had seen and felt the real thing, a real goddess, with life's blood pumping through her veins? She was out there, somewhere, beyond his reach. A second long pull on the bottle came so naturally, and then he reluctantly screwed the cap back on.

Chapter 12

A week later, Abigail sat having dinner with Roger in a restaurant at Peachtree Center in Atlanta. He had made the reservations two weeks before and planned it to coincide with his return from another trip to Houston. They sat at a table for two in a private corner on the mezzanine level under dim, seductive overhead lighting.

Quiet background music filtered in from somewhere. The entire dining room looked very modern, with abstract art expertly displayed on each wall. The color scheme throughout appeared warm, with interesting patterns and textures.

From their vantage point, they could look down and see the entrance and most of the main floor below them, where diners sat with candlelight at their tables. The tuxedoed waiter had just brought their appetizers to the table. The conversation with Roger did not flow as freely as usual that evening.

"How many more trips do you have to take to Houston?" she asked.

"Not sure," he said. "Maybe one or two."

"Can you tell me anything about the project?"

"It's, ah, a government thing. Very much under the radar. Can't talk about it yet."

She took a sip of wine and gave him a long look over the top of her wineglass. "Well, I'll look forward to hearing about it."

Roger suddenly appeared focused. "So, let's talk about the wedding. How big is the guest list, so far?"

Abigail inhaled deeply and sat up straighter. "About seventy.

Mom's still working on it. She's waiting for your input, too. I have some ideas about our honeymoon. Have you ever been to the Bahamas?"

He cleared his throat with a slight nervous tremor and said, "I'll - I'll have that list to her shortly. Yeah, I need to get on to that. Bahamas, ah - no, I haven't. I'm sure it's beautiful. Perhaps - " His eyes had wandered down toward the front door on the main level and suddenly locked onto a developing situation.

The maîtred's voice suddenly became prominent over the soft din of the dining crowd. "Madam, you do not have a reservation! You cannot just walk in!"

A woman's coarse voice replied, "This won't take long. I didn't come to eat!"

The main entrance was beyond Abigail's line of vision, and she could not see the source of the disturbance, but Roger could. She noticed a controlled look of shock and terror on his face.

As she turned to see what had captured his stare, a tall woman appeared coming up the steps toward them, with blonde ringlets hanging down to her shoulders. She wore a sleeveless, one-piece green sequined dress that extended to about mid-thigh and molded to her figure.

On her feet, Abigail saw pale, tan knee-high boots with high heels. Her bright blue eyes matched the eyeshadow she wore. She stopped at the table inches away from Abigail's chair.

She pointed to Abigail and said in a loud voice, "Who's this?"

Meekly, Roger answered, "Simone, this is Abigail Blessing. She's, ah, a friend." He paused to glance at Abigail, then back at her. "What brings you, I mean, why are you -"

The woman pulled out a fuzzy, out-of-focus, pixilated picture and tossed it on the table in front of Roger. "This, you turd! This is what brought me all the way from Houston to find you."

Abigail was stunned at Roger's abbreviated manner of introducing her to this woman, and now shocked at what she immediately saw in the image lying on the table.

Roger looked around to see who was listening. He picked up the photo and looked at it, trying to look sincere. "What is it?" he asked politely with an empty smile. Abigail noticed his cheeks beginning to flush.

Simone could not keep her voice down. "It's a picture of a drugstore pregnancy test, you idiot! See what it shows? It's positive!" She bent down and looked closely into his face. "I'm knocked up with your kid!"

Roger stammered, searching for the words and finally said, "How do I know that's your test? It could be anyone's!"

"No, it's mine! I've been trying to call you for five days! I left you three phone messages, and you never returned any of my calls, including one today!" With those words, she picked up Abigail's water glass and tossed the contents in his face. While Roger sputtered and caught his breath, she turned and walked down the stairs and toward the front exit.

Abigail hadn't moved throughout the entire encounter, shocked beyond simple, sheer amazement. She searched for words, but her disbelief of the incredulous scene she had just witnessed blotted out any clear thinking she could summon. As Roger wiped his face, she peered at him with cold eyes and hissed, "What is she talking about?"

He stood and partially regained his composure, wiping the front of his shirt and trousers. Ice cubes crunched beneath his feet.

"She's crazy if she thinks I'm going to believe that's her pregnancy test. I used to know her a long time ago and she's just trying to grasp at any straw she can. She's really off her rocker, Abigail."

"That's not the point! Why would she come here to talk about a pregnancy test? How are you connected to any of this?" She held up the photo and waved it in front of him.

Roger could only shrug and shake his head in denial.

"Wait here," she said.

Roger continued to mop up the water with the help of a waiter and a busboy while Abigail walked down the stairs, out the front exit, and looked in both directions. She saw Simone standing a few yards away, trying to hail a cab, and hurried to catch up with her.

"Simone, wait! I'll pay for your cab if you will give me a couple of minutes to talk. Is that okay?"

She looked at Abigail cautiously and then agreed.

"Start at the beginning. First of all, are you from Atlanta?"

"No," she said, "I'm from Houston. It took me a week to figure out where to find him."

"How long have you known him?"

"Two years. I see you're wearing an engagement ring. Is it like this one?" Simone extended her left hand and the diamond on her ring finger looked twice the size of Abigail's. "He called me two weeks ago and said we were done seeing each other. Do you know where we were when he gave me this rock? Right there at that same table where I found you. You better dump him, sweetie, before he decides to take what he can and then runs out on you."

"How far along are you?" Abigail asked timidly.

"Not much. Seven weeks, maybe eight. I got suspicious when certain things didn't happen on time, so I bought that pregnancy test just on the off chance that, well, you know." She stopped talking long enough to light a cigarette. "But, I got to get back home. My mother's watching the kids and I promised to be back in a few days."

"You have children?"

"Yeah, twin girls. God only knows where their daddy is by now. Seems like I have a bad choice in men. Roger broke up with me right after he found out I had two kids."

"I don't know what to say." Abigail found herself caught between empathy and rage. "I just hope you will do okay."

"Don't worry. I'll land on my feet. You still have a chance to get rid of that bastard without any loose ends like the one I got. Do it now!"

Abigail asked Simone to wait and not leave yet, then turned and re-entered the restaurant. She climbed the steps again and stopped at the table where they had been sitting. She took off her engagement ring and laid it on the bread plate in front of him. He stood and started to speak. She picked up the freshly filled water glass and threw it in his face. The entire company of diners applauded as she walked out. Outside on the sidewalk, Simone was nowhere to be seen.

Abigail's cab pulled up to her parents' house around 11 PM. The house lights were off except for one lamp in the living room. She tiptoed into her room and went to bed and slept fitfully all night.

The next morning, John and Barbara rose up early. They greeted Abigail with smiles when she walked into the kitchen. Their smiles faded when they saw the downcast look of despair on their daughter's face.

"I've seen that look before," John said. "It means something's not right."

Barbara crossed the room and gently hugged her. "Want some coffee? We didn't hear you come in last night."

Abigail sat at the breakfast table across from both of them and tried to collect her thoughts.

Impatiently, John asked, "So, what's up, Abbie?"

Barbara silenced him with a look.

She took one sip of her coffee and said, "I need some time to myself."

John and Barbara glanced at each other.

"Okay," her mother said. "Whatever you need."

Abigail left the table and went back to her room. An hour later, she came out fully dressed with car keys in her hand.

"I need to go to the mall. It may be a while."

"Take your phone," Barbara said quietly. "Will you be home for lunch?"

Abigail just shrugged and left.

Moments afterwards, John said, "What do you suppose that was all about?"

Barbara looked at him with a frown and pursed lips. "John, connect the dots. She spent the evening with Roger and now she's upset about something. Ten dollars says she and Roger had a disagreement. Just give her time."

Lunchtime came and passed. Around 3 O'clock, John could not restrain himself. "Barb, this isn't right for her to not tell us anything. She's had plenty of time. We don't know where she is or what she's doing! Maybe she's had car trouble. Maybe - I'm going to call her!"

"You will do no such thing! She's a grown woman. She said she needed some time to herself, so you will give it to her!"

"Aren't you worried?" he asked.

"Yes, I am worried about what's troubling her, but you seem more concerned about the fact that she hasn't come home. She told us where she was going. Go stay busy with something in the garage and DO NOT call her!"

An hour later, Abigail pulled into the driveway. She got out carrying three shopping bags full of merchandise from the mall.

Both her parents sat in the living room and tried to act casual when she came in.

"So, the shopper comes home at last! What did you buy?" her dad asked, clapping his hands together.

"Just some stuff I needed."

"Like what?"

She looked at her father with an irritated face and began pulling items out of the first shopping bag and waving them at her father. "Clothes, Daddy, see! Just some clothes! Don't make a big deal out of it! I told you on the phone where I was!"

John's face began to turn red, and Barbara glared at him. She finally said, "Come into the bedroom, honey, and let's try on the things you bought. I can't wait to see them."

John rose to go with them and Barbara waved him off with a look. He stopped and stood motionless like a kid who didn't get picked to play ball.

As Abigail began spreading her purchases on the bed, the two women communicated silently. Finally, Barb thought the time was right. "You want to talk about it?"

"What, the clothes?"

"You know what I mean. What happened last night?"

"I really don't know. I'm still trying to figure it out. Mom, may I have the room to myself?"

In the kitchen, John looked at Barbara with a huge question mark on his face. She said solemnly, "Did you notice the engagement ring is missing?"

An hour later, she emerged with red eyes and tear-streaked cheeks. She sat on the couch and her parents came in from the kitchen. No one said anything for a full five minutes.

Finally, she said tearfully, "I feel so stupid! All his grand talk about what we were going to do and all his plans, I just feel so…" She stopped and looked at her father. "Daddy, have you made a deposit on the reception hall?" She then turned to her mother and asked, "Mom, have you mailed the invitations yet?"

Both nodded yes to both questions.

Abigail sighed and continued, "Then see if you can get your deposit back and don't mail out anymore invitations. There's no need to. Not after last night."

Barbara and John listened with focused attention as Abigail retold the episode at the restaurant. When she finished, they looked at her with their mouths open.

John responded first and said boldly, "Well, I'm glad you found out when you did. He had us all fooled. What should we do if he calls or comes by?"

"I simply want him out of my life. I won't take any calls from him and if he comes anywhere near the house, I'll call the cops!"

John squirmed in his chair, a little startled by Abigail's visceral response to his question. He started to make a further comment, but Barbara interrupted him. "You won't need the cops, honey. We get the message," her mother said. "He won't bother you at all, not if we have anything to say about it."

Abigail excused herself and went into the bathroom to wash her face and brush her hair. She came out looking only slightly improved.

John remembered something and abruptly said, "Oh, this letter came for you yesterday. I meant to give it to you before you went out on your, ah, date." His last word 'date' seemed to fade as his lips formed the sound of the word. He handed the envelope to her and waited expectantly.

"Who is it from?" Barbara asked.

John leaned forward and pointed to the envelope in Abigail's hands, "There's no return address, but it's postmarked from Alexandria. Mailed less than a week ago."

Both women looked at him, wide-eyed, but realizing he was only acting like the father he always was. "Are you going to open it?" he asked.

"Later Daddy. I think I recognize this handwriting. I think it's from Granny."

"But, if it's from her and the postmark was that recent, then someone mailed it after she died. So, she must have written it before she…"

Barbara interrupted, "Honey, open it when you want to. It's addressed to you."

An hour later, she had showered and changed. Barb and John tried to encourage her to eat some supper, but she only picked at her food.

Shortly thereafter, she announced she was going to bed. John looked at his watch. It was only 8 O'clock.

She needed solitude more than sleep. Somehow, she had to make sense of what had happened. Had she been so blind to Roger's real self? What red flags had she missed? Thinking back, she tried to piece together every conversation she had had with him and came up empty-handed, imagining what she should have known and what she would have said. Around midnight, she sat on the side of her bed and opened the envelope.

The next morning, she walked into the kitchen and announced, "If you can spare it, I need one of the cars. I have to drive somewhere, and I'll be gone a few days."

"Where are you going?" her father asked.

"Louisiana. Please don't press me for details. I don't have all the answers myself. I just know I need to go."

Chapter 13

Abigail arrived in Tioga on Sunday afternoon under an overcast sky and a prediction of light showers later in the day. She made a laser straight course for Sophia's house. The shop door stood open, and she saw someone, a man, busy at work inside. When he turned around, she saw a flash of red hair and a beard.

"Help you, ma'am?"

"I'm looking for Cash. Cash Ratliff, is he around?"

"Sorry, not at the moment. Can I take a message?"

Remembering her manners, she extended her hand and said, "I'm Abigail. Would you know when to expect him back?"

Oscar tried to wipe the grease off his hands, but just smiled and rubbed his palms together. "Sorry, I'm Oscar Kelly. I work for Cash. You know, it's Sunday and I never know when to expect him to come home. He goes to the community church over on MacArthur Drive and then sometimes he gives rides to different folks trying to get home. You know, old folks who don't drive anymore. I saw him there this morning." He paused and looked at her with arched eyebrows.

"Sorry, I didn't catch your name, ma'am."

"I'm Abigail," she said with a forced smile and waited for his response.

Oscar seemed to be searching his memory. He shrugged and said, "Well, okay. Nice to meet you, Abigail."

"Did Cash ever mention me?"

Oscar shrugged again and shook his head. Then his eyes widened. "Wait, on second thought, I'll bet he's at the cemetery.

He often goes there on Sunday. You know where Miss Sophia was buried? Did you know her?”

Hearing the word ‘cemetery,’ Abigail immediately turned and walked fast toward her car at the head of the driveway. When she reached her car, she turned around and waved.

Cash stood looking at Sophia’s gravestone next to Donald Blessing’s. An ancient oak sheltered the two graves and a tangle of large roots at the base formed a crude seat where he sat during his weekly date with her every Sunday afternoon. He leaned back against the tree trunk and spoke as though a piece of granite could have ears.

“Sophia, things at the shop are going as well as expected. Fall is definitely here, winter’s not far off, and we’ve got crews out raking up leaves. That’s going good, and it keeps the employees busy, so I don’t have to lay anyone off. I think I told you that we’re doing parking lots now. We bought some big vacuum machines. They call them goats ‘cause they gobble up anything in the way. Then we paint new stripes for the parking places. I never knew there was any money in that sort of thing. Oscar put me to thinking about it.” He grinned to himself as he continued, “He’s a good man, that Oscar. Found himself a girlfriend. Met her at church. She likes red hair and they both have a ton of it, but she convinced him to get a haircut.” He looked at the grave as though expecting it to answer.

A car door opened and shut behind him. He paid no attention to it. Visitors always filled this place, especially on Sundays. A few seconds later, he heard a twig snap close behind him and turned to see a perfect angel walking toward him. She wore tan jeans and a red plaid shirt. Her clothes looked a little wrinkled, but Cash spent no time on that detail. He found himself taking a deep breath as she slowly closed the distance between them. She stopped about a dozen feet away from him and stood with her fingertips in her pockets.

"Hi, Cash. Good to see you."

Cash stood and looked around as if to find some missing piece of a puzzle that would explain this angelic vision standing in front of him. "Ah… yeah. Good to see you. You come alone?"

"It's just me. Got a minute? I wanted to talk to you."

"Me? In your busy schedule? I guess I should feel honored."

"Cash, I drove here from Atlanta just to see you."

He looked straight at her for a moment, shifted his feet, and replied, "Okay, I got plenty of time. What's up?"

She took a deep breath and asked, "Did you and Granny ever have conversations about me and, you know, me and - Roger?"

Cash paused to measure his words carefully. The reality of the vision that stood in front of him still felt like he was dreaming. "Your grandmother and I had a very confidential line of conversation. We talked about a lot of things. What specifically do you want to know?"

Abigail took a deep breath and continued, "Cash, I've just finished a long drive and I'm tired. I didn't come here for any reason other than to talk to you about this. Will you please just answer me?"

He stuck his hands in his back pockets. "It would have been a lot easier to just call. You had my number."

She rubbed the sides of her head and half shouted, "Look, this is pure bullshit. Please answer my question!"

A slow smile began to grow on his face. "Yes, you are Sophia's granddaughter. She had the same way of getting right to the point."

"And so?"

"Look, your boyfriend tried to get me arrested at the airport. And you saw your grandmother's reaction. I have no idea if you had any part in that. You can easily imagine what she and I might have talked about later that same day, and the next day, and the next. Yeah, we talked about the two of you. How is Roger, by the way?

"I have no idea, Cash. Roger and I are through."

Her words caught him off guard. "Bullshit! I saw the invitation to your wedding."

"No, my parents are in the process of cancelling everything – my decision."

"Sorry to hear that. I guess you found out the truth somehow."

"Are you? Are you really and truly sorry?"

Cash looked at her inquisitively. "Is that what you came all this way to ask me?"

"You knew something about Roger. Why didn't you tell me?"

"It wasn't my place to say. None of my business. Believe it or not, I could see that you drew the invisible line for me, and I knew not to cross it. Who am I to get in the middle of your life? Besides, I figured you probably knew him better than I suspected."

"Are we both talking about the same thing? Knew him? I only knew what he would tell me! Obviously, he told you something different."

"Like what?"

Abigail glared at Cash in frustration. "You're running out of excuses, Cash. Let's get on the same page and stop talking like we speak two different languages."

"Well, I speak English, not mind-reading."

"Look, I drove all day and night to get here. Doesn't that tell you something?"

Cash scratched his chin, pursed his lips and looked away from her.

She rubbed her eyes hard, trying to ward off a headache that had been brewing for the past two hours. She then reached into her back pocket and pulled out the envelope from Sophia. "Do you recognize this?"

Cash leaned forward and studied it closely without touching it. "Yeah, I mailed it. I was cleaning out a desk drawer and I found it all stamped and ready to go. I figured it was some unfinished business, so I mailed it. Glad to see you got it. It almost went out in the trash."

"Are you glad to see me?" she blurted. "You don't seem to be."

"Well, yeah. I already told you that when you first got here. I'm always glad to see you."

"How much?"

Cash felt his patience wavering. "How much? Abigail, what's your point? Why are you here? At Sophia's funeral, you wouldn't even speak to me. God knows you had the time. Maybe I'm not good enough for you, except for those times when it seems safe to make more than just a passing connection."

Abigail had a look of astonishment, then quickly recovered. "Not good enough? What makes you say that?"

"Hey, the only thing you and I had in common was Sophia. She's gone now. I mean, just look at you, college graduate, lookin' for a fancy job, nothing but good fortune waiting for you. I'm an ex-con with a dishonorable discharge who lives from day to day with a job that I didn't deserve, given to me out of the love and generosity of Mrs. Sophia Blessing and her family. What do I have to be proud of?"

"Granny thought the world of you. That should carry some weight."

"Weight for what? Make some sense, girl! Your grandmother never beat around the bush like this. Make your point."

"My point is that you have reason to think better of yourself. You deserve better than you give yourself credit for."

"You drove all the way here to tell me that? You could have written me a letter and saved the cost of gas."

"Cash, Goddamn it! I am trying to make a point! I have a high opinion of you and I'm not the only one who thinks that way!"

Almost at a loss for words, he asked, "Like who?"

"Granny says so, right here," she said as she practically jammed the envelope in his face.

He took a step back. "So, what's with the letter? Why did you bring it?"

"I'm trying to decide if I should show it to you."

Her statement caught Cash by surprise. He responded slowly, "It's a letter from her to you. Why should I see it? I can't help you decide what to do with it. When you do, you'll know where to find me." He took a step towards his car.

"I just told you why you should see it!" She stopped and composed herself. "Granny would never tell me how to live my life, but this letter is about someone very special, without mentioning his name. She knew I would read between the lines and clearly see what she meant."

Cash felt a moment of hope and caution. He responded, "Very

funny. If you think I'm going to let you bait me like this, then think again. You made your opinion of me quite clear weeks ago." He turned again and started to walk away.

As he did, she shouted, "She would want you to see it. Come back here and look at this!" Her voice quivered, pleading. She had promised herself to avoid saying, *please.*

He turned back and paused, looked at her and then at the envelope. He had no intention of being set up for another disappointment. But something pricked his conscience, maybe a small crumb of hope, and he retraced his steps back to where she stood. With tears on her face, she put the envelope in his open palm.

Cash looked at her with a furrowed brow. He turned the envelope over several times as though looking for a secret clue as to its contents. He felt a mild tremor in his hands as he opened the single page Sophia had written:

Dear Abigail,

I have a boatload of grandchildren, your cousins, and for some unknown reason, you and I have the strongest connection of any of them. There are times when I feel like you are my late-life child, although we both know differently. Maybe it's because you are the daughter of my youngest child. Whatever the reason, your life and happiness mean a great deal to me. I don't want to see it go to waste. You have such potential, and I want you to live your life so that you never miss a thing, and that no one ever tells you that you are limited because you are a woman.

The only problem I see is your choice of men. There is something about Roger that makes me uneasy. I'm not sure how genuine he is. Please look long and carefully before you take that step down the aisle with him. He doesn't have the heart of gold like you do.

This may sound trivial to you, but ask him about Houston. I have it from a good source that you should ask him that question.

Speaking of golden hearts, there is one other person besides you who has such a heart. He's been very close to me for the past several months, and I have come to know him so well. You know of whom I am speaking.

With all his boldness, he has a genuine shyness that hides his real feelings. I see him as a work in progress. If I was fifty years younger, I would finish the job. He's the real thing, and he thinks you are, too. Look in his eyes and you'll see. He's genuine. I'm not making your choices for you, dear child, but I don't want you to overlook what's right in front of you. Life's too short to dance with the wrong man.

All my love,

Granny Sophia

When he finished, he looked up at her and she said, "Granny wrote that the day after you two got back from New Orleans. I could tell by the date."

Cash folded the letter, put it back into the envelope, and handed it back to her just as a drop of rain fell between them. "Makes me feel like I'm a hobby project to be finished in someone's spare time, like painting by the numbers." Without looking at her directly, he asked, "When did you open this?"

"I opened it the day before yesterday," she replied. "Why do you ask?"

"Didn't take you long to switch gears, did it?"

"Wha- what do you mean? Switch gears?"

"When did you break up with Roger?"

She cleared her throat and said hesitantly, "Ah, four days ago." Grey clouds rolled in, and distant thunder rumbled. The sparse shower slowly began to take on the face of a genuine rainstorm.

"So, in the span of less than a week, you broke up with your wonderful, precious boyfriend, saw a letter from your dead granny, and then came looking for me. Have I got the timing right?"

In her usual fashion, when stuck with an impossible question, Abigail folded her arms and tightened her jaws. Cash could see rage building up in her eyes.

"So, why don't you just get back in your car and go home? There's nothing here for you."

"I can't believe this! I drove all the way from Atlanta to see you face to face with all my vulnerability exposed and you won't even…"

"Even what? Come running to you with my arms open like a lost child? Can you change your loyalty that quickly? And don't tell me you had some endearing image of me on the back burner the whole time you were dating Roger! You were so wrapped up in him, you couldn't see past all his lame excuses. What did he tell you about Houston, huh? You didn't ask, did you? That's because you didn't want to know, right? Now you're in full rebound mode. How do I know you won't be gone in another week looking for someone else?"

"You think I'm that fickle? I'm not some teenager who can't make her mind up! I outgrew that years ago."

"Could've fooled me."

They both stood looking at each other with raindrops running down their faces. The sprinkle suddenly turned into a downpour, and they both began walking hurriedly to their own cars.

After a couple of minutes, Abigail started her engine and drove away. Within seconds of her departure, the rain stopped like someone turned off a huge faucet.

Cash opened his car door, got out, and walked through the wet grass back to Sophia's grave. He found his usual seat on the tree roots and started to sit, but lost his footing and plopped down in a muddy slop that instantly covered the seat of his pants. He felt the dampness soak through.

"Ah, shit! Look at this mess! What else is going to happen today?" He had almost decided to leave and head for a change of clothes, but something stopped him.

For some reason, he couldn't take his eyes off Sophia's headstone. The smooth granite came into sharp focus and clutched his attention like a gigantic magnet. In its grasp, his thoughts heard a voice saying, *"Okay, something's eating at you. I can tell."*

Where had he heard that? Whose voice was it? A slight breeze whistled through the bare branches of the old oak, sending rain drippings to land on his head and shoulders. He sat motionless.

Suddenly, like the release of someone hypnotized, his focus snapped back into his control, and he looked around as though he wasn't sure where he was. His thoughts distilled, and it came to him as he reflected, *"Sophia! That's the voice. She said those exact words the day I met Roger. We were looking out the living room window as he was leaving."*

Okay, he should answer the question. What's the problem?

Cash grabbed an old towel from the trunk of his car and laid it on the front seat, hoping to control a portion of the mud on the back of his pants. In mere minutes, he arrived back at the house and saw a strange car parked in the driveway with Georgia plates on the rear bumper. The question of the owner became obvious as he entered the house and saw Abigail in the living room holding an overnight suitcase.

"You just don't give up, do you?" he half shouted. "What are you doing here? I thought you had left."

"No, I'm not dumb enough to try driving all the way back after I drove nonstop to get here. I could use some sleep."

Cash chuckled then said smartly, "Well, be my guest! Make yourself at home!"

"I will. It's my family's house, remember? You got the business, but you just rent the roof over your head." She paused to let it sink in. "What happened to you? Wallow in the mud somewhere?"

"Don't change the subject. So, you're staying here? How long?"

"Just long enough to get some sleep. Just pretend I'm not here. That shouldn't be too hard!"

They both heard the back door open and slam shut. Seconds later, Oscar stood in the kitchen door, wiping his hands with a greasy rag.

"Oh, good! I see you found him. Ya'll get caught in that shower?" It took Oscar a moment to realize he had walked into an exploding drama. Considering his next move, he said, "I need to clean up. Cash, the Chevy truck needs a new fan belt."

Cash nodded, and Oscar disappeared down the hallway. Abigail looked at Cash with a question on her face.

"He lives here with me. He works for Argyle and rents his own room. I got the okay from your dad a couple of months ago."

"Speaking of my dad, does he know how filthy this house is?

Have you looked at the kitchen?"

"Every day," he replied.

"And piles of dirty clothes in that last bedroom? When's the last time this living room heard the sound of a vacuum cleaner?"

"That last bedroom is mine. Like you said, I pay the rent for that room AND for this kitchen. So, you can just keep your nose out of it. We're doing just fine." He paused and almost shouted, "I thought you were going to bed."

"My God! This is my family's house, not some kind of man-cave! Daddy will definitely hear about this." She turned, walked down the hall, and slammed the door to her room. Cash reached down with two fingers, picked up her overnight suitcase and gently put it outside the door she had just closed.

Oscar finally emerged, looking somewhat improved over his previous appearance. "Where'd she go?" he asked.

"Who was that? She came here looking for you and I sent her to the cemetery. Never got a chance to talk to her."

"That's Sophia's granddaughter."

"Really? What's she doing here?"

"It's a long story."

"Uh-huh. You want to tell me about it? Seems like you need some counseling on your personal life. Go ahead, I got all day."

An hour later, Cash had retold the events of first meeting Abigail, then Roger. Oscar remembered the scene at the Pelican Cottages, and it all fell into place in his mind.

"So, you still haven't told me why she's here."

Cash sighed and said, "I think she's got this inflated idea that, all of a sudden, we are meant for each other."

"Oh, I see, and you said to her…"

"Oscar, we could never make it together. She is leagues above me. She'd be tired of me after about two weeks."

"I don't get it. Is there something I don't know?"

"Well, I mean, she's educated and got all her sophisticated ways, and I'm just, I don't know. I just don't see how she could -"

"You mean she couldn't fall for a guy who's an ex-con? You're preaching to the choir, boy. Don't give me that crap, Cash. You done your time. You're a different man now. Don't never sell yourself short. You're smart, you're tough as nails, and I know there's a soft spot inside somewhere."

Cash shrugged and looked at the floor. "I have nothing to offer her. My future is a blank page. I mean, what would people think? What would she say when people found out about me?"

Oscar continued, "What do you care? Anyone who holds that against you ain't your friend anyway! Aren't you getting close to thirty years old? How long you going to wait before you find the right woman? Speaking of which, I know lots of guys who would give anything to have a chance at that wonderful bundle of womanhood I just saw standing here. You hear what I'm saying?"

Cash stood spellbound at the intensity coming from Oscar.

He continued, "Man, I know you got this big empty hole in you just waiting to be filled. Your life is so empty right now. I've seen how you talk to people, take care of business, and direct traffic. You got more going for you than most guys who never spent time in the joint except you don't know what to do with what you got! I wish I had half the class you got. You understand me?"

Cash gave Oscar a perplexed look. Finally, he said. "I'll sleep on it. I can't decide right now." He gave a soft chuckle and said,

"Like I really have any say in it. I may have burned that bridge, Oscar."

Cash had always been good at keeping his inner thoughts bottled up where no one could see them. Now, those thoughts seemed to have found cracks in the walls he built and he wasn't sure how much longer he could keep them contained.

"Change your clothes," Oscar quipped. "Let's go get some burgers."

Chapter 14

The next morning, a furious pounding on his bedroom door woke Cash from a dead sleep. At first, he thought he was dreaming. He looked at the clock and saw that it was not quite 6 AM.

He rolled out of bed and yelled, "Yeah, what?"

Oscar burst into the room in his underwear. "She's gone, man! I just saw her pull out of the driveway!"

Cash rubbed his eyes and said with a tone of resolution. "Well, that's her choice, I guess."

"Hey! Did you give her an option? Did you promise to talk to her this morning?"

"No, I didn't, but…"

"But you said you'd sleep on it, didn't you?"

"Oscar, why are you pushing me?"

"Because, right now, I know you better than you know yourself. So, get your lousy ass in gear! You got things to do!"

Cash looked at his friend, and Oscar raised one eyebrow.

"Okay, she's gone. What can I do?"

"She was pretty anxious to see you when she pulled up here yesterday."

"Yeah, so?"

"On her way here, I doubt that she stopped on the edge of town to get gas, you know?"

It took Cash a few seconds to see what Oscar was saying. "So, she probably needs gas on the way out!"

Oscar jumped way ahead of Cash's thoughts. "There's a big

truck stop on the Monroe highway. She needs gas, and she's probably hungry. If you hurry, you can catch her there."

"Can you come with me?"

"Naw, I'm going to sit this one out."

The old, rusty Dodge Cash had inherited from Sophia had rolled daily and slowly on its last leg, but like an old horse, it could turn better than a mile a minute when you asked it to. Traffic proved to be moderate and moving at a fast clip. In his rearview mirror, he could see a hint of smoke that told him the old horse was burning oil. The speed limit was 65, but that didn't apply to him that morning.

The truck stop lay ten miles outside of town, and Cash saw it coming into view about 6:30 by the clock. He could not remember what kind of car she drove, but he knew a Georgia plate would stand out if he looked close enough.

Still rubbing the residue of sleep from his eyes, he began to wonder about Oscar's predictions of Abigail and the truck stop. Maybe. What if Oscar was right, but the timing was wrong? What if… what if?

He pulled into the station, and there it was, a late-model Toyota with the gas pump hose still attached to the car. She had just finished filling up and he saw her replace the nozzle on the pump, get in and start the engine, while stuffing a Danish pastry in her mouth. He leaned on his horn and cut off three drivers trying to exit so he could block her path to the highway.

She got out of her car, slammed the door, and stomped toward his old jalopy. Her voice could have cleared a logjam. "What the hell are you doing?" She was still chewing on her breakfast snack while he stumbled out of the driver's seat. "Who the hell do you think you are?"

Cash half-sprinted between cars, struggling to find the words to explain himself to her and to the other drivers he had violated as they attempted to maneuver onto the highway.

"Hey, shithead! What are you trying to do?" yelled one driver.

"Move your ass out of my way!" bellowed another.

"Sorry… sorry.. I just have a little personal business to tend to. Can you back up and go around the other way? Yeah, like that, thank you!"

Abigail took long strides toward him with her fists clenched. If Cash had never seen fire and rage in her eyes, he saw it now.

"You idiot! What were you thinking? You almost caused a dozen wrecks right here in this gas station, and you come at me like…"

"Like you came at me yesterday?"

She stopped at his words and stammered, "Yeah, yeah, like I did yesterday."

"Okay, it's my turn. Where did you think you were going so early in the morning? You didn't even say goodbye."

"I didn't see the need!" she shrieked.

Cash rubbed his eyes and said, "Okay, fair enough. I'm giving you the need. Right here at this gas station with all these people watching and blowing their damn horns. Are you saying goodbye?"

She hesitated a few seconds, then said, "I'm not sure." Her face was still a portrait of hell's fury.

"Could have fooled me," he quipped.

"What do you want?" she demanded, stamping her foot.

"Maybe a second chance?"

She waved her arms and said, "At what?"

"I'm not sure. Maybe what Sophia had in mind."

"What?"

"In the letter. You said read between the lines."

Three men approached from the small traffic jam he had created. Cash saw them, turned to Abigail, and said, "Look, let's get our cars out of the way, and then we can talk. I promise, if you still want to leave, I won't try to stop you."

Abigail quickly found a parking spot and slipped her car into it. Cash parked near the air pump where a man had just finished checking his tire pressure. She walked to where he stood and waited for him to speak first.

"Do you still have the letter?" His voice almost sounded pleading.

She reached in her back pocket and pulled out the crumpled envelope. Cash noticed the curve of her hips when he saw that she wore the same jeans as the day before. He held out his hand and she gave him the letter.

As he reached for it, she said, "Her words made time stand still for me. It gave me time to realize what I had overlooked. The last few days seem like years."

Cash went over the written page like it was the gospel, word for word, rubbed his eyes again, glanced at her, and said, "Do you really believe everything she tells you?"

She looked at him with piercing eyes and said, "Ever since I was a little girl, she never lied to me."

"Okay, how do you know she's talking about me?"

She crossed her arms and said stiffly, "Don't be silly. I can connect the dots. You did more for her than any of us could have. Who else could she be talking about? She knew what I would be thinking." Her tone began to mellow. "You must have broken some speed limits getting here. I thought, I thought you had written me off."

Cash folded his arms and just looked at the ground. Finally, he said, "Why would she know what you were thinking?"

"Granny and I had this private line of communication. We shared likes and dislikes. We thought alike." She stopped and took a step toward him. "Cash, have you ever really loved someone? And don't say Sophia, because that was different."

"If you put it that way, I can't say that I have. Well, maybe once, but it was quick."

"Not even a hint of something serious?"

"I said maybe. I'm not in the habit of risking my heart twice."

"What do you mean?"

"It hurts too much when someone breaks it off, especially when it's my own fault."

Her voice became almost a whisper now. "Sounds like you don't trust yourself. And yet, here you are. Like you're still trying to decide something. That's what she meant – *a work in progress*."

"You mean a *project*. And when someone else is done with me, what then? Go to the next project?"

"That's not what she meant."

"And so -"

"So -"

She had her next thought on her lips when Cash interrupted

her. "I'm still trying figure out what changed your mind about Roger. What confession did he make to you?"

Her face turned red. "He didn't. I saw the evidence myself and he had no excuse. The last time I saw him he had water dripping off his face."

Cash tried to stifle a smile. "You got him? You really got him? I wish I could have seen that!"

She tried to maintain an indignant manner, but Cash saw a small grin creep onto her face. "Yes, he got it twice. The other woman got to him before I did."

Cash chuckled when she mentioned another woman. He could see she was beginning to soften. "Where were you when it happened?"

"At a restaurant in downtown Atlanta. We had just finished appetizers, and he was acting weird, distant. I thought it was strange he hadn't done anything to help plan the wedding."

"I'm sure you'll find someone else. Just fill in the blank spot with a new name."

His comment caught her off-guard with her mouth open, but she recovered quickly. "Maybe I could." She stepped closer to him until their faces were inches apart. "Cash, do you love me?"

He looked at the ground, took a step back and shrugged nervously.

"No! Damn it, I want to hear you say it! Yes or no!"

"I don't know! We – we haven't known each other that long, you know."

"We can fix that," she said.

"What do you mean?"

"We need a starting point! Now stop stalling and answer my question. Do you have any feelings at all for me? Why did you follow me here to this gas station?"

"Yeah, I'm still trying to make sense of that part. Something inside told me to come here. Sophia's old car almost threw a rod out there on the highway. But I'm not sure. I mean, Oscar said you had left, and the next thing I know, I'm in the car trying to get here before you left for good."

She took a step closer and said, "Yeah, keep going -"

He rubbed the back of his neck and said, "My God, you're as stubborn as your grandmother."

"And….?" She looked at him with beckoning eyes.

He finally looked at her point-blank. "Okay, I guess right here in front of all these people is as good a place to start as any." He swallowed hard and continued, "Abbie, you need to know, the very thought of loving you scares the hell out of me." Taking her into his arms, he whispered in her ear, "But I'm willing to take that chance. Yes, from the very bottom of my evil, lousy, felonious heart, I really think I love you."

"You think?"

He nodded.

"Can you get beyond that?"

He turned his face so she could see him and said, "Only if you promise not to throw water in my face."

"So, don't give me reason to." She wrapped her arms around his neck, pulled him closer, and kissed him with no shame or hesitation. Cash could taste the frosting from the Danish.

Oscar was standing near the shop door, helping a work crew load up their equipment for the day. He saw two cars approaching from a distance, but thought nothing of it at first. As they got closer, he recognized them, chewed on his toothpick, and stopped to watch as they parked in front of the house.

Both drivers left their cars, oblivious to their surroundings, walked arm in arm to the front porch, and went inside. A broad grin spread over his face.

Yeah, this was going to be a good day. Merry Christmas!

www.ingramcontent.com/pod-product-compliance
Lightning Source LLC
Chambersburg PA
CBHW061056100726
47911CB00012B/255